PRAISE FOR THE LAST CHANCE HOTEL

'This mystery
a jolly,

T

'[*The Last Chance Hote*
ages nine to 12, with a twist: it will appeal to fantasy lovers, too
.. Thornton, like [Agatha] Christie, can turn murder into a
thoroughly comforting bedtime read.'

THE TELEGRAPH

'[A] hoot of a genre mash-up ... Talking cats, mysterious
notebooks full of ancient wickedness; what's not to love?'

THE OBSERVER

'Nicki Thornton's debut novel is wonderfully atmospheric
with a cast of eccentric characters.'

DAILY EXPRESS

'A magical blend of murder and mystery for super-sleuthing
fans everywhere.'

SUNDAY EXPRESS

'[A] mash-up of murder mystery and fantasy that celebrates
food and cooking, and is full of great characters, plot twists
and intriguing detail.'

METRO

'Murder mystery meets magical fantasy in this highly
entertaining debut, rich in inventive world-building
and eccentric characters.'

THE BOOKSELLER

A MESSAGE FROM CHICKEN HOUSE

Calamity, crime and . . . a cat! Yes, Nicki Thornton and her feline sleuth Nightshade are back and ready to tangle you in a brand-new tale of magic and mystery. Nightshade shines in the second of her categorically brilliant criminal-busting escapades as she helps out the unluckiest boy in the world! Together, can they get to the bottom of the sinister misfortune befalling Oakmoss, before it's too late? There's only one way to find out!

BARRY CUNNINGHAM
Publisher
Chicken House

THE POISONED PIE MYSTERY

NICKI THORNTON

2 PALMER STREET, FROME, SOMERSET BA11 1DS

Text © Nicki Thornton 2022
Illustrations © Héloïse Mab 2022

First published in Great Britain in 2022
Chicken House
2 Palmer Street
Frome, Somerset BA11 1DS
United Kingdom
www.chickenhousebooks.com

Chicken House/Scholastic Ireland, 89E Lagan Road, Dublin Industrial Estate,
Glasnevin, Dublin D11 HP5F, Republic of Ireland

Nicki Thornton has asserted her right under the Copyright, Designs
and Patents Act 1988 to be identified as the author of this work.

Cover and interior design by Steve Wells
Cover and inside illustrations by Héloïse Mab
Typeset by Dorchester Typesetting Group Ltd
Printed and bound in Great Britain by CPI Group (UK) Ltd, Croydon CR0 4YY

1 3 5 7 9 10 8 6 4 2

British Library Cataloguing in Publication data available.

PB ISBN 978-1-913322-71-7
eISBN 978-1-913696-64-1

For Oliver, Simon, Sam, Emily and Matthew –
all the cousins

Also by Nicki Thornton

The Last Chance Hotel
The Bad Luck Lighthouse
The Cut-Throat Cafe
The Howling Hag Mystery

PART ONE

1. The Unluckiest Boy in the World

When something terrible is about to happen, it's helpful to know in advance. So Oakmoss Hornbeam always kept a lookout for signs. His best friend Veena said he was an accident waiting to happen, usually as she handed him back his broken glasses.

Today, as he walked down the lane through the woods that led from his home to the school bus, the wind was setting up a blustery dance. Twigs, leaves and even branches frolicked past him with such joy

it was as if they were on their way to a party.

They were certainly heading in the opposite direction to the school bus.

That had to be a sign, Oakmoss thought. A sign that he should abandon going to school today? A sign he should go fishing instead?

Even the clouds were in a feverish mood, whipped up into a frothy race across the skies. That one was shaped like a pig and it was running ahead of one that looked like a velociraptor. If the pig won . . .

You couldn't ignore a sign like a pig outrunning a velociraptor.

Trees either side of the lane stretched and bent their branches. Were they trying to touch their toes, or . . . trying to whisper an urgent message? *Danger! Oakmoss Hornbeam, beware! Head home, Oakmoss! Don't go to school today! Goooo fiiishiiing . . .*

No, it would take more than a strong wind, wild branches and clouds behaving excitedly to make him abandon Veena to the 'banter' dished out on the Dogberry Academy school bus. Usually by Flanagan.

And then a black cat dashed right across the path in front of him. A black cat crossing your actual path was the very worst sign of bad luck you could possibly get. You could not ignore that.

Something bad was about to happen.

The cat stopped. It turned. It looked right at Oakmoss with unblinking green eyes and Oakmoss froze.

From above came a sharp splintering crack.

'Look out!' came a cry.

And Oakmoss did look – in shock – right at that black cat. Cats didn't talk. That had to be a—

'Look UP!'

This was the last thing he heard before an enormous branch came crashing down right on top of him.

2. A Trip To The Hereafter

Oakmoss was aware of something chewing at his hair and tugging. Something was also unpleasantly rubbing his face with what felt like wet sandpaper.

Bravely, Oakmoss blinked open his eyes and found himself staring right into a pair of intense bright-green eyes, centimetres from his own.

'Ah! Thought you were never going to join us,' came a lilting female voice.

It was the cat who had shouted a warning. She was

sitting on his chest making it impossible to move and difficult to breathe.

Twigs and leaves still danced around Oakmoss, trees still bent gracefully, trying to touch their toes. It appeared to be just as it had been before that huge branch fell on him. But surely he was now dead? Was this the hereafter? If so, it was remarkably like home. He hadn't expected that, but then he'd never thought much about it before. He'd thought there would be more astonishing things, like talking cats. Or clouds shaped like pigs (say).

Was he now a ghost, perhaps? Was he destined to haunt this familiar bit of lane for ever? That was going to be a bit desperate.

'Am I dead?' He was speaking to a cat. As signs went, surely talking to a cat was a bad one.

People would weep for days, shaking their heads after hearing how that tree had done for him. His parents should have let him skip school, how they'd wish they'd told him to go fishing more often.

Veena would be on that bus on her own. But Flanagan would probably start to be nice to her, what with the guilt and all. Oakmoss could even feel a little sorry for Flanagan, having to carry around that guilt for never being nice to him.

He found himself wondering what it was going to

be like here. Would there be cake, for instance? Did ghosts eat? Because apart from the fishing (which he would miss) and Veena (of course), what he found himself thinking about was how much he would miss cherry bakewell pie. And he supposed his parents, Uncle Erasmus, Hyacinth the cook . . .

'Would you mind stopping tugging at my hair with your teeth?' he said.

'Ah, you can feel that, can you?' said the cat. 'That's good.'

'Are you one of those black cats from the fairy tales? You know, the ones who appear to give warnings and then disappear into thin air? Or are you more of a portent of bad things about to happen?'

'That is a lot of really quite rude questions, if you don't mind my saying.' The cat sounded properly offended. 'Cats are good at many things, but I have to refute that all cats are some sort of bad omen. Huh. By the way, I think you're lying on your glasses.'

The cat shifted from his chest and Oakmoss was able to struggle on to his elbows. His head hurt, and his lip. An eye. His nose. In fact his whole face felt like someone had socked him with a giant fist. His elbows were about the only thing that didn't hurt.

The cat was right – he retrieved his glasses. They were bent and no longer sat straight on his ears, but at least he could see the cat clearly. She was glossily black with a bushy tail and a delicate pink nose to go with those big green eyes.

He dusted off hands that were painful, gritty and scuffed and had suffered a bit of skin damage. He tried to move, but everything was sore and he didn't really want to get up.

'Thanks for trying to save me. So what happens now?'

The cat dug a very sharp claw into his leg. 'Feel that?'

'Yes.'

'Well then, whiskers and white mice, you're not dead,' said the cat.

He wasn't dead? He really wasn't.

He experimented with rising gingerly to his feet.

'Well, I guess that's lucky. My best friend Veena tells me I am the unluckiest boy in the world,' said Oakmoss. 'I think she assumes it's helpful, as if somehow it will make me stop having accidents. But it never does.'

'Good and bad luck, it's mostly in the mind, you know,' the cat answered thoughtfully, licking a paw. 'It's lucky you stopped that branch flattening you. Lucky you're not dead.'

Oakmoss considered. Things weren't so bad as

he'd thought. It might even not be too late to get on the school bus. Was that lucky or unlucky?

He staggered to a handy gatepost and leant on it heavily. The cat leapt on to it, gave him a once-over, then poured off again as effortlessly as ink and trotted happily down the path. Oakmoss pushed off the gatepost with a grunt and followed her gingerly. They were only a few steps away from the main road when the cat leapt backwards as the school bus roared past in a spatter of fumes and grit. Right at the back, a girl with a lot of unruly dark hair and an extremely cross face was looking out at Oakmoss as the bus belched its way down the road.

'Are you all right?' asked Oakmoss.

'I think we've both had a lucky escape,' said the cat. 'As well as not being dead, it looks like you've missed having to spend the day in a hot classroom trying to concentrate on a lot of things that I'll bet don't interest you in the slightest.'

'I think you're probably right,' said Oakmoss, considering.

'You'll find I usually am,' replied the cat.

3. TWIN OF DESTINY

Oakmoss had to walk (painfully) much faster than he would have liked to if he wanted to keep up with the cat. 'When I saw you I thought you must be a sign of bad luck. Now you've saved my life, I guess it means you are bringing good luck?' he said. 'Maybe that makes you my spirit cat and you're committed to protecting me for ever.'

'I sincerely hope not,' said the cat.

'If I'm not dead and I can't go to school, I guess I can go and spend the day on the river, and that is

lucky,' said Oakmoss. 'The wind looks as though it's dying down. I must say you are doing a really good job. I like having a spirit cat already.'

'I am not your spirit cat.' The cat sounded cheesed off. She fell into step alongside him. 'I'm Night-shade, by the way. I assume you're too dizzy to be polite and ask.'

He tried to think of the right thing to say, how to help his spirit cat be a little less grumpy. The last thing you wanted to do was be rude to the cat who'd just saved you. 'Perhaps we're like twins,' he said. 'Twins of destiny.'

'Twins of destiny?' Nightshade paused to scratch at a hard to reach place in the middle of her back. 'Well, then, you could at least tell me your name.'

'Oakmoss Hornbeam.'

'Well, Oakmoss Hornbeam, quite frankly the last thing I fancy doing is hanging around with someone incredibly unlucky. That's not a great offer, is it? I mean, let's face it, what did your friend call you – the unluckiest boy in the world?' Nightshade looked at him, blinking her big green eyes. 'Strictly speaking, I didn't save you – you did that yourself. I can spot a rudiment when I see one and I can see you're a good one.'

'Rudi—what?' Oakmoss responded. Yet he knew

exactly what she meant.

He didn't know much about magic, even less about his own magic. But he knew Nightshade was telling him he was a sorcerer who had an affinity with the natural world, someone who could move things like air, or the earth, or water.

Which would be pretty cool, although it didn't seem very likely.

'How does a cat know about magic?' Oakmoss said. Dad always frowned and changed the subject if ever Oakmoss tried to bring up the subject of magic. 'You're absolutely sure you're not a fairy-tale cat? Was that an ill wind? Did you cause it?'

She stuck her pink nose in the air. 'Do you know anyone with enough magical power to summon up a storm?'

Oakmoss answered with a shrug. Shrugging hurt.

But imagine. If he could move things with just his magical powers. If it were true – Oakmoss darkly imagined the joy of it – for once, he could make Flanagan arrive for the bus with a swollen nose, or tip face-first into a muddy puddle. But no.

Oakmoss knew there were definitely uses of magic you got into trouble for. Causing people you didn't like at school to have accidents was very probably one of them.

'You want to know if I appeared because I'm a bad-luck symbol?' Nightshade said, leading onwards, bushy tail up in the air. 'Am I a warning there is worse to come? I don't know about these magical vanishing fairy-tale cats you speak of, but I haven't disappeared, have I? Maybe it's not the first time someone's called me a portent of doom. But I think I'd prefer to be a twin of destiny, as you put it.'

'I didn't mean to be rude,' apologized Oakmoss. 'Where are we going?'

'I was thinking you'd probably want to offer me something for shouting that warning, something beyond being your twin of destiny.'

'What sort of something?' asked Oakmoss suspiciously.

Nightshade paused, one paw raised. 'I find things always look better after, say, an ice cream.'

'Ice cream! I don't think cats eat ice cream! They do serve dogs ice cream at Marge's cafe, but I'm not sure of the flavours. Or are you joking?'

'Never mention dogs.' Nightshade looked at him solemnly with her big green eyes. 'And I never joke about ice cream.'

4. IN NEED OF ICE CREAM

It is one of life's biggest unsolved mysteries. No one knows the answer: Why are cafes so happy to serve dogs? And yet completely ignore cats?

'I can never get to the bottom of it,' I told Oakmoss. 'Cats are extremely clean. Dogs are big, hairy, dribbly and often muddy creatures, and some of them can't actually eat without dragging their ears in their own food – why would you ever want that in a cafe? But oh no, it's always the dogs that get the bowls of fresh water, the special treatment, the

jars of dog treats on the counter. I am not even kidding.'

Oakmoss just blinked owlishly as he pushed his glasses up his nose, which I took to mean he agreed with me entirely.

He had hair the colour of mud. I liked the kindly eyes behind his lopsided glasses, one brown, one green. I hadn't missed that they had looked fearful as that bus passed and I knew that look. It was just how I felt when I passed those sorts of alleys where certain cats hung out.

We carried on walking along the hot mean streets of Dogberry. Dogberry? Dogs again! Worming their way even into the names of towns.

'You seem to know about magic,' Oakmoss said, picking up our earlier conversation. 'I thought cats only had opinions on things like mice and naps.'

'You'd be surprised what cats have opinions about.'

'Could you tell if I was under a spell?' Oakmoss pressed. 'Uncle Erasmus is convinced I must be under some *ill-wishing spell*.' He mouthed the words in a low voice, darting an anxious look about.

I didn't particularly want to be his protector, even less his twin of destiny. But whiskers tell you when someone is in trouble and needs help. I can't imagine how anyone manages without whiskers.

Or maybe it's just my whiskers. I am an exceedingly special cat.

'Finding out if someone is ill-wishing you would require magical investigation, and that is tough,' I told him. 'But funnily enough, magical detection is something I'm exceedingly good at.'

'Well then, guess I'm lucky again.' Oakmoss was still staggering a bit. I kept looking back to make sure he was keeping up.

'Detection involves digging out secrets. You can't tell people's secrets just by looking at them. I doubt people look at you and think, *Now there's a boy who can move the air powerfully enough to throw off a tree with his hands.*'

This comment seemed to hit a nerve, as his jaw jutted perceptibly. 'Is that because I'm a little small for my age? Is it the freckles? Or the glasses?'

The trouble, really, was that I couldn't see why anyone would go to the bother of ill-wishing some untidy small boy with an inordinate amount of freckles. But I didn't wish to insult him by saying so.

'What about that girl with the mean face at the back of the bus?' I suggested. 'Could she have it in for you?'

'What? Oh no, that was my best friend, Veena – the one I told you about. She'll be cross because we hang out together and today she'll have to put up with people like Flanagan on her own.'

We paused at a bus stop plastered with flyers urging people to support a charity fairy-tale gala (COME DRESSED AS YOUR FAVOURITE CHARACTER – PRIZES!!!) in aid of an unlikely organization called the 'Rescue All Toys Society'. You couldn't read the details, as they were obscured by some fresh graffiti – mostly the words 'The Flan', written over and over in aggressive pointy bubble writing and with the letter 'l' drawn as a dagger dripping blood.

'Does this Flanagan like to be known as the Flan?' I asked.

Oakmoss winced and I guessed this meant yes. 'You're very good at working things out.'

'I am actually. So the Flan is a bit of a menace. The sort of person who might have got hold of an illicit charm from somewhere? Sometimes witches aren't fussy enough about who they sell to.'

Oakmoss shuddered. 'I don't even want to think the Flan has got hold of an illicit charm. Do witches really sell them?'

'If you know the right places to go. Well, let's call Flanagan a prime suspect. If someone is casting an ill-wishing spell over you I'd say it's most likely in something you eat or wear. How about something sneaked into your school bag? That'd do it.'

Oakmoss pushed his glasses up his nose again. 'I lose everything in my school bag almost every day. It disappears and I find it empty. Once it arrived back with the words "twit-twoo" chalked on the side. It gives everyone a laugh when Flanagan hands around peppermints and takes bets on whether I can twist my head around completely. Says I look like an owl,' he finished, as if I hadn't got that. 'And the Flan thinks it's hilarious that my dad makes toys.'

At last we headed down a side road where I could smell more than exhaust fumes and the grittiness of tyres on roads, away from things whizzing past in an urgent blur, replaced with the pleasant, soothing aroma of takeaway; nice fresh bins.

Oakmoss was starting to intrigue me.

From that demonstration of powerful sorcery back in the woods, I'd had him fixed as someone born into one of the illustrious magical families, not the son of a toymaker. I wondered about him.

I also wondered where this ice cream was going to appear from.

Frying Tonight looked a good bet for a fish supper – it was closed, but still held on to the whiff of cooking fat and vinegar. Next was Marge's, which Oakmoss already said had a dubious and discriminatory attitude to animals. Yet its aura of friendliness, a brightly striped awning and a big sign outside announcing sweets gave me hope . . . until I saw it. A bowl of fresh water on the pavement outside, with prints of graceless paws and the word 'DOG' printed on the side. I stopped and lapped a little. Just to show them.

Oakmoss started rummaging in pockets, went inside and returned with a crinkly bag of something.

'Liquorice wheels for Veena,' he explained, looking pleased with himself. 'They're her favourite and she'll be mad at me.'

'She gets liquorice wheels for being mad at you? I saved your life and I get nothing except a quick lick at a bowl of water put out for dogs?'

'I haven't forgotten. I'm working on it.'

We carried on past the promising shops and were reaching the dismal and disused part all towns have, where building fronts are boarded up and a general air of neglect coats everything, along with the dust. Bits of rubbish being blown along the street were more plentiful than shoppers and definitely more abundant than my fading hopes of that ice cream.

'Maybe you should just go home?' I suggested. 'Don't worry about that ice cream.'

Oakmoss put a hand to his head and seemed

surprised when it came away bloody. 'Are you always this full of good advice?'

'Always, although not everyone appreciates it as much as you do.'

We stopped at the most dismal-looking shop of all and Oakmoss surprised me by reaching for the door. Cats aren't surprised often.

The name 'Erasmus Collectibles' was painted in flaking gold on the faded green shopfront. In the grimed-up window sat a hopeless jumble of sad old things.

'Collectibles? Are collectibles things people are desperate to unload? Looks like the sort of thing they'd drop in the doorway in tatty boxes and scarper before anyone could stop them. Kind of like a reverse robbery. What are we doing here?'

'This,' Oakmoss winked at me from behind his big glasses, 'is where we get ice cream.'

5. A CLAW IN THE LEG

Oakmoss pushed the door and a waft of dust lazily escaped into the warm air outside. An old-fashioned bell clanged a low and soulful warning, as if any arrival brought only trouble.

Once you get accused of being a portent of doom you find yourself starting to look for signs. Oakmoss paused before going in and so did I. Was he sensing the same as me?

Cats.

I paused in the doorway, lifted my nose and sniffed.

Two.

You know how it can be with cats. Some are simply adorable – pussycats, you might call them. But some are like those annoying folk on the bus. You want to keep on their right side, but it's difficult sometimes to know what the right side is. Or whether there is one. Some of them are simply nasty, vicious fighters that will unexpectedly turn and claw you in the leg even when you think all you are doing is being friendly.

'Nice cats?'

No way was I venturing any further until I got the all-clear. I wasn't going to end up with a bloody pink nose. Particularly if I might be the twin of destiny of the unluckiest boy in the world.

'Gisborne is my uncle's cat and it's his shop. Grimalkin technically belongs to my dad, who is Erasmus's older brother. Grimalkin's got a torn left ear, it's how you can tell them apart,' Oakmoss said, seeing me hesitate.

'How did he get a torn ear?'

It was Oakmoss's turn to dither and I'm pretty sure he muttered something about fighting before telling me he'd check with his uncle that they were both definitely out.

He must have received a positive reply about

Gisborne and Grimalkin because he ushered me in, even though there wasn't a great deal of space to even tread a paw gingerly. It wasn't reassuring, either, that from somewhere in the gloom came some heavy wheezing.

From a counter at the back someone was busy making a lot of noise with a hammer and plenty of enthusiasm.

I pressed my nose up against a low chair with a once-cushiony top that had definitely been home to a family of very nibbly mice. Maybe this collectibles shop would be fun. I slunk under a table populated with china figures arranged so that one sharp movement from Oakmoss Hornbeam's unlucky elbow and they'd go over like a line of dominos. Under the table I was met with a dented coal scuttle and a dead spider.

I'd been expecting the owner to be hunched and whiskered, wearing a shabby jacket with patched elbows. I wasn't expecting Uncle Erasmus to have a mouth full of terrifying metal teeth like a shark who had spent too long at the dentist.

Then I realized he was holding nails in his mouth.

He had a shock of hair, mud-coloured like Oakmoss's, and the same narrow bony face, but Erasmus had a pale complexion that hinted he spent a lot of time in this dim place.

He was clearly pleased to see us, as he took out the nails, improving his appearance no end. He was able to smile, showing very white and straight teeth, but then the smile dropped when he saw the blood.

'Oakmoss! Not another accident.' He raced around from behind the counter and shoved the boy into a faded chair that creaked but managed to hold together. 'What happened?'

'I hit a tree.'

'Well, I'm sure it deserved it.'

'Actually, I think the tree hit me.'

'Either way, let's hope this tree's also got an understanding uncle to tidy it up before its parents see it.'

I liked Erasmus straight off, as the first thing he did was offer Oakmoss a sweet from a small striped paper bag.

'Have a zingtasco, it'll take the edge off.'

Oakmoss popped one of the big purple sweets in his mouth. 'Edge off what?'

Erasmus pushed Oakmoss's fringe out of his eyes and reached for a stinging antiseptic that smelled of catnip, but not in a good way. It was thick and yellow and poured slowly from the bottle. 'Your choice. Either you go to hospital,' he said, 'Or I patch you up.'

I knew it was stinging from the way the boy

winced and drew in breath noisily through his teeth. At the second dab Oakmoss lashed out, taking out the first of the figurines. An ugly pug shattered on the floor.

'Oh, sorry.' Oakmoss blushed to the roots of his hair, although I'd imagine the size of that sweet made it difficult to say anything.

'Never mind, it was hideous,' said Erasmus easily. I liked him even more.

One of the many really great things about being a cat is that humans assume you either can't understand their conversation, or that you aren't listening in. Erasmus tutted affably, made jokes and said he was experimenting with the zingtascos to give them extra zing.

'Don't add peppermint,' said Oakmoss. 'Can't stand the smell of peppermint. Flanagan eats peppermints.'

Listening is often where you find out things. My whiskers twitched when I learnt this was not the first time Oakmoss had stumbled into his uncle's shop covered in blood. Could Erasmus be right that Oakmoss's luck was so bad someone must have ill-wished him? Had someone here in Dogberry, maybe even someone on that bus, found a way to do this kind of curse?

Ill-wishing. It's a simple charm, the sort that can

done with the aid of a book and only a dollop of magical talent. Those kinds of spells that claim to change your fortune are often peddled by low-grade witches. Sold as an amulet or potion usually, and definitely sold to the non-magical. Do those kinds of spells really do anything?

I'd say belief is a big part of it and that good and bad luck is mostly in the mind. It's all pretty harmless low-level sorcery. Not the sort to get you noticed and in trouble with the authorities, by which I mean the Elysee (which runs the sorcerers' world).

But if someone was ill-wishing Oakmoss, maybe they were doing a pretty sound job of it. And maybe I had a case of a serious illegal curse to investigate. It would be tricky to track down or prove and it would also definitely be a misuse of magical power.

'At least you didn't fall out of a window. I never knew how you survived that,' Erasmus chattered on. 'And had barely a scratch on you.'

'I was fixing a home for sparrows to the roof,' Oakmoss explained. 'They like to nest in a colony so you need a special long box. Anyway, now I've got someone to help me be lucky.' Oakmoss looked at me and Erasmus's gaze followed with a comment that I'd need to be very good at my job.

'If you need any more good luck, Oakmoss,'

added Erasmus, 'I've got just the thing.'

And he slid across the counter the most hideous thing I had seen in the shop so far, among some pretty stiff competition.

It was one of the weirdest things I'd ever seen (I'm being kind – it was totally, awfully creepy). It was black, about the size of your average rat, made of cheap material, with blank-looking green eyes, a leering grin and a painted gold bell around its neck. It had a loosely waving giant paw and tail.

And the very worst thing about it was that it was shaped like a cat. A black cat.

When Erasmus set it down on the counter, the tail and paw began to wave. Around its bottom were stamped the words '*A Good Luck Fortune Cat brought to you by the Hornbeam Workshop*'. Its paw and tail kept moving long enough to be irritating. It kind of drew your attention, waiting for it to stop.

Oakmoss treated it with a suitable snort of derision. 'Think I've already got one.'

My exploring revealed that Uncle Erasmus took a relaxed view about what he put on sale to the general (non-magical) public of Dogberry. In a second-hand bookcase I'd seen *Pranked! Hilarious Magic to Trick Your Friends – They'll Never Know What Hit Them* stood spine to spine with *Best Book of Birds*. And

Mind-bending Meld Magic had been jammed unceremoniously on top. I was pretty sure at least one of those was an actual magical text written for sorcerers

I'd had a busy morning and spent some time considering which chair to settle into for a little sit-down. I made my selection and got comfortable, stretching out first one back leg and then the other.

Of course, I wouldn't take a nap. Things looked like they might be serious for the boy. I took a vow to keep a careful watch, to not take my eyes from Oakmoss Hornbeam, not even for a second, not until I'd got to the bottom of this mystery.

It certainly looked like his luck had changed this morning – he'd met me. I am sure I am a bringer of good luck. But he was now doubly lucky. I am also exceedingly good at investigating.

6. Sensing Prey

Oakmoss had to prod the cat awake. Well, it had saved his life, he couldn't just leave her here, particularly as Grimalkin and Gisborne would likely be back soon. And how often did you get the chance to chat with a talking cat? Never mind a talking cat that had saved your life.

And she'd nodded off so quickly she'd missed the part where he'd had ice cream.

'Wake up.' Nightshade looked at him with resentful green eyes. 'I'm off home,' he nudged her.

She followed him to the front door and, over the sound of Erasmus hammering again, Oakmoss asked if he could take *Best Book of Birds*.

'Thought I saw a red kite this morning, just wanted to check,' he said, patting the bird book, which was small enough to fit in his pocket.

His uncle must have seen that Oakmoss's eyes also lingered on the magical books. 'D'you want these too? Your dad may need convincing that there's any point in you learning about magic, but my guess is you might be interested in finding out the basics. Maybe just don't tell him, OK?'

His uncle blew dust off other books with a wink. 'I'm probably too casual about having some of these magical titles on display – but they can't be used by anyone if they don't already have a spark of magic, can they? You may as well have them if you've a safe place to keep them. *The Power of How to Say Exactly What You Mean*. It's all about the importance of the mind when casting spells.'

'Are you sure you want to just give them away?'

''Course, you can take anything. Most of it comes from your mother taking pity on me and donating things.' Erasmus looked around at the packed shop and gave a chuckle that made Oakmoss suspect his uncle might prefer it if his mother didn't shower him with so many of her old unwanted things.

'And take what's left of these.' Erasmus topped the pile with a candy-striped bag. 'But go careful, these have extra zing, remember.'

Oakmoss accepted the zingtascos and added everything to his school bag, swinging it around to put it on his back as he said his thanks and farewells.

As it swung, his bag thwacked a vase almost as tall as him and covered in squiggles of Chinese writing. It wobbled and would have toppled if Erasmus hadn't dashed to save it.

Erasmus wiped his brow as he steadied it back into place. 'That was nearly unlucky – it's about the only valuable thing in the whole shop.'

Oakmoss scuttled to the door, embarrassed, eager to get out of there before he caused any serious damage. But his eagerness meant a costly mistake. He'd barely got the door open when he realized he should have been a lot more cautious. Out of the corner of his eye he saw two huge lumbering orange shapes, low and menacing, strutting towards the shop as if they owned the town.

Gisborne and Grimalkin had the same predatory air, the same square faces and strong chests. They paused and lifted their big, ugly heads, noses raised, immense paws planted on the hot pavement, standing watchful and proud and sniffing the air like a couple of prison guards.

Then it was as if everything happened in slow motion.

Oakmoss looked around anxiously for Nightshade. On his lips was a warning. But it was already too late. Nightshade had slipped out slightly ahead of him.

Grimalkin opened his yellow eyes wide and flexed his claws.

Oakmoss's warning died on his lips.

In less than a second, Gisborne and Grimalkin turned from being threateningly slow into predatory streaks of tiger-like hunting menace, all teeth, muscle, attitude and claws.

There was no time for Nightshade to turn and get safely back inside. She ran. And all Oakmoss could do was watch as the three cats raced out of sight.

7. A FROWNING FACE

Oakmoss looked up and down the street, his heart worrying for Nightshade. If she had never met Oakmoss she'd be curled up somewhere warm and safe right now.

But he hadn't simply met Nightshade; that cat had saved him. Now it was his fault she was in danger.

Oakmoss accepted he was pretty clumsy. But it was the first time it felt to Oakmoss as if he really did have an ill-wishing curse that hung over him so thickly it could spread to someone else.

He scoured the streets of Dogberry. Every step he took, peering down side alleys, looking up trees, Oakmoss kept imagining two orange faces, and paws smeared in blood.

The roads were dusty and hot, the buildings stretched and tall. It always felt like Dogberry town had been jumbled into a slightly too small space and the houses were all craning their necks to see past each other.

Nightshade was a smart cat. She was quick, he tried to reassure himself, but he hated this feeling there was nothing he could do. Despite Dad's lack of enthusiasm and hinting magic brought nothing but trouble, Oakmoss was sure magic must be useful for some things. There would be some spell to track down friends – there was magic for a lot of things, if you only knew how to do it.

Oakmoss did not know any useful sort of magic. He didn't know any magic at all. He thought about his haul of magical books in his backpack. Should he have been braver, ignored Dad's wishes and asked his uncle before if he could borrow some books?

Erasmus had once demonstrated a simple spell. He had waved his arms madly, chanted a bit, frowned and sweated a lot and seemed to need to make everything complicated.

To Oakmoss magic seemed . . . well, nothing like that. Because lately, it felt as if magic had started calling to him. It was like something was waking inside, something that had been ignored for too long, something restless and ready. It felt as if his magic was right there, waiting to burst out of him.

He wanted to feel that discovering his magic would be like finding a beautifully wrapped present under the Christmas tree. But what it really felt like was as if the more he ignored the magic growing inside him, the more restless it became. As if his magic was a trapped creature plotting how to finally escape.

It didn't take long to search the small town. He moved to where houses thinned out, leaving more room for things to grow, swoop and flutter. Finally, he escaped into greener spaces, hoping Nightshade had done the same.

And all the while Oakmoss asked himself: What if all these accidents that kept happening to him weren't down to anyone ill-wishing him? What if his accidents were a warning sent from his own magic, letting him know it would not stay squashed and buried for ever? What if it was his own magic sending a message that it was fierce and dangerous and he'd better watch out?

He kept searching for Nightshade until he reached an imposing grey wall of rough stone, which he followed until he arrived in a wide, tree-lined road. Today it was filled with a line of delivery lorries waiting to go into two black gates.

On a scrubby bit of grass verge was pitched a colourful tent, as if someone had chosen this road as a great place for a holiday. Outside the tent a small man was sitting and sipping a steaming cup from a thermos and eating some sandwiches from silver foil.

It was a glorious day, yet the camping stranger was dressed in a bright blue windproof jacket that colour-matched his tent and was zipped right up to a big moustache that gave him the appearance of a walrus. His grey hair was being ruffled by a light wind.

He caught sight of Oakmoss staring and put down the mug so quickly it slopped a little on the grass, and there was no chance for Oakmoss to pretend he hadn't just wandered up to get a closer look.

'Are you here to hear my complaint or are you bringing refreshments?' the man asked. He placed the foil-wrapped sandwiches carefully on the ground and got to his feet.

'Er, I don't have any refreshments, so I could hear the complaint? I mean, why are you camping here? Who are you?'

'My name's Mustard, and I'm here to make sure I'm not ignored and that everyone knows that name and hears my complaint,' he began with the air of someone who has told a story many times before.

'The trouble all started when my wife and I were on holiday and popped into one of those shops that sells sticks of rock. There were key rings made of seashells, that kind of thing, and my wife was very taken with a black cat toy with this waving paw and tail. I thought it was rather annoying. But I bought it for her as a present.'

Oakmoss asked if he meant one of the fortune cats. 'They sell them in loads of places. It's the Hornbeam Workshop's bestselling line.'

'Well, that cat turned out to be a proper *mis*-fortune. That cat tricked me,' said Mustard, the colour of his face rising. 'I want my money back and I'm going to stay here until I get it.'

Oakmoss was astonished. This man was camping here because of a complaint about a toy cat and wanted his money back? He was saved from making any comment by a welcome claw in his leg. He looked down to see a pair of big green eyes gazing quizzically up at him.

'Nightshade! Are you OK?'

Oakmoss made his excuses and quickly left the man with his strange complaint.

'I haven't finished yet,' Mustard yelled after him. 'In fact, I've hardly started.'

But Oakmoss wanted to know exactly what had happened to Nightshade and he could only do that where no one would hear her talk.

'I've seen off worse,' Nightshade answered when she was able. She flexed her claws.

'You fought off Gisborne and Grimalkin by yourself?'

'I know the value of staying out of trouble. Something I'd like to teach you.'

'You ran away and hid. Very sensible.'

Nightshade blinked up at him. 'At least I didn't end up covered in blood. I think it's time you told me about *your* accidents.'

Oakmoss led the way, doubling back, retracing some of his steps along the forbidding high wall, Nightshade trotting alongside.

'My worst was when my brakes failed as I was cycling down the hill. I was lucky I ended up in a really muddy ditch. The bike wasn't so lucky.'

'Brakes failing, falling out of a window – and that huge branch falling on you today. You are definitely getting more than your fair share of bad luck,' mused

Nightshade. 'Your good luck seems to be that you've survived them all.'

They followed the wall to where it met the sludgy River Dogberry.

Over the wall lurked an impressive house with four floors of dull grey stone, four rows of windows and a dark slate-tiled roof that jutted out like a frown.

'You're not thinking of climbing over this wall and going anywhere near that ugly house, are you?' Nightshade protested as Oakmoss found a foothold on the lowest part of the wall. 'If you ask me, that awful house looks like it was built specifically to resemble some menacing creature. I'd take the message and steer clear if I were you.'

'Yes, but I—' Oakmoss dropped down from his attempt to climb and scratched at the side of his face.

'Whoever thought to put those terrible turrets either side?' went on Nightshade. 'Bad decision. They're like the pointy horns of an evil goblin or a demon. Don't you think?'

'Yes, the turrets,' Oakmoss said. 'They're only there for show. They've got no stairs up to them, you can't even get up to the top.'

Oakmoss kicked at a stone, which instead of being as loose as it looked, was embedded deep in the ground. He hopped around grimacing, holding his toe.

'That was a bit unlucky,' commented Nightshade as she watched him. She blinked twice and peered at him with her big green eyes. 'This is your home, isn't it?'

'Don't worry,' said Oakmoss, squinting up at the glowering house. 'I think Hornbeam Hall looks like an evil face too. At least,' he muttered as he approached the wall again and felt for familiar hand holds, 'you don't have to live here.'

8. IMMINENT DANGER

There was more than one mystery here I'd like to get to the bottom of. But then there usually is when a magical family is involved.

'First, let's talk imminent danger,' I suggested, raw from my narrow escape from Gisborne and Grimalkin. 'Any unpleasant pets I should know about?'

'There's another cat, but she's one you definitely don't need to worry about.'

I'd make my own judgment on that. 'You live here

in this big house and your father's a toymaker?' My whiskers were twitching like antenna picking up an urgent secret signal. Whiskers do that.

On the one hand, you will find your average magical family do tend to keep themselves and their magic secret from the rest of the world. They pass on their magic and their secluded homes with high walls. On the other hand, in my extensive experience, not many people from long-standing magical families choose to make toys.

Oakmoss dusted off his hands after a pretty efficient scramble over the wall.

'My dad's from a long line of sorcerers and inherited this house from my grandfather, but whatever magic Dad inherited is not strong. But it's OK, because he just loves making toys.'

My whiskers were telling me that Oakmoss was one of those rare cases where a family has become resigned to their magical line fading away – then a whole surge of magical energy focuses in one member. I wondered if they even knew.

'What about your mother?' I wanted to know. 'Is she a toymaker too? Who else lives here?'

'Mum runs a charity. And we have help. There's Hyacinth, who cooks. She also sorts out the garden. And she does odd jobs. Trapmole is Dad's apprentice and is keen on anything to do with the workshop.'

'Well at least you're heir to a successful family business. That's pretty lucky.'

'Lucky? Having your future all mapped out?' responded Oakmoss glumly. He suddenly burst into an angry speech. 'Most people don't have a destiny of spending their life churning out horrible black cats to pay for an ugly house that's too big to live in. Having a dad with the lamest job in the world is bad enough for making me stand out at Dogberry Academy. But I'm also the only person posh enough that the cook is sent to bring in my PE kit when I forget it.'

Oakmoss was dragging his heels and prodding at things in the river.

'They've never even tried to encourage you to see if you have magic?'

He shook his head.

This was tough on Oakmoss.

'You don't think they'd want you to use it?'

Another shake of the head.

It was clear he had that sort of natural sorcery that was going to start happening whether he wanted it to or not – and that means trouble. That kind of magic is likely to start exploding out of him and I knew he best start learning how to control it as soon as possible. What you really need when that happens is people around you who understand.

What he didn't need was a mystery over whether someone might be ill-wishing him.

We started to walk up a gentle incline towards the back of the house, approaching like a couple of burglars through the cover of some trees.

'When people learn I've been involved in clearing up high-profile cases involving some very dangerous sorcerers,' I began, 'they always want to know how I do it.'

(If he'd asked, I'd have explained that the key to investigating a magical crime is to treat it the same as any other. You establish facts, you look for motives, narrow the suspects. You sort the truth from the lies and then work out which secrets are important. It takes time and a lot of skill, but luckily I have plenty of both.)

I needed to begin with a question: Who might want to ill-wish Oakmoss? My first suspicions leant towards the trouble on the school bus. Young Oakmoss was marked out as being slightly different. Someone might have found a way to do more than just pick on him.

'You'd be surprised,' I said to Oakmoss, thinking aloud as Hornbeam Hall began to emerge from above a line of trees, 'how often in the very tricky and high-profile cases in which I've been involved, there is often one thing at the root of the crimes.'

'I know what that's called, you're talking motive. People hating one another, I suppose. Covering up murky secrets from the past?'

'I wasn't thinking of that—'

'Power grabs? Evil sorcery? Blackmail, I suppose? Ooh – revenge? I guess there's jealousy, that's a big one. Those love triangle things like our tragic teacher Mrs Bootle and the Scrabble affair – Mr Bootle could have easily turned nasty towards Mr Skinner— Oh, I probably haven't told you about that, have I? That was Veena's big scoop. She's editor of the *Dogberry Academy Times*.'

'Oakmoss, I wasn't thinking you're being targeted with ill-wishing because you were involved in a tragic love affair, even one involving Scrabble.'

'Oh. I hadn't realized you were talking about me.'

We'd arrived at the monstrous rear of Hornbeam Hall. Severe, rambling, imposing, utterly unfriendly were the words that sprang to mind. But however you described it, now we were right outside looking up, its grandeur was impossible to ignore. I waved a paw.

'You, Oakmoss, have something that people

would go to great lengths to get their hands on.'

The unlucky heir to the Hornbeam legacy blinked slowly.

'Money,' I said. 'We are talking *serious* money here, aren't we, Oakmoss? And money's at the root of so many crimes.'

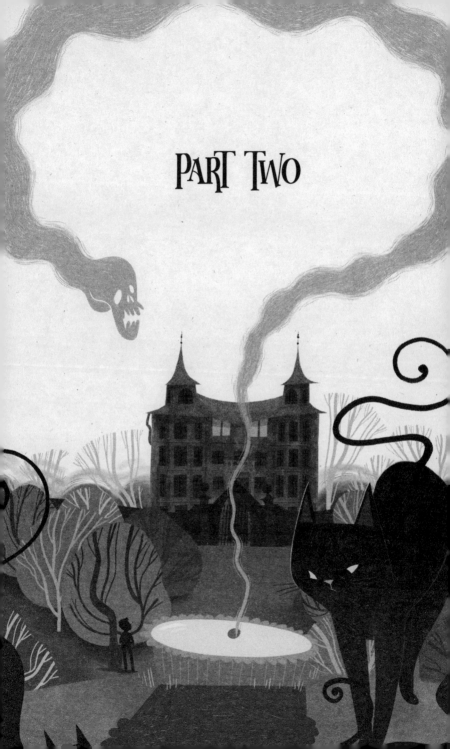

PART TWO

9. A Top-Secret Project

We had approached splendid yet forbidding Hornbeam Hall by nipping over its high wall, going along by the river, looping up a hill and arriving at the back through some trees. We arrived in a courtyard behind the house.

'I wasn't expecting all this,' I said as we wove our way past lorries unloading.

'Yes, that'll be deliveries for RATS,' answered Oakmoss.

'You what?'

'Mum has set up this charity and devotes all her time to raising money.'

'Your mother raises money for rats?'

Oakmoss turned to grin at me. 'It stands for "Rescue All Toys Society". Dad's into making his toys. Mum is planning a toy hospital where toys are repaired and recycled. She thinks it's a great idea to buy some place and turn it into a toy rescue. Tomorrow's a big fundraiser. You might have seen the posters? A fairy-tale gala.'

'That's here?' Magical people tend to be secretive, so it surprised me that the Hornbeams were letting people inside these high grey walls and throwing open the hall's grounds to the public.

'Yep. You can bounce on a fairy-tale castle, win coconuts and there's a prize for the best fancy dress,' said Oakmoss.

There was something else unexpected at the grim grey of the back of the gaunt and unfriendly house. It was softened by an elaborate long room made mostly of windows and light wood, and it was filled with things growing. Pleasingly pretty bits of stained glass scattered rainbows. 'Someone's spent a lot of money on a nice room for plants.'

'Oh, Mum's garden room? Yes, she's forever making changes. She's nuts about these orchids and ferns, things that like the heat and the damp, so had all this built. Gives her an excuse to spend all day in a hot place, I reckon.'

So he had a father who had inherited this house from a long-standing magical family, but whose own magic was weak and who preferred to make profitable toys. Oakmoss's mother was a charity fundraiser who grew orchids, and he had a faintly magical uncle who ran a junk shop. None of this was what I'd expected. But there was even more to interest me in this courtyard.

If you hang around with sorcerers, as I do, you get used to seeing some unusual sights. You learn that if you see something odd, there is very often something magical behind it.

I have spent my whole life around magical folk, but I don't have that thing that's often called a sorcerer's eye, you know – that ability to see when magic is being done. But then very few people do. I very nearly missed something.

To one side of the courtyard you could see a low whitewashed wall, all festooned in rambling roses and one very small wooden door. Most people would think that beyond that whitewashed wall were just trees and beyond them, the very high stone wall that surrounds Hornbeam Hall.

So why was it that every time I tried to look directly at it, my gaze kept swooping away and I found myself fascinated by some pigeons having a nice dirt bath by the kitchen door?

It was if there was some distortion of the air that was making me not want to look closely. I had a strong suspicion what that meant. We are talking glimmers.

A glimmer is a magical method of concealing something. It's not invisibility – that requires extraordinary magical skill, although I don't pretend to understand the science of magic. It's more confusion of the mind. An illusion that convinces people that something is not there.

Or, as in the celebrated Case of the Butterfield Crow (not an investigation I was involved in, but people still talk about it) – it can fool people into thinking something *is* there. In that case a glimmer fooled an entire museum into not noticing a small but valuable gold statue had been removed. MagiCon (that's the magical police service) weren't brought in until the thieves had a three-month head start. Not a case that ended well.

I'd never seen a glimmer as big as this before. Mr Hornbeam might be frowny and forbid magic, but that glimmer meant someone around here possessed some decent magical capabilities. Someone who could also perform an ill-wishing?

I found my thoughts turning to kitchens. Obviously a snack wouldn't be out of the question, and my keen senses could detect the aroma of recent baking in the air. After all, it'd been a busy morning – saving lives, escaping certain death at the jaws of Gisborne and Grimalkin.

But mostly, I wanted to meet the person who made Oakmoss's sandwiches. Because the easiest way to slip someone a spell is to put it into food.

All of this was entirely wiped from my mind, not by confusion magic, but by someone rushing out of the kitchen door with a plate of thick and very richly buttered toast.

Oakmoss was walking towards the kitchen, but watching the dirt-bath pigeons. You didn't need to have magical insight to guess that the unluckiest boy in the world would cannon into the rushing figure at such a pace they both ended up sprawled in the same dirt as the pigeons. Or to predict that the toast would hurtle upwards in one moment of joyous freedom and return to earth. One, two, three, four slices – all butter-side down in the dirt.

10. The Mark of Botched Magic

'Can't you, for once, look where you're going?' snapped toast boy. 'Particularly when you are anywhere near me.' He gave an angry squint at the buttered toast that was now languishing in the dust. But he saved his biggest glare for my new friend.

He looked a little older and bit taller than Oakmoss. It was difficult to be sure, as he was sprawled on the ground, but at least that gave me a good opportunity to inspect him; often all I get to see of people is shoes.

'Oh, hello Trapmole,' said Oakmoss, retrieving his glasses from the dirt and giving them a quick wipe. 'Sorry, Trapmole.'

So this was the apprentice. Trapmole's hair was slicked down over his narrow forehead, and was dark save for a stripe of white to one side of his fringe. That stripe could be there for many reasons, but I know people reckon it's the mark of a witch. I don't think it was a serious attempt to look like a badger. I'd call it the mark of botched magic, because I'd seen it more than once – evidence of a clumsy attempt at a spell that has gone explosively wrong.

Trapmole was trying to grow whiskers, but failed whiskers are not a good look. Humans really don't have a clue what whiskers are actually supposed to do.

Oakmoss crawled forward and made the mistake of handing him back slices of very grimy buttered toast from the dirt. Even a cat would turn up a pink nose at toast that grubby.

Trapmole got to his feet and dusted down his black trousers with a slow and deliberate air. He tossed the toast disdainfully in the direction of the lucky pigeons, who fell on it in a frenzy of grateful pecking.

'Can't you do anything without turning it into a disaster? And why are you not at school again?'

Oakmoss was wearing what could still be identified as a school uniform, but it was torn, and crusted with the remains of tree moss and blood. The crash into Trapmole had sent a recurrence of blood oozing from the cut on his forehead and it had dripped on to his once white shirt.

Instead of offering sympathy, Trapmole's dark little eyes were frowning with intense dislike, reminding me of a few cats I'd got on the wrong side of.

'I had an accident on the way to school,' admitted Oakmoss sheepishly.

'Well, if your dad finds out he won't be pleased,' sighed Trapmole without an iota of concern, even with a hint of glee. He was playing with a chunky ring he wore on his thumb – silver with a heavy skull design. 'You really can't do anything well, can you? Except have accidents.'

Trapmole gave Oakmoss a superior look, which shot the apprentice to the top of my suspicious customers list.

Oakmoss recovered an upright position without a friendly hand up. 'Should I make you some more toast?'

'You'd probably burn it. No one trusts you to do

anything without ruining it. I bet your dad hasn't even told you we're working on a really exciting top-secret project in case you manage to spoil it.' He puffed out his chest and tapped the side of his nose.

'Er, sounds great, Trapmole.'

'Yes, well, what with the visitors tomorrow, your dad has put me in charge of putting in extra security measures. The last thing we want is someone bumbling in where they shouldn't! And I even showed your mum some of our latest developments and, yes, she was amazed. She said how lucky it is your dad chose me to be his apprentice.'

'Mum visited the workshop? Well, that's, er, good, Trapmole,' Oakmoss responded.

'Well, we're all busy-busy, aren't we? All making sure tomorrow makes as much fundraising money as it possibly can. Is Veena coming?'

'Tomorrow? Yep.'

'Does she like lemonade?'

'Lemonade? Yes, I should think so. Why?'

Trapmole tapped the side of his nose again. 'Tell Veena to look out for lemonade. I –' he pointed to himself – 'am in charge of lemonade.'

Trapmole waited, giving Oakmoss a chance to say what he was doing for the charity gala.

'Er, yes, well I've got plans too, of course,' Oakmoss faltered.

The boy might be good at hiding that he was a powerful sorcerer from his family, but he was a pretty poor liar.

11. Pudding

Even before I put a paw inside the house, I could smell that the air was loaded with the dizzying scents of sugar mixed with butter and eggs, fruit and chocolate.

But there was something else I almost missed.

Cat.

Oakmoss saw me pause. 'You really don't need to worry about the other cat. Come on, Hyacinth does the best cherry bakewell pie. Maybe I'll be lucky today and she'll have made one. You do eat pie,

don't you – not just ice cream?'

'I am a cat at my peak. You don't get a physique like mine by just eating ice cream.'

I could have mentioned that, so far, I hadn't eaten any ice cream. But my main objective was to assess this Hyacinth: with her worryingly tempting cakes, she sounded highly suspicious to me. Any cook working for a magical family will surely have at least a hint of witch about her, so she too was already high on my list of suspects for any ill-wishing.

'Oh, catacombs! What happened to you?' A whirlwind with flaming red hair twisted into two long plaits swooped over and enveloped young Oakmoss in a huge hug of concern. 'Double catacombs! You look like someone tried to kill you! And you've brought a new friend for the cats to play with.'

I guessed she was talking about me.

The hug was brave, as the boy was crusted with various remains of accidents.

'Got into a bit of fight with a big branch, Hyacinth. For a moment I thought I was dead, and do you know what I was thinking of?'

Hyacinth shoved Oakmoss into a kitchen chair before bringing out a bottle of a familiar yellow lotion. She made a few quick swipes that brought more wincing from Oakmoss.

'I was thinking that I would never get to eat one of your cherry bakewell pies ever again.'

'You are a kind boy, Oakmoss, but sadly, even to cheer you up, there's no cherry bakewell today. Priority baking is for tomorrow's tea tent.'

She popped a couple of thick slices of white bread into a toaster. Within a short space of time, she delivered two slices of crisp and evenly browned and buttered toast and shoved a jar of honey at Oakmoss. Even better, without having to ask, I got a saucer of milk and a tail of mackerel on the side. On the floor, but I'm used to that.

Hyacinth might be doing a clever job of appearing kindly, being good at cooking and noticing when people needed a hug. But nothing much gets past me, and my superior detective senses said this kitchen could very well be the source of some nasty spells. I was going to keep a careful eye on everything.

A small ball of white fluff hurtled in from somewhere. I turned, mesmerized by startling blue eyes, and in that split second the evil monster snatched that mackerel tail right from under my pink nose. I hardly knew what had happened.

'Hello, Pudding,' greeted Oakmoss, tickling the invading creature under the chin and even rubbing her ears. A shedding of white fluff floated into the still, sultry air and deposited itself slowly on to the kitchen floor as the kitten purred appreciatively. 'Meet your new friend, Nightshade.'

'Please can you get those cats out of the kitchen,' said Hyacinth, as we all watched fluff floating lazily about the room. She gestured at a tower of cake tins in the middle of a long table and fruit scones racked and cooling alongside a plate of miniature pastries. 'I'm still baking.'

Pudding looked up at Hyacinth, giving the big old eyes (all cats know that trick, but she was pretty good at it). She even added a very convincing piteous miaow and Hyacinth fell for it. She slid a second bowl right in the farthest corner and I lunged at it, determined to get there before the annoying fluffball this time.

'Do make sure your new cat lets Pudding have a chance of some food,' said Hyacinth.

Pretty rich. So far, I hadn't got my jaws around anything. I gave the cook a disdainful look and that annoying cloud Pudding did it again – swiped the best piece of fish.

You get used to unusual things happening when you hang around with sorcerers. You get used to expecting the unexpected and today had been exhaustingly full of it.

But even in that day of expecting the unexpected, nothing could have prepared me for what happened next. There is no easy way to say it, so I'll say it quickly.

Humpty Dumpty walked into the kitchen.

And I quite forgot to fight Pudding for my mackerel tail.

12. YOU CAN'T POSSIBLY WEAR THAT

An egg, human-sized, with a face and wearing short, red tartan trousers took a step further into the kitchen, waggling his hands in an excited manner.

Oakmoss halted his piece of well-buttered toast just short of his mouth. 'Dad?'

The curved side of the egg clipped a rack of scones. Hyacinth had to do an impressive dive to save them.

Humpty Dumpty attempted to swivel to see what

was going on and Hyacinth shouted at him to keep still. 'Sir,' she added quickly, moving a precarious plate out of the way. 'Is this your costume for the gala?'

'You think I'm dressed as an egg for fun, Privet?' said Mr Hornbeam.

He edged as close to the table as he could manage, reaching for a pastry on a plate, but in the costume his arms were only half their usual length and he couldn't make it. Sweat was starting to creep down his face.

Behind him, a substantial woman in an insubstantial and very gaudy orange swimsuit tottered in on high heels.

'Mum?'

She was carrying a long, silvery fish tail of sequins over one arm and had a tower of dark hair studded with little shining fish and sparkling seashells. She struck a pose. 'And this is mine.'

'Are you both trying to kill me?' said Oakmoss, his voice coming out unnaturally high. 'Because I am going to die of embarrassment if these are costumes you are seriously suggesting wearing in public for the fancy-dress gala. Just kill me now before anyone discovers my parents are actually Humpty Dumpty and . . .' He paused and addressed his mother. 'And a monster of the deep?'

Mrs Hornbeam patted at her hair with a plump hand heavy with rings. 'The Little Mermaid,' she answered a little stiffly.

'If anyone around here is going to die, it'll be me,' groaned Mr Hornbeam. 'I'm going to starve. Adeline, can you help?'

Mrs Hornbeam tottered across the kitchen in her high heels, her fishy tail slithering behind. How she did not trip was beyond me. She put her husband out of his misery by popping a custard tart straight into his mouth, the sparkly jewellery at her fingers and wrists twinkling. 'You can't wear that costume, sugar plum.'

'Thank goodness, someone is talking sense,' glowered Oakmoss.

'True, I might boil. Boil – geddit? That was a dad joke.'

'You're a nursery rhyme, honey pie. You're a nursery rhyme and the theme is fairy tales.'

Oakmoss was gripping the table and his voice came out a little strangled. 'So the only reason you are thinking it may not be a great idea for Dad to go out dressed like a giant egg in public, wearing the most ridiculous tartan shorts, is because he's a nursery rhyme character when he's supposed to be a fairy tale?'

'Oakmoss, have you got a black eye?'

Oakmoss hunkered down in his seat, head low, and rather than answer he took a bite of toast slathered with butter and a comforting, thick layer of honey, chewing carefully so as not to reactivate the blood from his split lip.

'Have you been in a fight?'

'Only with a tree,' answered Oakmoss. 'I missed the school bus.'

Adeline sighed and fed a second custard tart to her husband, who had got himself wedged between the table and the wall. 'Well then, you can help – I'm not having you swanning off, going on about pigeons nesting.'

'It's kingfishers.'

'I've been so busy getting my costume just right I am exhausted. Tomorrow is all about the costumes.'

'I thought it was all about the fundraising,' muttered Oakmoss.

'This RATS gala is nothing but trouble,' grumbled Dad.

'Don't call it RATS,' said Adeline with a thin smile, plonking herself heavily on the chair next to Oakmoss and pulling the rack of scones towards her. 'When did these chairs get so uncomfortable? Erasmus can have these. We need new ones.'

Hyacinth slid a cup of frothy coffee towards her and the scones further away from her in the same movement.

'How many scones do we have for the tea tent, Privet?' asked Adeline, helping herself to one with a dimpled arm before Hyacinth could quite put them out of reach.

'One hundred and thirty-two,' Hyacinth announced proudly.

'One less than that, Privet!' giggled Dad. 'Two less if I can reach!' He rocked forward.

'Well, that's not nearly enough!' said Adeline, reaching for a knife and cutting her scone deftly in two. She bit into it as Hyacinth muttered about being busy with a lot of post. Adeline shifted aside a black fortune cat that was lurking behind the tower of cake tins. It was the second one I'd seen since stepping inside the house. Were they following me around?

'It's for the children, Privet. We must only think of the children. I haven't even visited my orchids today.' Adeline twitched her mermaid tail out of the reach of Pudding, who was following it with a keen intensity, swiping a claw at it every now and again. 'And we must get these cats out of the kitchen. Where did that one even come from?'

She was fixing me with a less-than-friendly look. I gave her the big old eyes and a seriously loud purr that is always guaranteed to work.

'Post?' Adeline stirred two spoons of sugar into her coffee, but was still watching me with suspicion, so slopped some on to the floor.

'A sack full. Some lovely letters from children desperate to find out when they can send their broken toys to the new toy repair hospital,' answered Hyacinth. 'They're hoping it's soon.'

Adeline clasped her hands together. 'For the dear children. Anything else?' She raised a thin eyebrow.

'Donations. I've put them in the usual place.'

'And what have you done towards the fundraising?' Adeline's quizzical gaze turned to Oakmoss. I kept myself out of the way under the table.

'If you and Dad are dressing up, I will be hiding in my room, because I will be toast, I will literally be mincemeat, if I ever face the Dogberry Academy bus ever again if anyone sees you dressed like that.'

'Silly! Dear heart, nobody eats mincemeat on toast,' replied Adeline, evidently not having really listened to her son's fears about the bus. 'How about a fishing competition, Oakie – that might bring in a few donations.' She leant in closer, her eyebrows drawing together and her eyes and lips narrowing.

'These custard tarts aren't my favourite, Privet,' Dad said to the empty plate. 'I prefer a cream slice. We are having cream slices for dinner, aren't we?'

'I can teach people to fish. If you promise to ditch the costumes,' said Oakmoss, sounding desperate.

'A fishing competition,' insisted Mum, stirring her coffee.

'If you lose the costumes.'

'This egg's no good,' declared Mr Hornbeam. 'I'm so hot you could fry an egg on me.' He stretched up and removed the entire costume. It appeared to be made of some sort of light foam and came off in one go, just leaving the oversized tartan shorts and his own tummy, which was still round.

'What *are* we having for dinner tonight? I want something really special to celebrate this wonderful gala,' said Adeline. 'It's so unfair of you to leave these in front of me, Privet.' She twirled the plate of scones. 'Isn't there any cream and jam?'

'Maybe we could have fish and chips from Frying Tonight and give Hyacinth a night off,' suggested Oakmoss.

'Fish and chips! Privet'll think you don't appreciate her delicious dinners!' Adeline lifted her entire tower of dark, fish-studded hair, revealing her own cropped blonde hair underneath. She placed the hair on the table.

'I'm simply exhausted even thinking about tomorrow. I may have to go for a lie-down.' She moved her cup, leaving a dark ring on the table, and rose. 'I'll be in the garden room. I must not neglect my orchids. Dinner at six, Privet?'

'Well, if . . . I can – yes, of course. A special dinner. By six.'

13. WARNING: DEEP WATER

Oakmoss had to prod the cat awake.

She'd leapt straight on to his narrow bed and had been asleep the whole time he'd been taking a shower and putting his school uniform in the bin and wondering if there was any chance of there being something other than simply bad luck at the bottom of all his accidents.

He arranged the books from his uncle on a shelf in a nook under the eaves, worrying about what Nightshade had said – that a spell would most likely

be in something he wore or something he ate. It put any ill-wishing uncomfortably close to home.

Nightshade finally moved into a very slow stretch and clawed at Oakmoss's bed covers. Her hackles were suddenly bristling in a line all along her back as her big green eyes met a fortune cat's unblinking ones.

'I think this is following us around,' she said disdainfully, batting at the toy that sat on the bedside table alongside a stack of spare glasses. 'Is it haunted?'

'Nah, we've just got a lot of them. They're everywhere.'

Oakmoss tried to fuss her ears, but she padded to the window and stuck her pink nose out curiously. There was a tree just outside the window with a wide branch that grew almost inside the room.

'This room is nice. Your parents seem nice,' said Nightshade.

'I guess by nice you mean weird and eccentric?'

'I'm sure most children think that about their parents. This is where you fell from?' she asked. 'It's a long way down.'

'Yeah, I was just fixing a bird box under the eaves. This is the best room in the house, as I can use that tree to go in and out really easily. It's such a faff going down all the stairs.'

Plus, he was woken by birdsong every morning. And sometimes he could sit here and enjoy a view right over the long grim grey wall. He could see the peeping rooftops of all the other houses in Dogberry and he would wonder what life was like for the people who didn't live in houses where you couldn't even hear if anyone was even in. Where you didn't have Hyacinth Privet to make your meals and wash your clothes.

'Anyway, ready to go? I've got something to show you.' He pocketed the bird book and the bag of zingtascos, swung himself over the windowsill and on to the broad branch, Nightshade following him effortlessly as they climbed to the ground.

Oakmoss took a winding route that avoided the courtyard and went along the slow-moving River Dogberry until it drifted into the still greenness of Dogberry Lake.

'This is my favourite place in the whole world.' He gestured to a small building almost hidden beneath trees leaning towards the water, branches stretching as if to conceal it from prying eyes. 'I don't show many people. What do you think?'

Nightshade was a little slow to reply as they both stared at the rickety shack nestling in the dappled shade of big leafy trees. 'This is your favourite place?' she said eventually, lifting a paw. 'A shed on sticks?'

'It's a boathouse. It's got a boat and everything.' The boathouse did look a little like it was magically suspended over the water, as the legs were spindly and worn away to almost nothing. Oakmoss was actually a bit relieved to find it still here after that terrible wind this morning. Above, the skies were now clear and blue.

'One of the previous Hornbeams must have liked fishing. I probably take after some great-grandfather Hornbeam or something. No one ever uses it except me.'

'Can't imagine why.' Nightshade gestured a paw at a hand-painted sign:

Warning: DEEP water. No fishing. No swimming.
No boats and Definitely NO DIVING.
PRIVATE
YOU SHOULD'T BE HERE ANYWAY
Can't you read? This is DANGEROUS!

'For someone struck by some sort of ill-wishing, maybe this shack isn't the safest place to hang around,' Nightshade said, following Oakmoss into the boathouse gingerly, as if each step might make the whole building give way.

'I can't think why anyone would want to ill-wish me. I've always been a little clumsy, so it almost doesn't seem worth their while.'

'That's what we need to investigate. Does the badger-boy with the toast—'

'Trapmole.'

'Could he be ill-wishing you? Or do you think the woman who makes the perfect pies is more likely?'

'Why are you so convinced someone is out to get me? I guess, Trapmole . . . he is always looking for improvements, ways to make more money, to impress Dad. I think one of the improvements he'd like to make is to get me out of the way. Otherwise, I'm supposed to take over when I leave school.'

'Hmm. I've not ruled out the not-very-friendly crowd on the bus either. And just because someone bakes you delicious desserts doesn't mean they're not a suspect. And please tell me someone under an ill-wishing is not planning to take that hunk of rotting wood on to the lake?'

'The rowing boat is safe enough,' Oakmoss responded stiffly as Nightshade poked at it carefully with her paw. 'But we can fish from the veranda if you prefer.' He was rummaging in a stash of fishing gear in a corner of the boathouse, which also contained a good few snacks.

'So safe that the boat's got a bucket under the seat,' replied Nightshade drily. 'Is that so you can make sure the water is going out faster than it comes in? If you take that on to the lake, you're braver than most.'

Oakmoss grabbed what he needed and headed on to the veranda that ran around the outside of the boathouse. His foot landed on a slippery piece of green weed and he only saved himself from plunging into the green depths by clinging on to a fragile handrail.

'See, didn't fall in – you are still bringing me good luck.'

Nightshade dipped a paw in the water's edge before risking following him on to the wobbly veranda. 'So is this where you're running your fishing competition tomorrow?'

'You don't think anyone's actually going to want to do fishing at the fairy-tale gala, do you?' he sighed. 'It won't be popular, will it?'

'Let's hope not,' said Nightshade. 'When fund-raising for a children's toy charity, it's not great if a child falls into the lake.' She finally stopped her disdainful padding about and found a place to park her bottom.

Oakmoss ignored her grumbling. Nothing could stop him loving the way the boathouse nestled into the trees, and the way its veranda jutted out to where the water was surprisingly deep. It was sheltered, so he could sit here even when it was nippy. He could fish. Or just watch the birds flitting, bobbing and diving, and listen to them calling to one another.

'Do you catch anything? I mean apart from weed, which is tasty only if you're a duck. I can't remember the last time I had a freshly caught fish for my supper. Anything to do with fish is fine by me. Particularly if I get to eat them.'

'Sometimes.'

Oakmoss dangled his legs and Nightshade tucked her paws beneath her. Her ears twitched as they watched the small orange float on the end of Oakmoss's fishing line bobbing on the surface of the water. Oakmoss wedged the rod into a gap between two of the veranda boards and started gesturing idly with his hands.

It was all pretty peaceful, until Nightshade ruined it by asking: 'Why don't you want your family to know what a good sorcerer you are?'

'I'm really not a—'

'Well, you've been turning leaves into winged creatures and sending them skidding across the lake for the last ten minutes. That's an advanced spell.

How do you know how to do that?'

Oakmoss shrugged. 'I really don't know, it just happens.'

'That is exactly the trouble with untrained magic.'

'I . . .' Oakmoss didn't know what to say, so instead he checked his bait – a little piece of bread and a chunk of sweetcorn – and cast his line again. There was a sudden flash of electric blue and Oakmoss pointed. 'Kingfisher!'

He dived into the boathouse again and reappeared with binoculars, then rummaged in his pocket for the bird book he'd seized from his uncle's. 'I want to find out more about them. They like high banks to nest in, just like here.'

'If I have a superpower,' began Nightshade, steadily washing a paw, 'and I am a cat, so I mean in addition to the climbing, the claws, the whiskers, the super-senses, the ability to nap on demand and in places you humans don't even expect—'

'And the incessant talking.'

'—it's that I am an amazing detective. So, tell me about your friend Veena.'

'Veena definitely doesn't want to hurt me.'

'You say that, but funnily enough, when you investigate a crime, it very often turns out to be the person you least suspect.'

'Veena would never do anything bad; she has principles. She's editor of the *Dogberry Academy Times*. The school tries to take a hard line, says people only want to read about sporting fixtures and exam success. But I don't think that can be right, as circulation soared when Veena ran an exposé revealing that Mr Skinner and Mrs Bootle were dying for love of each other and were meeting for secret lunchtime games of Scrabble.'

'That doesn't seem very smart.'

'Oh, you're wrong there – Veena's really smart. They told her there were ramifications when you print that sort of news. Veena's the sort of girl who didn't even have to look up what "ramifications" meant. She explained it meant Mrs Bootle transferring to another school. Veena even manages to dodge the school banter as everyone's pretty terrified they're going to make the next front page.'

'I was actually thinking more of you having a determined and inquisitive best friend who wants to make her name as a news reporter when you are secretly a powerful sorcerer from an ancient magical family.'

'Well, she's never going to find out, is she?' He didn't even bother to argue the powerful sorcerer bit.

'Oakmoss Hornbeam!' called a voice. 'How dare you abandon me on the bus *again*. And who *exactly* are you talking to?'

14. ELEPHANTS DON'T USE PLATES

Veena Vale could spend the whole of a sweaty day at school and look just as cool and neat at the end as she had at the beginning. She would grow up to be one of those people who could karate-kick six bad guys out of the way and arrive on the terrace unruffled and equally ready for cocktails or tennis.

Oakmoss thought he would grow up to be the person people muttered about in worried tones and wanted to keep an eye on.

'Yeah, well, things nearly got a bit tragic this

morning,' said Oakmoss, giving an experimental grin and wondering just how mad Veena was. 'I was just talking to myself. And I'm really sorry about abandoning you.'

He got his apology in quickly. Veena always thought people should be honourable and interested in things like truth and justice. It meant she was constantly disappointed, particularly going to Dogberry Academy.

'You don't look tragic. Looks like you've had a fun day fishing.' She pointed an accusing finger at him. *Very mad, then.*

He should have asked Nightshade if he could let Veena in on the secret that he had today made friends with a talking cat. He longed to share that with her, and his other secrets.

How did you go about breaking the news that you were a sorcerer?

She was his best friend, and you shouldn't have secrets from best friends. They tend to notice. Particularly Veena, who noticed everything, Nightshade was right about that. Best friends like Veena tend to start wondering exactly what you're not sharing. And then they might decide to go off and be friends with someone else who trusts them.

At least she trusted him enough to join him on

the unsteady veranda and squeezed herself between him and Nightshade. 'Did you know you've got a cat following you? She's very black, except for her pink nose, which is the only thing that gives away that she's not actually just your shadow.' She tickled Nightshade under the chin, who responded with an indignant look with her green eyes.

'This is Nightshade – she's a nice cat. Not like Gisborne and Grimalkin. And she saved my life when I had an accident on the way to school.'

'Yeah, right.' Veena rolled her eyes. 'Like cats do that. If I put that on my front page no one would even believe it.'

Oakmoss dug around in his pocket for the liquorice wheels he had bought at Marge's. He had the last of the zingtascos gifted by Erasmus. And he had the best of the boathouse biscuit stash. Veena must be feeling brave, as she looked at the choice he offered and took one of Uncle Erasmus's home-made bright purple zingtascos.

'Don't crunch it,' warned Oakmoss as she peered at it curiously and then popped it into her mouth. He was alarmed when her face took on an expression as if the sweet had just exploded. Her eyes watered. She spat it into the lake.

'Well, that was a mistake. Give me one of those

liquorice wheels quickly.' Her face resettled itself as she chewed. 'So, you had an accident on the way to school. What was it this time?'

'A tree really had it in for me. I might have died, only Nightshade was there and noticed and just in time she shouted—'

'Nightshade *what*?'

Oakmoss pocketed the zingtascos and crunched a ginger nut. 'What I meant to say is, she's my lucky charm.'

Veena looked at Nightshade with a forensic and sceptical gaze. 'She looks like those hideous fortune cats your dad makes.'

Nightshade gave a low hiss.

'You could really do with one. You'd need a really good lucky charm. You've had more accidents than an elephant balancing plates on his head.'

'That's just silly – elephants don't use plates,' said Oakmoss. 'Hey, how does an elephant ask for a cream cake?' he asked, offering the liquorice again.

Veena shrugged and Oakmoss waggled his arm in front of his face like a trunk and said, 'Can I have a cream cake, please?'

Veena grinned. Her nose crinkled and transformed her face when she smiled. 'Your jokes are so lame.'

'All the best jokes are lame.'

'So you keep telling me. I still say that's just you not facing up to the fact you need better material.'

Oakmoss couldn't help grinning too, knowing Veena joking with him meant he was forgiven for abandoning her to the Flan and the gang on the bus, and to a day at school without him. 'Let's go out in the boat,' he suggested.

'Hmm. An offer to go out in that boat with the unluckiest boy in the world. I am never doing that. Anyway, we've got work to do. You do know you've got an angry man on your doorstep hurling accusations around? I want to ask him for an exclusive interview.'

Oakmoss pulled a face. He passed her the binoculars and helped himself to another ginger nut. 'I think I've worked out where the kingfishers are nesting.'

'I don't think that's good enough for the front page.'

'Kingfishers nesting is amazing! Sometimes you've got to tell people why something's amazing. All Mustard's done is pitched a tent.'

'Yes, but he's done it right outside Hornbeam Hall! That's something we really don't want to miss!' Veena was getting to her feet. 'Even the Flan's taking bets on how long he's going to be camping for.'

'Bets?' echoed Oakmoss hollowly. 'How long are people betting he's going to stay?'

'I believe the best odds are for anything over three weeks.'

'Three weeks!' Oakmoss nearly spat out the ginger nut. 'I don't think I can cope with the thought of an angry man hanging outside my house for weeks. You're always telling me I'm unlucky, Veena. Well, just to warn you, this may be a sign my bad luck might be spreading.'

'I don't think bad luck can spread,' Veena said matter-of-factly. She was getting ready, taking out her notebook and a smart and shiny red pen. She beamed. 'Although that would make a good story. Whichever I go with, it's going to make a great front page!'

'No, Veena!' Oakmoss felt a rare spike of anger, as if something was starting to boil inside of him. 'I know all about truth and justice. But you can't put something horrible happening to my family on the front page.'

'I can't help the fact it's happening to your family,' responded Veena in a small voice. 'That's the trouble with the truth, you really can't just ignore it because it's happening to someone you like. That's not how truth works.'

Oakmoss tried to calm himself. This wasn't the first time he'd had this strange churning feeling inside and he was sure it was magic threatening to explode out of him. It was a reminder that Oakmoss felt his calamitous accidents were not a result of ill-wishing by anyone else, but a reminder that hidden magic could be dangerous. And he needed to keep it under control, even though keeping it squashed down was getting harder and harder to do.

He felt a claw in his leg. Nightshade miaowed and pawed at him. Oakmoss looked right into the cat's green eyes, grateful for the distraction.

Then Oakmoss heard the smallest, pitiful miaow. 'Ah, Veena, look what's behind you!' he said, pointing.

Veena put her hands on her hips and was about to speak, when fluffball Pudding started rubbing around her leg.

'Oh, what a beautiful kitten.' She immediately crouched to pet it. 'Where did you spring from?' She stroked and fussed over Pudding, getting white fur all over her jeans. The arrival of the world's cutest cat distracted Veena, but only for a minute. 'I need something for the front page. People are relying on me to break the next big story.'

'Not Mr Mustard!' Oakmoss felt his anger return. 'Imagine the Flan's jokes on the school bus if Mustard's demands for his money back for a fortune cat go on the front page.'

Veena glowered and was not backing down. 'Everyone was talking about it at school today. If I ignore it everyone'll know it's because we're friends and I suppressed the news. You can't ask me to do that. I have to investigate.'

'If we're friends, I wouldn't have to ask.'

'Fine. You don't have to help me. I'll go on my own.'

'Give me your lucky pen and that notebook.' Oakmoss made a grab for it, but she snatched it out of his way. They tussled until he cried out and put a bloodied finger in his mouth. 'Paper cut!'

'If you get blood all over my notebook and lucky pen, I'll never speak to you again.'

'And if you put my family on the front page, I'll never speak to *you* again. You'll be on the Dogberry Academy bus facing the Flan alone FOR EVER!'

Oakmoss felt rage like boiling liquid about to explode inside of him and he shoved her aside in his desperation to get away. He went into the welcome dim and damp gloom of the boathouse, gulping down deep breaths.

He made a futile effort to slam the door behind him, but it closed with an unsatisfying soft and saggy whump and swung open again, revealing that Night-shade had padded in after him.

He really was the unluckiest boy in the world, there was no doubt about it.

There was an ominous creak. He looked to see where it was coming from.

He looked down and heard Nightshade yell: 'Look out!' for the second time that day. 'Look DOWN!'

With a splintering crack, the boards gave way beneath him and for the second time Nightshade's warning was too late.

He plunged into the depths of the cold green lake, weed tangling around his limbs. He struggled in vain as the water closed over his head and the weeds clung to him like watery fingers that wanted to keep him there for ever.

15. NO POINT PRETENDING

'Oakmoss!' Veena screamed. She raced inside the boathouse and threw herself full-length along the planks, her nose almost touching the scummy water.

I sidled up and dipped my own pink nose towards the water. The surface was still, not even a ripple to show it had swallowed up my new friend moments ago.

I was cursing myself. I was supposed to be protecting my doomed twin of destiny and this omen could

have been literally read by anyone – there was a huge sign warning this water was dangerous and deep. Why had I not insisted we stay away?

Veena's gaze alighted on me, but there is one thing cats are famous for that's actually true – we're not good around water. I wish I'd asked if Oakmoss could swim, because there was nothing I could do except peer hopefully at the water beneath the splintered edge of the floorboards and keep hoping something would surface. And he was gone so long. So long that I almost jumped in after him with no thought for my fur.

Then a jet of water spouted upwards like a geyser, and bouncing on the top, riding the spray like a partying mermaid, was young Oakmoss. He was covered in weed and dirt and he'd lost his glasses, but he was alive!

He managed to control the water, did a shimmy like he was surfing, and crash-landed with a thump. He lay there gasping, while Veena pulled away the tangles of stinking weed around his legs, arms and neck.

'Oakmoss! You're alive!' said Veena. I thought she was going to cry. Then I thought she was going in for a hug, but backed off at the last second. He really was filthy and smelly.

He coughed up a bit of green water. 'I'm OK.'

Veena rummaged in Oakmoss's emergency stash and found a moth-eaten red tartan rug which she threw around him. I think he'd been hoping for a biscuit.

Jettisoning himself out of the water was a use of rudimentary magic I hadn't seen before. But I was positive that if Oakmoss Hornbeam hadn't been able to summon his magic, then he wouldn't be lying on the floor of the boathouse covered in rotting weed and gasping like a fish. He'd be at the bottom of the slimy lake. I'd been right here and I'd let it happen. I'd known there was something more than simple bad luck behind all Oakmoss's accidents.

Then I felt Veena's gaze turn to me. 'Your cat –' she said, her eyes narrowing unpleasantly – 'she spoke. She shouted a warning. Is that what you meant when you said she saved your life before?'

'You probably imagined it,' said Oakmoss, hiding under the rug.

'It was clear as anything,' said Veena, folding her arms in a way that told me we weren't going to get away with this.

'You can talk. Cats can talk? All cats?' Veena said to me, slowly reaching for her lucky pen like it was a weapon. 'Or just you?'

I said nothing. A bit late for that, I realized.

Oakmoss busied himself pouring dirty water out of his shoes.

Veena's dark eyes looked deep into mine. 'Are you part of a science experiment gone wrong? Have you escaped from some underground laboratory?' She was talking to me slowly and clearly, as if I was hard of hearing. Her pen was poised.

I said nothing, but my hackles started to rise.

'I think maybe it was just a dream,' Oakmoss tried lamely. Underneath his blanket he was subtly using magic to dry himself. Not the best timing, with someone like Veena around.

But then someone like Veena was going to work things out sooner rather than later and I had a feeling she might take it better if we explained things to her first. Oakmoss needed a friend he could talk to, and not just his uncle, not just me. Someone he could confide in. Someone who was on his side at school. But someone who also knew about magic. Plus, clearly, the boy was in serious danger.

'Or are you an alien who's come to Earth disguised as a cat? Is it because cats have such an easy time of it?'

I could see why she wanted to be a writer. She had the imagination for it.

'You have to let me know how you can speak, else I may have to kill you.'

I didn't like to point out that this threat wasn't based on very sound logic, plus I felt she'd probably follow through on it. I'd known the girl only a matter of minutes, yet she struck me as the sort who wouldn't let it drop until she found out the truth.

'You try never saying a word the whole time. It's really difficult, you know, especially when someone's in danger.' I settled down on the warm boards and crossed my paws. 'I was kind of hoping you'd just overlook it.'

'Overlook a talking cat!' Veena's response was so loud it hurt my ears. She knelt down so she could look me directly in the eyes. 'I've got so many questions I don't even know where to start. I've never interviewed a cat before. Is it just you?'

'I cannot speak for the entire feline population, but my guess is yes. Well, have you ever met a talking cat before?'

Her face told me she was having several inner struggles. I could tell she was trying to work it out, didn't believe this was happening, was looking for the trick.

'I'm still fine!' came a small voice from behind us. 'I could do with a biscuit.'

Pudding sneaked under the blanket. I was happy to leave her to the job of comforting Oakmoss. She could get her fur all wet and mucky.

'Can we do this later? Oakmoss could do with one of those hot sugary drinks and a piece of toast.'

'I don't think a cat who can speak can wait – this is the big-time. The name Veena Vale is going to be known everywhere. You have to tell me everything.'

'I doubt we've got time for that.'

'I've just had another brush with death,' Oakmoss said from underneath his blanket, teeth chattering. 'I lost my glasses.'

'What a surprise,' said Veena, without taking her eyes from me. 'Nightshade, I can get you interviews. I can get you television. Talk shows. Stardom. Maybe even a film deal.' She almost squeaked with delight.

I unsheathed my claws and started to clean them. 'The thing is, Veena, I'm going to have to swear you to secrecy before I tell you anything. If you reveal I can talk, you might be endangering all sorts of people.'

'What people? I can't be part of a cover-up. This is something the world needs to know.'

'It really isn't.'

'I'm offering you fame and fortune.' She was

writing down everything with a deep and furious intensity.

'I'm offering you the truth. Although ... what was that about a film deal? No. you're right, this can't wait. Not if we want to protect Oakmoss. He's in serious danger. But journalists are bound by secrecy of their confidential sources and such, aren't they?' I wasn't sure, but it sounded right. 'I can tell you, but only if you promise that you never print a word.'

Veena's pen stopped scribbling. 'Truly? That's the deal? This is a monumental decision,' she said, biting the end of her pen and beginning to pace, making the floorboards creak menacingly. 'I find out, but have to keep the secret? There's no news story, no film deal, no future career?' She stopped chewing her pen and gave me a penetrating look. 'And it involves Oakmoss?'

'Veena, you're Oakmoss's best friend and you need to know this.'

'All right, what's the truth?'

'I only discovered it recently myself. The truth is, I can talk because I was hit by a rogue speaking spell by a sloppy witch when I was a kitten.'

Here they came. The questions.

'*Spell?* So the secret I have to keep – the one that has put Oakmoss in danger – is magic?'

16. EXPECTING MIRACLES

Veena was looking at me, her dark intelligent eyes widening with quiet disbelief. 'Whoa, that's . . . that *is* what you are telling me, right? Magic is real?'

I looked towards Oakmoss, who was still in hiding under the blanket – I was getting no help whatsoever from him. I had a feeling he was still using magic to dry himself.

'Yes, but so incredibly rare that sorcerers are utterly secret about it. I mean, at one time, sorcerers were common, often called the cunning folk; the

people you went to for a good-luck charm or cures if you were sick. People stopped believing, so there's not much call for it these days. Today's sorcerers tend to keep a very low profile.'

Veena began to tap an irritated foot on the soggy floorboard. 'This is a deal as rotten as these floorboards – I get the inside track on magic, but I can't shout about it?'

'I wouldn't bounce up and down quite so much after what happened to Oakmoss,' I advised.

Veena stopped tapping and quickly stepped to a drier patch of floor. 'But . . . sorcery . . . witches are real? I have *so* many questions.'

'I think we might have to limit how many more questions I can take. I've done my best to answer.'

'I think you'll find so far it's been one main question and some supplementary questions, because your answers so far are lousy. I want proper answers. I can't believe I am uncovering the best news story of my career and I'm agreeing not to print it.'

I settled in one of the dry corners where the sun was shining, the warmest bit of the shack. It's a cat thing.

'Sorcery has dwindled so much that if you try to print that it's still around, you'll probably find that people will just accuse you of making it up.'

Veena's eyebrows shot up so far I thought they were going to launch off the top of her head. 'You're saying if I try to break the news on magic, instead of seeing the name Veena Vale on billboards around the world, I'll sound like Mr Mustard who's raving outside Oakmoss's front door?'

'Exactly. I'm saving you from the embarrassment, really.'

'Mustard just wants a refund for a fortune cat.' Oakmoss had finally finished drying himself and emerged from under the blanket. He was now rummaging among the fishing rods at the back. He managed to produce a fresh pair of glasses and an untouched packet of something that might be chocolatey and might be coming my way.

Veena came up really close and bent down to my level, eyeball to eyeball. 'So you're magic. Can you fly?'

'Fly? I'm a cat. Surely that's even less likely than my being able to talk or play the piano. But you see, here is where magic gets complicated. Technically, you might call me magical, but I can't do any magic. And flying is a very advanced form of sorcery.'

'But possible?'

'Possible, yes. Likely – no.'

'But making cats speak is easy?' Her dark eyes

were lasering into mine. It was difficult for me to look away. 'That happened by accident. So there are experienced wizard people who can do things like ... turn pennies into gold?'

'They prefer to be called sorcerers. And why do people always think magic can do things like that? That's advanced transformational magic, less magic, more miracle. The last thing magical folk need is people seeking them out thinking they can force them to do miracles.'

I'd got to my feet and I knew Veena was thinking I was trying to slink away from her questions because as I padded softly towards the door, she told me she had tonnes more.

'So how many people are sorcerers?' she asked.

'Not many.'

'Vague answer.'

'Yes. Sorry.'

'Levitating this pen? Easy or advanced?'

'Middling.'

She looked at her pen. 'Speed writing?'

'Seriously advanced.'

'So most magical people can't even make a pen fly? What's usual in magic?'

'It depends on your natural magical affinity, and the amount of training you can be bothered to do. I guess even a novice with poor magic could learn to do a basic curing spell, or maybe to shut a door.'

'People need magic to shut a door?!'

I shrugged, which is actually difficult for a cat. 'I'm not saying magic is always useful.'

My ears had tuned in to a small scratching outside.

Were we being spied upon? Oakmoss wasn't the only one in danger around here. I'd been chased halfway around Dogberry and I wouldn't forget that in a hurry. I sniffed the air.

Pudding gave a very loud miaow right in my ear that stopped me hearing anything. The Hornbeams really had a poor selection of cats.

I risked getting my nose bloodied by sticking it outside. But no one was there.

'Today's sorcerers keep their magic a secret not just because it's so incredibly rare, but because it's also incredibly difficult to master,' I went on. 'Magical people can't all just conjure fire or something with a click of their fingers. It's hard work.'

'Nightshade is absolutely right about everything, you should listen to her,' said Oakmoss.

It turned out I could not have picked a worse example, because as Veena and I turned to Oakmoss as he spoke, it was quite obvious he was cradling a small flame in the palm of his hand and using it to dry his socks.

'No!' Veena looked at me and then at Oakmoss. 'The reason Oakmoss knows a magical talking cat is ... Oakmoss is in danger because ...' She stared – a full-on stare with a wide-open mouth and a slackened jaw. 'Oakmoss isn't . . . Oakmoss . . . No! Oakmoss isn't magical. He can't be!'

17. A GRILLING

Oakmoss was trying and failing to open a fresh packet of biscuits, eventually resorting to tearing the packet with his teeth. He felt Veena looking at him in disbelief. He wished he'd prepared for the moment his secret was out. He wished it wasn't a moment he finally got the biscuits open and several shot on to the floor.

'The question,' said Nightshade, who had been doing a brilliant job of explaining, 'is not whether Oakmoss is an incredible sorcerer, but whether

someone is ill-wishing him. His accidents have got serious.'

Veena started tapping an impatient foot on the wooden floor again. 'That's just Oakmoss.'

'That's what *I* said,' Oakmoss said slowly as he picked up the biscuits and handed them around. Veena and Nightshade shook their heads. Oakmoss bit into one. 'I don't think I want to be magical. What use is magic? Makes you feel weird inside and having to keep all the secrets is hard work,' he said, chewing a fresh ginger nut carefully. A new packet always meant extra crunch.

'I'll grow up even more of a loner with no friends; someone who retreats further and further into themselves, living in one room and only eating cereal.' He realized Veena and Nightshade were staring silently at him and shrugged. 'Well, probably,' he finished.

'You can actually curse someone with, like, bad luck, or a *hex*?' asked Veena, reaching for the right word and sounding scathing and far from convinced.

Nightshade lazily speared a leaf that was fluttering past with her claw. 'There are rules about how and when sorcerers can use magic. A spell like the one I suspect Oakmoss is under is pretty serious stuff.'

'You use banned magic and there are punishments,' said Oakmoss. 'Nightshade reckons my accidents might be because someone's out to get me.'

'Like who?'

'Well, she started off thinking Flanagan.'

'Flanagan can cast a spell?!' Veena sounded horrified. 'How can Flanagan be magical? Nightshade said magic is incredibly rare.'

'It is,' answered Nightshade. 'But those who still believe might track down a practising witch and buy a spell. An ill-wishing isn't one of those really difficult magics. Although the one Oakmoss is under does seem powerful.'

'You are suggesting Oakmoss's accidents are down to magic?' asked Veena, who looked increasingly disbelieving and more cross.

'S'not my fault if the cat says I'm in danger. When we first met I thought she must be like one of those magical cats that appear to give warnings. But those floorboards just giving way like that . . .'

Just at that moment the wind whipped up and the whole boathouse shook dangerously. 'Or they could just be rotten,' muttered Veena.

'You investigate magical crime the same as any other crime,' Nightshade explained. 'I'd start by examining those floorboards. But be careful, if you want your fur to stay clean.'

Veena shot Oakmoss a suspicious and unnecessarily furious look, but she knelt down and peered at the broken floorboards. Then she lay on the wooden floor for a close inspection, putting her upturned nose right up close to scrutinize the raw edges of the splintered boards. Oakmoss, Nightshade and Pudding moved alongside and peered too.

'Rotten.' She got up, dusting off her hands.

'It's very specialized investigation to tell if magic has been used,' Nightshade explained. 'I've got sorcerer friends who work for the Sinister Speculation Services who are experts at tracking down where magic has been misused.' She busily gave herself a wash. 'They're like magical detectives.'

'You have friends who work for something called the Sinister Speculation Services?' Veena crossed her arms in front of her, one eyebrow raised, her voice as sharp as ice. 'That really doesn't sound likely.'

'They're known as S3, aren't they?' said Oakmoss, nodding furiously. 'My dad's told me about S3. They can detect the ripples spells leave in the air and that's how you get caught if you use banned magic.'

'They get tough on the wrong kinds of sorcerers,' went on Nightshade. 'Particularly those who use illegal spells on people who don't have a clue that magic is even real. Punishing the guilty can involve memory tweaking, harsh magical enforcement, a bit of blood, and enormous amounts of paperwork.'

'Yeah, right,' said Veena scornfully.

'Of course, you might be right that someone isn't ill-wishing Oakmoss, but I'd say the alternative is worse.'

'Would that alternative be that you've made all of this up?' said Veena.

'What alternative? How worse?' asked Oakmoss, who felt like pointing out that this was him they were talking about.

'The alternative is that someone isn't just generally ill-wishing you, but that someone wants to do you serious harm. It could be that your powerful rudimentary magic is the only thing protecting you.'

'Powerful magic? I don't think that's very likely,' said Veena, glancing at the biscuit crumbs collected on Oakmoss's T-shirt.

'You wouldn't say that if you saw the way he threw a tree away. Magic can be extremely helpful when someone is trying to kill you.' Nightshade raised a paw and dropped her voice to a whisper. 'Or when your whiskers tell you someone is outside, listening to everything we say.'

18. A LÉTHAL SECRET WEAPON

Veena opened her mouth and looked as if she was about to launch into another sceptical speech when they all heard the unmistakable snap of someone trying to move very quietly and then stepping accidentally on a dry stick.

'There *is* someone outside,' Oakmoss hissed.

Nightshade moved a paw to tell them all to be silent, looking worryingly like a waving fortune cat.

Oakmoss tiptoed to the door and flung it open, making the whole boathouse give such a dangerous

shudder it felt it was going to give up the effort of holding itself together and disintegrate gratefully into the lake.

'Show yourself – we know you're there!' called Oakmoss, trying to sound aggressive while holding steady in a wobbling building.

The last thing he was expecting was a sheepish-looking teenage boy to appear – and for Nightshade to leap forward, not to stick a warning claw in his leg, but to screech joyfully.

'Dexter Stormforce! What are you doing here?'

'Nightshade! Looking for you, of course!'

The boy bent down to fuss her ears and came gingerly into the boathouse. He was a little older than Oakmoss and quite a lot taller. He wore a brown leather jacket with an air of confidence and had a quiff of long hair that bounced as he walked.

He really could not look less like a swamp monster who was having an identity crisis, which is how Oakmoss felt – crusty, still damp and definitely bleeding, brushing crumbs from himself as he munched another biscuit. He extended the packet. 'Ginger nut?'

The handsome boy took one. 'Thanks! How the heck are you, Nightshade?'

Pudding leapt to nestle adoringly on the boy's

shoulder, looking rather like a pirate's parrot. Nightshade gave her traditional greeting, rubbing around the bottoms of Dexter's tight black trousers.

'Still following that pink nose of yours to whatever trouble it leads you to?' He had chiselled cheekbones and a charming smile that showed off a dimple in his chin. 'Well, this is lovely,' he said, looking about.

'Full politeness marks for finding anything nice to say about this place,' said Nightshade. She made the introductions, then went on, 'Tread carefully. Oakmoss just took a dive straight through the floorboards. Nice timing for you to arrive – we're just discussing magic being used irresponsibly, then you show up. I don't believe it's a coincidence.'

'So if you are speaking to this person,' Veena said quietly to Nightshade, 'does that mean this someone is . . .' she waved a hand around vaguely and finished by silently mouthing the word *magical*.

'Dexter Stormforce is one of the most courageous and brilliant magical investigators I've met.'

'Magical investigator?' repeated Veena, tapping her chin with the end of her pen. Her tone was still disbelieving, as if they had all colluded to play one giant trick on her.

'Oh, don't be fooled into thinking his most lethal

weapon is his charming smile,' said Nightshade. 'I've seen him fighting, and the biggest mystery about Stormforce is how he rushes in to deal with some spectacularly dangerous sorcerers in such ridiculously tight trousers. And now I want to know what brings him here just as we're talking about attacks by illegal magic.' She blinked up enquiringly. 'Which, of course, he is going to tell us even if it's top secret.'

'Wow – you work for the Elysee?' said Oakmoss enviously, in an awed voice. 'You must be seriously magical.' He carried on brushing crumbs off himself and extracted a large piece of pond weed from the end of his nose, hoping it didn't look too much like he was removing a giant bogie.

'I am an official magical investigator – I work for S3.' Dexter gave a little shrug, as if being a big-shot magical investigator was no huge deal.

'He's S3, Veena!' hissed Oakmoss. He knew Veena never let anyone get away with anything less than a full explanation. 'They work to make sure magical happenings don't leak out into an unsuspecting world.'

'Saving the non-magical from the magical bad guys is what we do,' grinned Stormforce.

'You're here to solve all my bad-luck problems?' asked Oakmoss in astonishment.

Veena pointed an accusing finger at Nightshade, who began to use a paw to wash one of her soft ears.

'She,' Veena said accusingly, 'told me magic is real, but you could go around the world twice and not trip over a single magical person. But here I am, in a small boathouse on the edge of a not very impressive lake, and I am talking to three magical people, one of whom is a cat.'

'Ah, yes. Well, Nightshade is quite right,' Stormforce explained easily, examining one of Oakmoss's fishing rods. 'But as there are so few sorcerers about, and they have to be so secretive, you know, you do find that magical types tend to hang out together.'

Veena's foot began tapping on the wooden floor again. 'And these very rare sorcerers hanging about actually have a whole – what? – system of government – this Elysee? And a department that makes sure sorcery remains a secret?' said Veena. 'So how can magic be all that rare?'

'It is rare. But you'd be surprised how often little bits of magic leak out,' explained Stormforce, taking a seat in the middle of the rowing boat and pushing the hair out of his eyes. 'People find ways to explain it away, like assuming they are imagining things. Which is handy, really, as it saves using a lot of that tricky adjustment magic. That's very hard work and it can leave people with a certain amount of memory loss. If people just explain it away themselves, it also saves an awful lot of paperwork.'

Nightshade continued washing her ears. 'I have just had to introduce Veena to the whole idea of magic. I still need to convince her that she doesn't need to put it in her newspaper.'

'Oh, you don't want to do that,' said Stormforce, blatantly giving Veena the full force of his smile.

'I think you still need to convince me this is not all a joke, Mr Stormforce,' said Veena.

'Call me Dex, everyone does.'

'Dexter, it's good to see you, but what has brought you to Hornbeam Hall?' asked Nightshade.

'Why are *you* here?' Stormforce responded evasively. 'For the same reason as me? Nightshade helps me out from time to time.'

Oakmoss thought he heard the cat mutter something like *do we really need help from way-too-talented and cocky teenage wizards*.

'Seriously?' Veena said in a voice still glowering with suspicion. 'In the magical world cats really do investigating?'

'That would indeed be a fine way to run things,' said Nightshade, unsheathing a single claw and chewing on it. 'But technically, no. I simply do what cats do best: sneak around, watch from hidden places and work out where the fishy smell is coming from.'

'All humans tend to underestimate cats,' said Stormforce easily. 'Especially Nightshade.'

'We were just discussing a very bad case of ill-wishing,' Nightshade explained. 'Oakmoss went through these floorboards and I thought he wasn't coming back up again. But I'm surprised it's come to the ears of S3.'

'That's absolutely fascinating!' Dexter turned to Oakmoss with a grin. 'I've never met anyone targeted by a really evil ill-wishing spell before. That's pretty cool.'

Oakmoss shrugged. He felt a bit proud, the way Stormforce said it.

He rummaged for the last of his zingtascos, wanting to offer one to Dexter, but only removed a soggy pink-striped bag from his pocket. The sweets were now at the bottom of the lake.

Oakmoss delved into his other pocket and stared at a sodden bird book. He'd been looking forward to reading that.

He felt particularly small, and very in awe of this amazing Stormforce person. Had he really been sent by some authority in the magical world to find out if someone had it in for him?

Stormforce was looking at Nightshade in confusion. 'I haven't been sent here to investigate an ill-wishing. I'm here on a top-secret mission. It's the usual – a quest for truth and justice.'

'But you can tell us,' said Nightshade persuasively.

Stormforce considered a moment then answered with a single nod. 'I've been sent to find out why someone is camping out on your doorstep, making a lot of noisy accusations. I'm here to investigate Mr Mustard.'

19. SAVING THE NON-MAGICAL FROM THE BAD GUYS

'I told you,' said Veena quickly. 'Told you we should go and interview Mr Mustard and find out what his problem is.'

'His problem is he's just a little . . . intense,' said Oakmoss.

Stormforce picked a stray leaf from the arm of his leather jacket. 'When there's a man camped outside the house of a magical family shouting accusations, the Elysee gets to hear about it.'

'Magical family? You mean Mr Hornbeam is magical too? Another one!' Veena folded her arms. 'Am I seriously the only non-magical person here?'

Veena looked as if she might stamp her foot and Nightshade hastily pointed out the floorboards were none too safe and they didn't want a group plunge into Dogberry Lake.

'You say that saving the non-magical from the bad guys is what you do,' went on Veena. 'So Mr Mustard's not just a bad guy, he's a magical bad guy?'

Stormforce answered with a shrug. 'When accusations are hurled about, I investigate,' he said smoothly. 'I need to do that as quickly and quietly and with as little fuss as possible, clear up any misunderstanding, and I'll be on my way.'

Oakmoss thought this sounded brilliant. Dad always grumbled about the Elysee being a bit of a nuisance. But they must really look out for magical folk if they sent in investigators when someone was being a pest on the doorstep. Nightshade must be right when she said the Hornbeams were an important magical family.

'And on the plus side,' said Nightshade, 'a new chief suspect for us!'

Everyone stared at Nightshade in silence.

'Think about it.' She stretched easily and began

methodically washing a paw. 'Oakmoss's reputation for clumsiness becomes nearly fatal just as someone turns up having a big issue with the Hornbeams.'

'Actually, good point,' nodded Stormforce. 'Mr Mustard has sworn revenge on the Hornbeams. So, yes, chief suspect!'

'Has he?' said Veena and Oakmoss together.

'I'd like to hear about these accidents, Oakmoss,' said Stormforce.

Oakmoss wanted to ask why anyone would swear revenge for being sold a fortune cat that they didn't like, but he sensed everyone's gaze on him.

'Well,' he shifted uncomfortably, 'I fell through these floorboards.'

The moment he said it, he considered that falling through rotten floorboards wasn't exactly sinister. He felt unconvincing in all sorts of ways. And he'd never had this many visitors in the boathouse before – everyone was sidling around the hole where the planks had given way and it made it seem even more crowded. Oakmoss was hot and bothered. He paused and could tell he was turning red. The air seemed particularly heavy and still.

Stormforce turned to him with a friendly smile. 'Go on,' he encouraged, removing something from his brown leather jacket. It was small and pointed –

it looked like a silver letter opener.

Oakmoss watched in silent fascination as Stormforce pointed the small object at the floorboards. It looked lethal now; more dagger than letter opener.

Veena crooked a sceptical eyebrow at Stormforce. 'You're going to see if these boards have been bewitched, aren't you? Bewitched? Is that the right word?'

'It'll do,' said Nightshade.

'With that?' she said, pointing to the object in Dexter's hand as he waved it slowly over the splintered planks.

There was a flash of blue light that hovered for a few seconds, shimmering over the boathouse floor, licking around the edges of the broken boards as if the light was alive and moving under Stormforce's command.

Veena's impatient foot-tapping stopped. Her eyebrows shot high in amazement and stayed there. 'Was that magic?' she breathed.

As the blue light faded, Dexter peered at the handle of the magical instrument. He frowned, his intelligent gaze sweeping the tiny ramshackle building.

What was he learning? Oakmoss watched, fascinated. Dexter crouched low, right down to the broken boards (it looked a bit uncomfortable in those tight trousers).

There was hardly even the sound of breathing in the warm, still air as Dexter carried out a detailed inspection. Everyone leant closer to the floorboards as he ran his slim hands lightly over the broken ends, flipping his long fringe out of the way as he stared into the scummy still water that shivered beneath them.

Stormforce frowned intently at Oakmoss, but that could be because Oakmoss could feel he was drying to a sort of brownish green crust that might, with a bit of imagination, have worked as a fairy tale costume for tomorrow's gala.

'Oakmoss, what else? How many accidents? How serious?' Stormforce prompted. His tone was still encouraging, but it now carried more of a demand for information.

'Umm . . .' Oakmoss thought quickly back over what had befallen him lately – moving through the everyday, like being the source of hilarity on the school bus, forever having to keep a stash of spare glasses, even in the boathouse, losing his homework, tripping over his feet, discovering his bag emptied again. Dexter wouldn't be interested in any of that.

Falling out of trees (twice), he volunteered.

Crashing into trees (more times than he could count).

Falling out of his own bedroom window (while fixing a nesting box for the sparrows who chattered in the tree outside his window).

'Trees seem to be involved a lot of the time,' said Stormforce thoughtfully.

'Is that important?' quizzed Oakmoss.

Stormforce didn't respond, but instead surprised Oakmoss by sending a shimmer of blue light out again, this time right over Oakmoss. He stood still and looked down at the magical light, which tickled slightly as it ran over him.

'You haven't mentioned your fatal accident,' said Veena.

Oakmoss pushed his glasses up his nose. 'I'm pretty sure I haven't had one of those yet.'

'You've come pretty close,' pointed out Nightshade. 'You would have been completely clobbered by that branch this morning. Told you, you were lucky.'

'I was thinking of that accident which was terminal for your bike,' said Veena.

'A non-tree accident,' mused Stormforce, tapping his face thoughtfully with his long fingers.

Oakmoss shrugged and tried to brush off a bit

more mud and weed. 'I hadn't checked my brakes. I really am quite clumsy.'

Stormforce frowned again into the small but lethal dagger. Was he about to pronounce that Oakmoss was under a dangerous ill-wishing?

'Sorry, Oakmoss,' said Stormforce. 'But I'm afraid Nightshade's right.'

'I usually am,' said Nightshade.

'You are very lucky to have survived, because these floorboards have been tampered with.'

'Is it a magical crime?' Veena breathed, instantly lying flat to peer at the boards. 'You can tell by . . . ?' She swooshed an arm, mimicking the movement he'd done to cast the magical light.

Dexter shrugged. 'One of the biggest problems with magic is that it is incredibly difficult to be sure.' He checked the dagger again. 'But I can't detect signs of Oakmoss being under an ill-wishing spell. I think there's someone keen to see you have accidents, however. Doesn't have to involve magic. These boards were cut with a saw, just enough so that they looked safe but would give way under someone's weight.'

Oakmoss stared at the boards. Someone had deliberately made sure he'd have an accident?

Veena turned to Oakmoss, wrinkling her nose as

she slowly pieced together what Dexter was saying. 'Have you seen anyone around here with a saw?'

Oakmoss swallowed drily. Hyacinth managed the grounds and did maintenance on the rambling house. She could often be seen sawing wood. There were tools in the shed off the courtyard, but that was never locked – anyone could have picked up a saw, he told himself.

Stormforce bent to remove a smear of pond weed from one of his boots. 'And Nightshade's right about another thing—'

'Again,' put in Nightshade.

'You've survived an accident that wrecked your bike, a fall out of an upstairs window and a plunge beneath these floorboards – that water is deep and dangerous. Whether someone is behind all the accidents or you are simply unlucky, one thing is for sure – your magic must be amazingly strong, Oakmoss Hornbeam.'

Oakmoss tried to shrug off this unexpected attention and praise, but wasn't able to stop himself blushing.

'We should investigate,' said Nightshade. 'There's something fishy going on. I can always tell when something's fishy. It's like my whiskers are radar for fishy business.'

'Exactly what I was about to say!' Stormforce was already heading to the door of the boathouse. 'Although not the bit about the whiskers. This is all so interesting! I love the fact you've got a prime suspect before you even know for sure if a crime's been committed.'

'Have the rules of magic been breached? Is Oakmoss in danger?' pressed Veena. 'What do you really think?'

'I think what you really need is an expert – someone who knows about this kind of case. Someone who is an incredible expert in investigating crime. You need someone who understands magical people and can stop anything really serious happening.' He pointed to himself. 'What we really need here, is me.'

20. THE VERY GRAVEST PUNISHMENT

'Er, but does anyone want to help me?' said Stormforce, tucking the magical dagger away inside his jacket.

'Investigate?' breathed Veena, not even trying to hide excitement. 'Investigate a magical crime? With you?'

'You've got it exactly. I could do with some help, quite frankly. Sometimes finding out the truth and getting justice is very hard work.'

'I don't think we can completely rule out an

ill-wishing,' put in Nightshade, polishing her whiskers thoughtfully. 'It could have worn off. A spell like that needs to be topped up, doesn't it?'

'Absolutely. A spell like that would be cast over something you carry, or food,' explained Dexter as Oakmoss tidied away his fishing kit.

'Well,' said Veena, 'it'd be absolutely no good giving Oakmoss anything to carry with an ill-wishing charm, because he loses everything all the time.' She made an exasperated noise. 'I think Nightshade's right as well – it seems she usually is – Mr Mustard has got to be our prime suspect. It'd be pretty easy to find a way to get over the wall and tamper with these floorboards. How do we prove it?'

Stormforce stroked his chin thoughtfully. 'Proving things is also very hard work.'

'My dad makes toys, and Mustard just wants a refund,' Oakmoss felt he should point out. 'It's unlikely Mr Mustard has got so fixated on my family that he's picking on me for revenge.'

'It was unlikely I'd start investigating magical crime with a cat who can talk,' responded Veena. 'We all have to make adjustments when presented with the facts.'

'We should go and—' said Dexter.

'Get some facts by talking to our prime suspect,'

Veena interrupted. 'Of course we'll help you, Dexter. I told Oakmoss ages ago we should talk to Mustard. Although Oakmoss has a point. I think we need to understand why Mustard's resorted to making threats against the Hornbeams.'

'Unfortunately, we've just missed the chance to ask him,' said Stormforce. 'PC Truffle was trying to move him along when I arrived. But I'm sure he'll be back before too long.'

Oakmoss was trying hard to remember exactly what Mr Mustard had told him. Hadn't he said his fortune cat had brought only misfortune, that it had tricked him?

'I've been keeping my whiskers to the ground,' said Nightshade. 'And I like Mustard as a suspect – but Oakmoss's bad luck began before he turned up.'

'I think I'm just a bit unlucky,' insisted Oakmoss.

As they walked back towards Hornbeam Hall, Stormforce explained Mr Mustard's accusations had started a while ago. 'It's possible he's been hanging around working out how to cause trouble before he pitched his tent. There's a lot we need to find out.'

They took a winding path along the river and up to the house. Veena (inevitably) started firing questions at Stormforce. Nightshade and Pudding followed and Oakmoss started to trail behind, grateful for the chance to think.

'What's the punishment if the Sinister Speculations Services find someone doing something illegal with magic?' Veena asked.

'Close watching, usually. Sometimes a fine, very few end up in jail, Veena,' answered Stormforce. 'For magical crime involving death and worse, the very gravest punishment is that the Elysee has power to limit the culprit's use of magic.'

'Investigating magical crime sounds really difficult,' said Veena. 'It must be easy to get away with a crime if you're magical. Especially as no one knows about magic and people find ways to explain anything unusual happening.'

'You've got it exactly.'

'I mean, how can you tell if someone is definitely a criminal?'

'You do ask the trickiest questions.'

'Thank you,' said Veena.

'I guess the main thing that makes someone definitely a criminal would be if they get caught.'

It was a hot day and they walked slowly. Oakmoss knew he'd always been a little clumsy. The very idea of anyone going to the bother of ill-wishing him, or even trying to hurt him, seemed unlikely. What would be the point? Plus Stormforce, an expert magical investigator, had failed to find any spell cast over him.

Despite the sunshine, Oakmoss suddenly felt chilled as he remembered falling in the water; desperately trying to hold his breath and work out which way was up until he felt his lungs would burst. He'd been panicking. Every struggle just made the weed wrap tighter around his legs.

But he'd certainly been lucky then. Because he'd remembered Nightshade's words and that had saved him. He'd known his only chance was his magic. Nightshade telling him several times that he was a powerful sorcerer had been a lifeline. He'd known he had to reach for his magic. Somehow, he'd found it. Somehow, he'd been able to summon the power to free himself.

He'd imagined himself free of the weed and shooting upwards. And somehow the water had made him do just that.

Otherwise he would still be there now, trapped under the boathouse, lungs full of water. Oakmoss was sure of it.

Stormforce unexpectedly clapped Oakmoss on the shoulder, making him jump. 'Timing is crucial.' From his back pocket he took out a folded sheet and waved it around. 'Can you explain this? This seems a spectacularly bad idea.'

Oakmoss was surprised to see a poster advertising the fairy-tale gala.

'Hornbeam Hall has been in magical hands for generations, and tomorrow it's throwing its doors open for the first time,' said Stormforce. 'The place will be swarming with curious, eager non-magical folk.'

'And when magical folk invite a lot of people into their home, it usually results in complete chaos,' put in Nightshade.

'Very true!' said Stormforce, waving the poster. 'However, it is brilliant cover to investigate!'

'It is?' asked Oakmoss.

'Of course. Magical crime investigation is always best done undercover.'

Oakmoss explained how Mum was trying to raise money for RATS. 'I mean, her charity to repair broken toys.'

'Your mum must have to work very hard to get anyone to donate actual money to a toy charity called RATS,' said Veena darkly.

'Do people really give money to rescue toys?' asked Stormforce.

'Lots.' Oakmoss remembered Hyacinth saying there was a whole sack of donations.

The ground rose gently as they walked up from the river. The moment they peaked the hill they could see that an amazing transformation was taking place. In the usual neat and tidy grounds of Hornbeam Hall, colourful tents were springing up, and stalls enticing people to try their luck at everything from hook-a-duck to hoopla. There was bright bunting strung between booths, and notices announcing everything from Rapunzel's lucky dip to Rumpelstiltskin's tombola.

Oakmoss was surprised to see Dad setting up a stall selling rows of the Hornbeam Workshop's fortune cats, a slogan painted above their staring eyes: EVERYONE DESERVES A BIT OF GOOD LUCK! Dad had his hands in his pockets and Oakmoss caught the punchline of one of his groaningly awful jokes about which side of the house Jack's beanstalk grew.

'On the outside!' guffawed Dad. Oakmoss was enormously relieved he wasn't still wearing those tartan shorts, or any sort of costume.

Veena had stopped at a Cinderella coconut shy. WIN ONE! IT MAY TRANSFORM INTO A FAIRY-TALE CARRIAGE (BUT ONLY UNTIL MIDNIGHT!) 'I don't think that was a coconut. I'm pretty sure that was a pumpkin,' she said with a frown.

'And you'll both be wearing costumes?' said Stormforce.

'No!' Veena and Oakmoss both said together.

'That's just for the kids,' added Veena.

'Sadly, nope, it isn't. Believe me, the adults are having way too much fun thinking up costumes,' said Oakmoss quietly, as they passed the podium where the prize for the best fancy dress would be announced.

'The theme is fairy tales,' said Veena scathingly. 'I can't even think of a good female fairy-tale character.'

'You'd make a good Maleficent,' said Oakmoss.

'Cheers. Exactly. All the best female characters are the evil ones. What a great theme.'

'What's this one for?' asked Stormforce, pausing curiously by 'Puss-in-Boots Throwing'.

'Erm, I think Mum said that's a competition to see who can throw a welly boot the furthest. I expect there's a prize – there usually is.'

Everything was making Oakmoss think that tomorrow was going to be totally cringe. He just hoped no one from school would show up.

'Fascinating! And do people enjoy that? Throwing boots? Do they pay money for that?'

'Well, Mum hopes so.'

Stormforce had slung his brown leather jacket over one shoulder and was sauntering through the unexpectedly lively grounds with an easy smile. 'Everything looks perfect for this fairy-tale gala; should make a lot of money for these rats,' he drawled. 'Unless something seriously unlucky happens. Oh, I forgot, you *are* seriously unlucky, aren't you, Oakmoss?'

21. The Pointy Horns of an Evil Monster

'Is the Hornbeam Workshop actually here in the grounds of the hall?' Stormforce asked Oakmoss. 'It's just that I haven't seen it. Which does make my plan quite tricky.'

'Plan?' said Oakmoss.

Stormforce paused with a puzzled expression next to a sign which read THREE LITTLE PIGS HOG ROAST. Although it might be that he paused because, at exactly that moment, Hornbeam Hall rose into sight in all its grimness above the colourful stalls.

'Has anyone ever said the twin turrets of your house make it look like the pointy horns of an evil monster?' said Stormforce. 'It looks like it's watching us.'

'Yeah, from this angle the house does look a little unfriendly,' agreed Oakmoss.

'Unfriendly?' said Veena. 'You mean evil. Forbidding is the word I'd use. Or hostile.' She'd always been good at words.

Baba Yaga's tea and cake tent was blocking the entrance to the courtyard and the back way into the house. Long trestle tables lined the insides and it was packed full of chairs that spilled out on to the lawn. They had to make their way laboriously through a tangle of guy ropes to reach the courtyard, where the earlier bustle had been replaced with a serene silence. The sun was bright behind the whitewashed wall rambled over with pink roses.

Stormforce shielded his eyes and cried: 'Oh, would you look at that!'

'At what? That wall and a small door?' said Veena.

'Someone's been busy with a heck of a big glimmer – that's one giant concealing charm,' said Stormforce.

'Don't look right at it. Try looking at it out of the corner of your eye,' Nightshade explained to Veena.

Veena turned her head a few times. 'Oh yes! That's incredible! There's a whole building hidden behind that wall, but when I try to look right at it, I just seem to want to look away. That's magic, right?'

'Hidden with a magical charm designed to work by confusing the mind and convincing people there's nothing worth looking at,' said Stormforce. 'Interesting.'

'The workshop used to just be in an old outbuilding,' Oakmoss explained. 'Trapmole was keen to expand, but Mum said no way was she going to look out at an ugly factory.'

Oakmoss also followed Nightshade's instruction and managed to take a good look at what was behind the low wall – a tall and extremely ugly building; blank and windowless. 'It's hidden so it doesn't spoil the view. I wouldn't want to look out at that every day, would you?'

'That's the workshop where all those fortune cats are made?' enquired Veena.

'When did you last take a tour around your father's workshop?' Stormforce asked Oakmoss.

'Er – not for ages. Why?'

'Well, magical protections can cause problems,' said Stormforce. 'Mustard's beef with your family is about a fortune cat and that's the workshop where they're made. I've got to take a look around. Now if you're investigating, say, a high-security bank to steal some diamonds – a nice, regular sort of breaking in – you could find blueprints and plans. You'd know in advance where the security cameras are, the lasers that trigger the alarm, the air ducts in case you need to make a hasty exit.'

'That glimmer is a bit of magical security so there might be more?' Veena frowned. 'Wait! Does this mean *Trapmole* is magical too?' Veena crooked a quizzical eyebrow at Stormforce. 'Seriously? And Nightshade tried to claim that being magical is incredibly rare.'

'It is, but magical people *do* hang out together,' muttered Nightshade.

Oakmoss was already heading across the court-yard to the kitchen thinking there might be cake. Thinking about cake seemed much more appealing than thinking about Mr Mustard wanting his money back because he hadn't liked his fortune cat. At least the Elysee had sent Stormforce to sort it all out and hopefully Mustard would soon be sent on his way. Oakmoss considered perhaps he should have paid more attention to Mustard's story. What had he said exactly? Something about . . . he'd been tricked, but *by the cat*? That didn't make any sense at all.

'I fear Mr Mustard will only leave once he feels his complaint is being investigated,' said Stormforce, who was still fascinated by the glimmer.

'By investigate, you mean you need to shine that blue light around, don't you?' breathed Veena. 'Like you did with Oakmoss and the boathouse?'

Stormforce was nodding. 'That's what I do. This is where you are going to be absolutely crucial, Oakmoss. I can't get rid of Mr Mustard without seeing inside the workshop.'

Oakmoss felt his shoulders droop. 'I don't think I can persuade Dad to show you around,' he replied uneasily. 'No one goes inside except family, and his apprentice, Trapmole, of course. And you'll never persuade Trapmole. With the gala and Mustard he's even put extra security in place. I don't think you'll be able to go in tomorrow at all. Sorry, Stormforce.'

'Oh, I agree, let's not bother your father.' Stormforce flashed a lazy smile. 'Trapmole will be helping out, impressing your parents, running his stall. Everyone will be distracted by all the brilliant games and the prizes. Tomorrow is the ideal and unmissable opportunity to slip into that workshop.'

'Slip in?' repeated Oakmoss.

Stormforce reminded him he'd said magical investigations always had to be done in secret. 'The sooner I carry out some covert investigations, the sooner I can get Mustard and his tent packed up and send him on his way. I'd like to do it without bothering anyone, particularly your busy family,' said Stormforce. 'It will be difficult and dangerous,' he said with relish. 'Which is why, Oakmoss, it's so brilliant for you to agree to be involved.'

Oakmoss was trying to remember at exactly what point he had agreed, particularly to something that very much sounded like breaking in. And he hadn't liked the difficult and dangerous bit either.

'We're just a wee bit short of up-to-date intel. Which is why I can't do it without you,' went on Stormforce.

'You need to do reconnaissance, Oakmoss,' said Veena. 'You need to find out what magical security Trapmole has put in place.'

'She means Stormforce is relying on you to make sure he doesn't get caught doing his undercover magical investigation,' added Nightshade.

'I know what reconnaissance is,' protested Oakmoss. 'But—' A feeling of dread crept over him, making his skin cool even in the summer sunshine.

No one was saying this was a terrible idea. No one was saying Oakmoss should not do this.

'This is how you do a magical investigation?' said

Oakmoss carefully. 'This is how you stop Mustard camping out on the doorstep? This is how you get him to leave my family alone?'

All he had to do was get Stormforce inside his family workshop and out again without anyone knowing. It seemed simple enough.

Oakmoss could clear the family name of any wild accusations. He could get Mr Mustard sent on his way. Maybe then Oakmoss's bad luck would lift, particularly if part of Mustard's revenge was ill-wishing him.

'Won't you need a lookout, while you do your thing with the blue light?' asked Veena.

'That would be a big help,' answered Stormforce.

'Then we *all* sneak in?' said Veena excitedly. '*Without permission?*'

Stormforce clapped Oakmoss heavily on the shoulder. 'It'll be fine,' he reassured. 'We won't get caught. As long as we know what we're facing, nothing catches us out and we don't end up on the wrong side of any security, magical or otherwise.' He looked at Oakmoss. 'We need to do this tomorrow, when the gala is in full swing, and that doesn't give us much time.'

Everyone was looking at Oakmoss.

'Who's in?' said Stormforce.

Veena's hand shot up. She giggled. 'Proper invest-igative journalism.' She looked at Oakmoss, her eyes shining.

Stormforce raised his hand.

Oakmoss felt Pudding clawing at the bottom of his muddy trousers, looking up at him imploringly with her big blue eyes as if saying she was in. Night-shade raised a paw.

Everyone was waiting. If this was how magical investigations went, he guessed he had no choice. Of course, if it all went wrong and Dad discovered his only son was involved in a covert magical investiga-tion of the Hornbeam Workshop . . . Oakmoss decided not to think about that.

Tentatively, he raised his hand.

'All right,' he sighed. 'I'll talk to Trapmole.'

What on earth had he let himself in for?

22. CHERRY BAKEWELL PIE

O akmoss couldn't believe how uncomfortable he felt as he stepped into the kitchen. It was mostly Nightshade's fault, not letting the idea drop that he was under an ill-wishing and pointing out it would be in something he wore or something he ate. She'd planted suspicion of Hyacinth.

Also, Hyacinth had already baked over one hundred scones for the gala. She'd been organizing deliveries and Mum had asked for a special celebratory dinner. What would Hyacinth say when, in an

already busy day, he suddenly turned up with unexpected friends? Especially as Oakmoss had never turned up with friends before.

'I try to give her as little bother as possible to make up for the fact that Mum doesn't seem to think Hyacinth needs to do things like sleep or sit down,' Oakmoss had tried to explain.

Veena was delighted she would finally get to see inside his house – in all their years of friendship, Oakmoss had never let her get further than the garden and she was even more thrilled now she knew it was a magical household.

'That is the exactly the problem,' said Oakmoss. 'That's always been the problem.'

It wasn't that the dinner table magically laid itself (very often), or there was a stack of smelly cauldrons full of old spells that needed washing up (only on Wednesdays). Most people, Oakmoss considered, would probably never notice this was a magical household. Nightshade had said most of the time if anyone saw any magic happening, they simply found a way to explain it away.

But if they had visitors Dad moaned that he found it a strain to constantly remember not to do things like light candles without using any matches. And Hyacinth just occasionally would get a vision and a shocked expression and she'd grip a visitor's arm and might tell them to watch out for ladders. Or adders.

Hyacinth's face was taking on a shocked expression right now as she turned from where she was bending to put something in the oven in the sweltering kitchen and saw Oakmoss, with Veena and Dex hovering in the doorway.

'Hello, Hyacinth – what can we do to help?' began Oakmoss nervously, but breathing in a comforting mix of chocolate, cream, almonds, pastry, coconut and icing. It was too difficult to stop his mouth watering, even with his heart beating fast.

'I am *fine.*' Hyacinth turned and pushed a stray strand of flame-red hair from her even redder, sweaty face and moved closer. '*You* on the other hand are very much not fine. You've already had one accident today. What happened this time?'

Oakmoss had forgotten that he was still crusty from his slimy dip in the lake. 'It's fine, no blood this time. I'll go and change.'

'Ooh! You've brought friends! How lovely!' exclaimed Hyacinth, clasping her hands. Her tone gave away that she might not think it was all that lovely.

Oakmoss quickly explained that Veena and

Dexter were here to help him set up his fishing competition for tomorrow and would not get in her way. He had zero intention of getting involved in explaining that Dex was magical and that this afternoon Veena had discovered plenty of the family's magical secrets. Oakmoss was good at keeping things to himself.

Veena was looking around with great curiosity and suggested she make everyone a cup of tea. 'If that would help,' she said to Hyacinth.

'I can manage,' Hyacinth said, struggling to add an enormous tray of potatoes to the oven.

Stormforce swung over and took the heavy tray from her with muscled arms. He somehow managed to look as dashing rescuing potatoes as he might if he'd just stopped a runaway horse.

'We're here now, so you don't have to,' he grinned at her.

'Yes, well, thank you, Dexter,' said Hyacinth, looking even redder, 'I am a bit behind. Those delivery drivers. You wouldn't believe how many cups of tea they drink.'

Stormforce slouched against the oven with his dazzling smile on full display, pushing his fringe out of his eyes. 'Oakmoss, you go and make yourself a bit more . . . a bit less . . .'

'I'm sure if you ask, your mum will want to invite them for dinner,' Hyacinth said, a touch anxiously. She leant closer to Oakmoss and added in a whisper, 'I've been making the house presentable to non-magical folk for tomorrow, just in case, you know, people do wander. I think it'll be fine if they stay.'

'Really? Only if it's not too much bother?' Oakmoss replied. 'We can definitely help you cook.'

'You know your mother doesn't like you doing that,' said Hyacinth pointedly. 'And, although I'd hate to say your help is more trouble than it's worth, last week a knife did slip when you were slicing tomatoes. There was an awful lot of blood. You nearly lost a finger.'

'Ah, yes, but I didn't, so that was lucky,' Oakmoss smiled. 'I didn't even need to go to hospital – not when Mum finally found that old book of emergency healing that she thought she'd donated to Erasmus.'

'Just leave the helping out to us, Oakmoss,' said Stormforce. 'Hyacinth, please tell us what to do. Staying for dinner sounds wonderful, but we'll be happy with a slice of bread and cheese, although it looks like you already have enough for twenty.'

Oakmoss put down a bowl of cat food and

Pudding went straight to it and ate hungrily. But Nightshade had not followed into the kitchen.

Oakmoss could not believe he'd forgotten Grimalkin! He'd almost led Nightshade directly into trouble again.

'Where's Nightshade?' asked Veena, handing around mugs of tea and watching Pudding wolf down all the food as Hyacinth bustled about doing fancy things with pastry and putting more things in the oven.

'Nightshade had a run-in with Grimalkin earlier. I guess she's hiding outside,' said Oakmoss, heading that way.

'I'm not hiding!' came a small voice from just outside the door.

'I'll go and make sure Grimalkin's not planning an ambush,' Oakmoss told her, then headed across the kitchen to the hallway.

'Oh, Oakmoss, you've got a tea leaf floating in your tea, that means a letter,' said Hyacinth as she swished past. 'Oh no, it's not a tea leaf, it's a small fly. Sorry. That doesn't mean anything except you're unlucky.'

'Who's Grimalkin?' asked Stormforce, grabbing cutlery, passing half to Veena and asking for directions to the dining room.

'My dad's big ugly fighter of a cat,' replied Oakmoss. 'His brother, Gisborne, lives with my dad's brother, Erasmus.'

Grimalkin was not difficult to track down. He was in one of his favourite places, sprawled over the window seat where the Hall's grand staircase turned around halfway. The window seat caught the late sun, and was the perfect place for an ambush and to claw anyone passing either up or down.

Grimalkin half lifted one of his yellow eyes but seemed too tired to play his favourite game today.

Oakmoss headed back to the kitchen and took a bowl of food and water outside to Nightshade, reminding her she could use the escape tree to get to and from his room.

Then he saw an array of desserts laid out on the wide kitchen windowsill to cool.

Oakmoss could not resist a closer look.

There was a tower of coconut macaroons, six flaky pastry puffs filled with a thick layer of cream, and in pride of place was his own favourite – a triumphant cherry bakewell pie. Hyacinth's speciality. She didn't make this little slice of heaven on earth very often as Oakmoss was the only one in the family who ate it. (He never understood how anyone could resist that smooth white icing and a ring of plump cherries.)

'Oh wow, Hyacinth, thank you so much!'

'Ach, no bother,' said Hyacinth, flying past. 'Luckily a little bird told me half the village are baking cakes for tomorrow, so I slowed the scone machine and found some time to bake your favourite.' She tweaked his cheek affectionately.

Dexter was at Oakmoss's elbow, putting his nose close to the cherry bakewell. 'How long did you say it was until dinner?'

'Leave those cakes alone,' said Hyacinth, stepping in to snap at Stormforce with a tea towel, 'particularly that cherry bakewell.'

'One cherry?'

'Not even one – that's for Oakmoss!'

'Yeah, hands off, Stormforce,' said Oakmoss, 'I can normally make it last a whole week.'

'That sounds like a challenge,' scoffed Dexter.

'Oh, Uncle Erasmus is here for dinner too!' Oakmoss said delightedly, noticing a fabulous three-layer chocolate cheesecake.

Hyacinth bustled over with one of the towers of cake tins. 'Yes. If he remembers. Now, I've got scones that didn't come out quite right, and a couple of custard tarts that were Mr Hornbeam's favourite but he's decided he prefers a cream slice – would you all like some of those?'

Veena, Stormforce and Oakmoss crowded around the tin of broken delicacies, mis-shapes and the last of the mini custard tarts, cramming an assortment of crumbly pastries into their mouths until Hyacinth took them away, telling them they'd spoil their dinner.

'We'd be glad to do real jobs, not just eating,' said Veena, licking her fingers. 'But not Oakmoss. Your priority is to remove the stench of decaying river weed.'

'I'm doing it!' Oakmoss whipped the final scone from under Stormforce's nose and headed up to his room to shower and bin his clothes for the second time that day before finally checking his freckled face for any remaining mud.

He put on about his third pair of glasses that day (Mum made him keep a ready stash of spares). He looked at his odd-coloured eyes and asked himself: was this the face of the unluckiest boy in the world? Or was Nightshade right (she was usually) and this was the face of someone being deliberately targeted by someone? Someone close to him, someone possibly even in the house right now?

23. Murderous Towards His Family

Alone in his room all Oakmoss's many worries crowded in. How had he managed to agree to help Stormforce take a look inside the Hornbeam Workshop? And he had to be nice to Trapmole and find a way to persuade the apprentice to show him around and reveal any security measures, magical or otherwise.

But probably the worst thing was to find yourself putting on fresh clothes, checking yourself in the mirror for any stray bits of lingering river weed and

realizing you are counting the number of people who might want to ill-wish you.

Oakmoss's heart had skipped a beat when Storm-force had declared those boathouse boards had been weakened by a saw, because who was regularly seen with tools and garden implements? Only Hyacinth Privet.

If Hyacinth felt vengeful, even murderous towards his family, well, that wouldn't surprise him, not really, given the strain his parents put on her. But it made Oakmoss incredibly sad to even think she might want to hurt him.

Oakmoss hadn't forgotten that Nightshade's first suggestion had been Flanagan, who could have consulted a witch to get hold of some sort of ill-wishing charm. Nothing would surprise Oakmoss about Flanagan. But Flanagan having access to spells was truly terrifying.

Of course Trapmole resented him. He'd been taken on as Dad's apprentice until Oakmoss was old enough to take over, which meant Oakmoss was destined to be Trapmole's boss one day. Awkward. Trapmole used every opportunity to demonstrate he'd make a far better head of the Hornbeam Work-shop. He wouldn't entirely blame Trapmole for thinking how much easier it would be if Oakmoss was simply removed from the picture.

Oakmoss found that he was hoping the prime suspect was Mr Mustard, with his frenzied accusations about a fortune cat tricking him and being owed money. He certainly seemed the sort who would stop at nothing to upset the Hornbeams. If they could just prove whatever was bugging Mustard was a lot of nonsense, then maybe, just maybe, Mustard and all the accidents, as well as any ill-wishing, would just go away.

It all depended on him successfully getting them in and out of the workshop tomorrow. Then Stormforce could say Mr Mustard's complaint had been investigated – and Mustard would be on his way, hopefully before the gala was even over.

Tomorrow loomed in a pretty terrifying way. But for now it would be enough if he could get through dinner and the rest of this evening without accidents, without discovering any more people who might want to cast a bad spell over him, maybe without anything bad happening at all.

Perhaps with Nightshade here, his luck would hold out just this once.

24. LETHAL TEETH

Oakmoss hurried downstairs, wanting to help, and arrived at the kitchen at the same time as his mother, who was asking a hot and tired-looking Hyacinth when dinner would be ready.

Oakmoss counted it as the first piece of jolly good luck (and a relief) that Mum had not decided to come down to dinner dressed as a mermaid. She was back to her own hair and her usual choice of a flowery skirt and a blouse with frills and ruffles up the front, with an assortment of colourful drapings

of a lot of sparkly jewellery.

Stormforce was outside the back door, dropping another morsel that Nightshade and Pudding began to tussle over.

'Exhaustion has really set in,' Mum said, slipping in close to Hyacinth's sweaty face and nodding. 'How will we ever be ready for tomorrow?' Mum placed a finger to the side of her face, making her jewellery sparkle. 'Can I suggest a little sit down, Privet, maybe in the garden room? And a drink.' She moved even closer. 'A teensy bit early, perhaps? Just a small one, it's after six after all.' She giggled. 'Or is it ever too early for a little drinkie-poo?'

'Oh, I'm fine, thank you, Mrs Hornbeam,' responded Hyacinth, stirring a big jug of gravy enthusiastically.

'Well, I'm glad you're fine, Privet! But it's me who needs to keep my strength up!'

'Oh yes, sorry, Mrs Hornbeam.' Hyacinth flushed even redder.

'I never knew writing my speech would leave me feeling so drained. But it's all for the children, all for their dear broken toys. Dinner's not going to be late, is it?' Mum looked pointedly at Hyacinth.

Stormforce appeared at her elbow as if by magic, moving in with a smooth and swift apology. 'It's completely my fault everything is behind. Veena and I, we've distracted Hyacinth. All we wanted was to help with the fundraising. I'm Dexter Stormforce, a friend of Oakmoss.'

'You're a friend of Oakie?!' Mum simpered, jangling her many bracelets. 'How incredibly kind of you to help with the fundraising. How very charming. I can't imagine why my boy has been keeping you such a secret.'

'And Veena's helping too, of course,' said Stormforce.

'Well, Dexter, you must come and tell me all your plans for tomorrow, it's very naughty of you not to come and tell me sooner,' twinkled Mum in a really embarrassing fashion, grabbing at Stormforce's arm and steering him away. 'I'm sure we can manage a couple of those miniature custard tarts as well, Privet.'

'I'm sorry, Mrs Hornbeam, those are all gone.'

'Gone? But they are Mr Hornbeam's favourites.'

'Mr Hornbeam said they're no longer his favourites and could he have a cream slice instead. There is a cream slice,' finished Hyacinth on a hopeful note.

'I am sure he said no such thing. What are we to do?'

'There are some coconut macaroons.'

'Just find something tasty, bring a few nibbles. We'll be in the garden room.' Stormforce was resisting, muttering about there still being lots to do and wanting to help, but Mum was dismissive. 'Oh, Privet will manage, but I need your help most urgently.'

She hurled an unfriendly look across the kitchen entrance to where Nightshade unfortunately had Pudding's tail playfully in her jaws. 'What is that cat doing? Get rid of it.'

Nightshade stalked magnificently into a corner and sat down.

'Now, Dexter,' said Mum, drawing Stormforce inexorably out of the hot kitchen. 'I am writing my opening speech. Do you know anything that rhymes with orange?'

Oakmoss was about to laugh at Dexter's discomfort when he heard a ferocious low hiss of warning. And then he saw a low, marmalade shape with menacing yellow eyes at the door to the hall; orange fur raised. Grimalkin.

'Look out!' Oakmoss called, but it was too late.

In one slick, black, shadowy movement, Nightshade sprang towards the open back door, followed by Grimalkin, who leapt right on to the kitchen table, the quickest route to reach his prey. His claws scraped, he lost his grip for a second and clawed and careered across it, scattering the tower of cake tins, which landed with a loud clang. He lunged after Nightshade like a marmalade-coloured shark, her black tail only centimetres ahead of his lethal teeth.

25. Lilies and Other Villains

There was no sign of Nightshade for the rest of the evening.

Oakmoss could hardly sit still as he was swept straight into dinner and could do no more than keep darting looks towards the dining-room door, hoping for just a glimpse that would tell him she was all right. He'd have to sit through several courses before he could be released to go and look for her.

At least there was no sign of Grimalkin either, no sign of blood.

He tried to laugh along with Uncle Erasmus, who'd arrived full of jokes and jollity and almost on time, apologizing about a chair he was fixing that wasn't behaving itself. He was wearing a crumpled linen jacket that suggested he'd decided he should dress smartly, but only at the last minute.

Erasmus had been surprised and delighted to discover they had unexpected guests, and had offered Oakmoss a small striped paper bag with a wink.

'Zingtascos! Don't tell me, you guessed I'd lose the first lot!' Oakmoss had fallen on the bag gratefully and popped one straight into his mouth.

Hyacinth had spotted him and told him off. 'Don't you go spoiling your dinner after I've worked so hard to do your favourites.'

Stormforce accepted one, but only out of politeness because he'd looked at the huge purple sweet and slipped it into his pocket when he thought no one was looking.

'How'd you lose the last zingtascos?' Erasmus had enquired, raising an eyebrow.

'Ended up in the lake.'

'That is unfortunate. How did they fall in the lake?'

'They were in my pocket.'

'Ah.' Uncle Erasmus had shaken his head, trying not to chuckle.

Stormforce might have a reputation as being excellent at investigating illicit magic leaking into an unsuspecting world, but as Oakmoss watched him during dinner, he decided it could not possibly equal his skill in charming Mum.

Mum refurnished the dining room often. Her latest change had involved chucking out the huge old carved table (now for sale in Erasmus Collectibles). It had been replaced with a long table of polished glass. She'd insisted Hyacinth light a row of tall candles along the centre and it was all quite lovely really; the way the candlelight reflected and the diamonds in his mother's jewellery sparkled as she gestured and helped herself to more wine.

It was passing with no actual disasters. Oakmoss hadn't even set anything alight. He even dared to reach across the table to help himself to more potato, and managed it without sending a candle flying. He mostly kept his elbows rigidly by his sides after that, not wanting to push his luck.

This dinner was almost enjoyable, but Oakmoss couldn't fully relax at having friends to dinner for the first time ever, not with darting anxious looks for his other friend Nightshade.

Erasmus and Stormforce were getting on brilliantly and seemed to be having a competition to see who could eat the most. Erasmus had motored through his first course and was on thirds, but still managed to try to beat Dad in telling the most jokes.

Veena was talking to Mum, and kept trying to turn the conversation to how plans were going for the toy rescue hospital.

'It's so hard. Finding just the right place,' said Mum, playing with a diamond necklace that twinkled in the candlelit room. 'It has to be right for the children, right for the toys.' She kept trying to turn her attention to Stormforce, who was sitting the other side of her.

'But the fundraising is going well?' Veena kept scratching the side of her nose. Oakmoss couldn't help but laugh as she was probably fidgeting as she was so seldom without a pen in her hand to write everything down.

'Oh, well, you can never have enough, can you?' said Mum.

But Oakmoss felt more and more uncomfortable not knowing what had happened to Nightshade. Was it him, or did the room seem to get hotter and hotter the longer he sat there? After arriving wearing a jacket, Uncle Erasmus had immediately abandoned it in a crumpled ball on the back of his chair, revealing a badly-ironed white shirt.

Oakmoss was also painfully aware that this was as good an opportunity as he was likely to get to speak to his father's apprentice. Trapmole was sitting the other side of Veena and next to Dad, and was gleefully recounting that sales of the fortune cats were up again and boasting how he'd made changes in the workshop that meant the machines worked even harder to keep up with demand.

'It's all going brilliantly with me there,' he said with a sly look at Oakmoss.

Dad couldn't look more bored at this attempt to talk business, and continued vying with Erasmus to make the best jokes. He made fun of the fact that Pudding had somehow managed to sidestep the no-cats-in-the-dining-room rule and was nestled in Adeline's lap. Oakmoss watched his mother cut her food with shiny silver cutlery and feed small, succulent pieces of chicken to her new kitten.

'You really must show me all these amazing improvements, Trapmole.' Oakmoss tried to sound genuinely interested.

Trapmole answered with a dismissive twist of his head and carried on boasting to Dad and Veena about how well everything was going.

'How much do you need before you start the hospital?' Veena asked Mum, also bored by Trapmole.

'Oh, my dear.' Adeline gave a dismissive chuckle. 'If only things were that easy. You couldn't possibly understand how difficult my life is, how hard I have to work before we can even think of beginning.'

Oakmoss wished it wasn't so hot in here. His mother loved the heat as much as Oakmoss loved being outside or having windows open. Oakmoss felt his cheeks growing redder and redder and there seemed to be no air in the room. They seldom had this many people to dinner and the room felt cramped and claustrophobic. Even now, at the height of summer, his mother frowned at anything like open windows or a cooling breeze.

'How come Oakmoss has never introduced you before, Dexter?' asked Mum, ignoring Veena's question about her views on Mr Mustard.

Stormforce answered that he was only passing through, and Adeline immediately insisted he stay, waving one of her hands, making her rings sparkle, and said it was no trouble at all.

'Privet will make up a bed in a spare room immediately.' She gestured to Hyacinth to pour more wine.

Hyacinth had just brought in a top-up of gravy from the kitchen, her orange plaits frizzing. 'Er, would it be OK if I leave that until after dessert?'

'Aren't you hot?' Veena whispered to Oakmoss.

'We'll be in the garden room next and that's even hotter,' Oakmoss replied glumly under his breath. 'Mum'll have got Hyacinth to put dessert and coffee in there.'

'Any hot chocolate?' asked Veena optimistically.

'I expect so. Hyacinth usually thinks of everything.'

'What exactly is the garden room?' asked Veena more loudly.

Mum answered her proudly. 'I built a big glass room at the back of the house for my orchids and ferns, they love it and so do I. I'm such a hothouse flower.'

'It's not even the heat that's the worst thing,' said Oakmoss darkly. 'It's the scented lilies that are out to get you.'

Veena crinkled her nose. 'Oakmoss, how can a plant be out to get you?'

'They have this pollen that's a seriously bright orange and it always ends up on you. Honestly, it's spooky. I swear they do it deliberately. You'll see.'

'Maybe that's just because if anything unlucky happens, it always happens to you.'

Hyacinth asked if it was all right to clear the table and Oakmoss quickly asked if she'd seen any sign of Nightshade. 'Or Grimalkin?'

Hyacinth shook her head as she balanced plates. 'Oakmoss, did you even stop to think if it was a good idea to bring another cat into this house?' she said wearily, exiting with difficulty, laden as she was with empty dishes.

It would be his fault that Nightshade had not been able to stay out of the way of the big, mean cat. What if there had been a fight? What if she was lying somewhere injured?

Oakmoss felt it was impossible to sit here any longer. 'I just need to . . .' he began his excuse, wanting to search right now.

He got to his feet too quickly and the idea of slipping away quietly disintegrated. He managed to tip his chair back and got his legs tangled up. Somehow, as he often did, Oakmoss found himself sprawling on the floor, looking up at a sea of faces where hardly an eyebrow was raised in surprise. His mother's face was just resigned and disappointed.

'Oakmoss, are you all right?' asked Uncle Erasmus.

Oakmoss scrambled to his feet and left without saying a word. At least nothing had smashed and not a single candle had tipped over. And the hallway felt cool and welcoming. He headed along the corridor, aiming for the kitchen first, although surely Hyacinth would have seen Nightshade if she was in there.

He noticed the door to the garden room was wide open. Mum liked to keep the air at what she called a carefully controlled temperature; what Oakmoss called sweaty and overheated. She said it was what her delicate plants needed, otherwise they'd wither and die. That door was never left open.

It was where Hyacinth would have placed the desserts ready for after dinner. Had Hyacinth left the door open? She'd be in trouble for sure.

As he went to close the door, he thought he should check inside, although mostly he felt a sudden urge to take another peek at his favourite dessert; that big cherry bakewell pie would be waiting in there.

He could not resist reminding himself of how tempting it looked, with its thick layer of smooth white icing and its perfect circle of glacé cherries hiding layers of almond and pastry beneath.

He tiptoed into the dark and overheated room, with its clammy air and overpowering perfume of the lilies he hated. He wanted to just take a sneaky peek at that glorious pie Hyacinth hardly ever made, then he'd carry on his search for Nightshade.

Fading sunlight warmed the glass, sending long

shivering sunbeams on to the damp black and white tiles. Oakmoss stepped quietly through the soft shafts of sunlight, through the tall palms, overblown ferns and delicate orchids, to a low table hidden in the shadows. He stood in front of the array of tempting desserts, all beautifully arranged, with a pile of plates and coffee cups waiting to one side. There was a big jug of thick cream that probably wouldn't be enough once Dad got started. He went closer, drawing in his elbows to avoid any malevolent lilies, but felt himself frowning.

Something was wrong.

He had seen all their favourites lined up on the big kitchen windowsill. Flaky pastry puffs filled with a generous layer of cream for Dad. Triple-layered chocolate cheesecake for Erasmus. Strawberry scones and coconut macaroons for Mum.

But where was his cherry bakewell pie?

He stepped forward, quite forgetting to draw in his elbows, and instantly, one of the evil lilies marked him. He now had a dark orange stain on his arm.

He peered around in the humid greenish gloom of the garden room, all his senses telling him something was not right. As his eyes adjusted to the dark, he saw exactly where that perfect cherry bakewell pie was.

The ill-wishing was not only real, it really was spreading. Because his favourite pie had met with a terrible accident. All across the black and white floor was a mess of pastry. The pie was reduced to a splattering of crumbs, icing and cherries strewn across the damp tiles.

Disappointment mixed with disbelief. How could this have happened? It was almost as if someone had deliberately smashed that pie to the floor. How mean. How terrible. The thought made him feel sad and scared at the same time. To be the victim of such a cruel trick. For someone to be so determined he wouldn't get to eat that pie.

But the destroyed pie wasn't the only thing sprawled across the floor in a dark corner. In among the crumbly mess of a once beautiful dessert, right in the shadows and under the long fronds of one of the big potted palms, a shape lay motionless. A shape with four paws.

PART THREE

26. It Was Meant For Me

Oakmoss hadn't resisted as gentle hands had steered him out of the garden room, even though he knew he was being bundled out like some naughty child being banished while adults cleared up a terrible mess in hushed voices.

Nightshade had tried to warn him. She'd sensed it all in her whiskers and he hadn't listened, not really . . . That terrible mess, those unmoving paws – it was all his fault. He staggered to his room, his thoughts a whirlwind.

The first thing he saw was a small puddle of darkness curled on his pillow.

'Nightshade!' he cried. He rushed across to bury his face in the soft fur of the sleeping cat. 'You're all right! You were here all the time! Something terrible's happened and I thought . . . for a moment I thought it was you. And I've been sitting there worrying all evening! And here you are, tucked up in bed without a scratch on you!'

He earned himself a baleful look from a half-open green eye, and a flex of a barely shielded claw.

'I'm not dead, I *was* trying to nap. You mean you were worried that ponderous freak Grimalkin caught me?' Nightshade stretched out her paws. 'Those big lumbering monster cats are too slow for a lithe cat like me. You worry too much, Oakmoss.'

'That lumbering monster is with the vet.'

He explained how he'd seen the smashed pie, and then found Grimalkin flat out on the floor, and leapt to the conclusion there must have been a fight. How he'd worried what state Nightshade would be in when he found her, how he'd looked at Grimalkin's yellow eyes, merely slits, not even flickering, but not quite closed, as if he was looking at Oakmoss and desperately trying to communicate something.

'I remembered the escape tree to your room,' said

Nightshade. 'So when Grimalkin came for me, I shot straight up the tree and watched him looking around for ages!' she purred. 'Whatever happened to Grimalkin or your pie, it wasn't anything to do with a fight.'

'But how did the pie get smashed if there was no fight? And what happened to Grimalkin?'

Oakmoss didn't know how long he'd been there, crouched on the damp tiles of the floor next to the motionless body, his hand on Grimalkin's chest, which had been rising and falling so slowly it was barely discernible to his touch.

He sat on the bed and talked as Nightshade snuggled into him. He calmed as he rhythmically stroked her silky fur.

They puzzled over it together – what could have happened?

'Nightshade. I've been thinking . . . these accidents, do you think it can be my own magic somehow twisting itself? I've never truly believed anyone was ill-wishing me. I've always been clumsy. And I wonder . . . could I be causing my own bad luck as a punishment? Nightshade, I keep having evil thoughts about how if I learnt how to use magic, well, I'd use it to make Flanagan have an accident.'

It had been worrying at him and he felt better to have confessed it, especially when she said easily:

'Oh, evil thoughts! We all have those. But you have never once acted on them, that's what's important. Do you think Grimalkin ate a bit of the pie?' Nightshade asked.

'You think there was an ill-wishing spell in it and that it was meant for me?'

'It'll be in something you wear, or something you eat, I said. And that pie was meant for you.'

'But Hyacinth—'

'Was not the only person in the kitchen today,' said Nightshade gently. 'You say the ill-wishing can't be in anything you wear because you lose everything. You even replace your glasses regularly,' she mused.

'Yeah, Mum makes me keep a stash of spares. Some in my bedroom, some in the boathouse.'

'You should seriously try to find a counter spell. Or do a strong protection aura. I don't know, you're the sorcerer.'

'A counter spell? Me?'

'Well, why not?' Nightshade clawed the cover on the bed. 'You are one heck of a sorcerer. Put all that natural talent to good use.'

'I don't think I'd be any good with that kind of magic; books and spells and things.'

'Yeah, you would be. You can move the air and water. It comes so naturally, you don't have to think about it. But who knows what magic you could master if you took some proper training,' encouraged Nightshade. 'You don't know what you can do until you try. Didn't you pick up a couple of books from Erasmus this morning? See if you can find anything that could help you break whatever spell is hanging over you.'

Oakmoss found *Mind-bending Meld Magic* where he'd put it on a shelf earlier. He flicked through uncertainly. 'Dad always warns me that magic brought nothing but trouble for my grandfather.'

Nightshade looked at him with her big green eyes. 'And that's awkward, because it means no one's teaching you anything. With magic like yours, that could be dangerous.'

Oakmoss flicked through the book. 'Dad gets so frowny at any mention of magic. I don't want my magic to be a big deal.'

'It's always a big deal when you realize you have a powerful sorcerer in the family. Not easy to tell your family that you have way more magical talent than they all do put together.' Nightshade was fixing him with her unblinking stare.

He was rescued from the uncomfortable

conversation by a tap on his door. Veena arrived, bringing a big glass of lemonade and news.

'The vet reckoned something Grimalkin ate disagreed with him – she took away a sample of the pie. How are you, Oakmoss? You didn't eat any of that pie, did you?'

'*Disagreed?!*' said Nightshade. 'Oakmoss told me Grimalkin was collapsed and hardly breathing. That cherry bakewell pie was meant for you, Oakmoss – it's time you realize the danger you're in. Or the next attack might very well leave you being the one flat out on the floor.'

27. EVIDENCE OF HER CRIME

Oakmoss fussed Nightshade's ears, his mind buzzing with questions. Everyone knew cherry bakewell pie was his favourite. How had that pie ended up smashed on the floor? Especially if there had been no fight?

Veena picked up the book he'd just put down. 'Oh – mind magic! What's that?'

'To be honest, I don't know. Nightshade was telling me I need to know more about magic. She thinks I could find a counter spell for all this ill-wishing.'

Veena flicked through the book. 'You have all the *interesting*, don't you? All the interesting magic, the interesting family . . .'

'All the interesting accidents and the interesting someone trying to hurt me.' It really was time to face up to the fact that he wasn't simply unlucky, but that someone was deliberately targeting him. But who?

'Is Hyacinth magical? She said that thing about the tea leaf,' said Veena, who never missed anything. 'Does she do prophecies and things? Is that magic?'

'I don't think her magic's very strong,' said Oakmoss, glad Nightshade had stayed with him snuggled on his lap. 'She's got magic in the family. Her mother's a hedge witch. Hyacinth's affinity, I think, is more with fortune-telling, the ability to see futures – and pasts.'

'What's a hedge witch exactly?'

'You know, someone with a lot of wisdom about the natural world.'

'I don't think I do know.'

'It's making cures mostly, using natural things – herbs, rocks and a little spiritual magic,' Oakmoss explained. 'Hyacinth says no one takes her mum seriously so she lives in the middle of a wood, cut off. Hyacinth decided that wasn't for her, so she works for Mum and Dad. Magical people do tend to stick together.' He looked at Veena, who was reading the mind-meld book. 'I do wish Mum didn't make Hyacinth work non-stop.' He sighed. 'And I hope it's not Hyacinth ill-wishing me to get back at my mother.'

There was another tap on the door. This time it was Dex, with Pudding at his feet and dessert in his hands. He was holding out a slab of chocolate cheesecake.

'You two can't palm me off with lemonade and cake,' said Oakmoss. 'Tell me what's happening.'

'Fair enough, I'll eat it,' responded Stormforce, looking for a place to sit, while Pudding leapt up to nuzzle against Nightshade on the bed.

Oakmoss shrugged and accepted the cheesecake, still sad about the loss of his favourite pie.

'I'm surprised anyone's eating any dessert,' commented Nightshade, watching Oakmoss take a large forkful. She gave Pudding an unfriendly look.

'Dexter – was there ill-wishing in that pie?' asked Oakmoss.

'Oh, good question,' said Veena. 'Did you manage to . . .' She mimicked the swishing motion with which Stormforce had sent a shimmering blue light over the boathouse and Oakmoss.

'There's been a lot going on in the garden room,

so it wasn't easy to perform a detailed magical investigation,' he said.

Oakmoss felt Dexter was being evasive and wondered if the magical investigator was going to keep what he really thought to himself. 'Nightshade thinks I should find a counter spell, Dexter, could you help with that?'

'Not entirely my area of expertise.' Dexter moved aside a pile of clothes from a chair in the corner to sit down. He stretched out to rest his booted feet on the bed. 'But there are quite a few mysteries around your family, and we have many questions that need answering.' He checked the small dagger hidden in his jacket. 'And I did manage a small but covert magical investigation.'

'I bet there was ill-wishing in that pie,' Veena said grimly. 'Hyacinth cleared up every single speck of it and it went straight in the bin. Was she covering up evidence of her crime? Oakmoss thinks Hyacinth is ill-wishing him to get back at his mother for treating her so badly. It's a possibility.'

'I said I hoped that *wasn't* it,' protested Oakmoss. 'We were investigating Mr Mustard as our prime suspect, or don't you remember? If he got into the grounds to tamper with those floorboards, what's to stop him having got to that pie? He could have been spying and doing anything under cover of all the bustle with the deliveries.'

'Absolutely. It's more important than ever to get to the bottom of what's brought Mr Mustard here.' Stormforce was looking at Oakmoss expectantly. 'Dinner was the perfect opportunity. What did you get out of Trapmole?'

'Er . . .' Oakmoss scratched at his head. It was the first time in a while this did not produce a fresh leakage of blood. 'I'm getting the tour of the workshop tomorrow,' he lied, not able to admit he had got nowhere with the unfriendly apprentice.

'Then we break in,' said Veena, rather too gleefully. 'Dex showers everything with that blue light of his, proves what he needs to and sends Mr Mustard on his way. Oakmoss's problems will be over. Yay! I'm sure it's not Hyacinth, Oakmoss. Anyway, it's going to be busy tomorrow – I should really go.' She put the book down.

'I don't believe there was any ill-wishing spell in that pie,' said Stormforce quietly.

'Seriously?' Veena said with a frown. 'I thought we'd all dodged a dose of this ill-wishing spell, except Grimalkin who is extremely ill. If any of us had eaten that pie . . .'

'Did he eat it? It looked more like he sort

of attacked it,' said Oakmoss, remembering the carnage.

'That's exactly what it looked like,' said Storm-force. 'It looked exactly as it was supposed to – that there had been a fight and it ended up on the floor.'

'And what do you think it looked like?' asked Nightshade.

'It looked to me like a plan that changed at the last minute.'

Veena shook her head. 'I don't understand.'

'I imagine Grimalkin found the door open, went into the garden room, found the pie already on the floor. I agree Grimalkin must have eaten some.'

'Destroyed already?' said Nightshade. 'But why destroy the pie? You just said it wasn't enchanted? You found no ill-wishing, right? And how do we have one very ill cat? None of that makes sense, sorry Stormforce.'

'It does if you remember that everyone knows Oakmoss is usually the only one to eat a cherry bakewell pie,' replied Dexter. 'And that something unexpected happened – you had guests.'

'Suddenly other people might eat it?' Veena raised an enquiring eyebrow. 'That's what you mean by plans having to change? That pie had to be destroyed once it was clear Oakmoss might not be the only one to eat it?' She chewed her lip thoughtfully. 'We really did have a lucky escape.'

'You mean cats were meant to take the blame?' said Nightshade huffily. 'Everyone was meant to think that we destroyed it.'

'No one could guess you'd tell us there never was a fight!' Oakmoss said to Nightshade.

'So, backing up a bit,' said Veena, 'why would the pie be destroyed if there was no ill-wishing in it anyway?'

Stormforce rubbed his chin and looked thoughtful for a long while without answering.

'And what do you think happened to Grimalkin?' pressed Veena, who had got to her feet, ready to leave.

It *was* late. The summer evening had tricked Oakmoss into thinking it was still early. 'Shall we walk back with you, Veena?' he offered.

'Ah, that's all right. Erasmus is going the same way,' said Veena.

Stormforce spoke slowly, as if still thinking everything through. He looked serious. 'I started off asking myself, if we *had* eaten the pie and all suffered just a bit of bad luck, what would have been the harm? Everyone has a bit of bad luck, we probably wouldn't have thought anything of it. But then I was confused because I couldn't find any curse on that pie anyway. Yet, you're right, we have one very ill cat. So there's only one conclusion that makes sense.'

He looked at them all in turn and spoke so quietly Oakmoss had to strain to hear. 'When the vet reports back on her findings, I have a feeling we're going to learn Oakmoss was incredibly lucky,' he said slowly. 'Grimalkin less so. That pie had to be destroyed because if anyone had eaten it things would have been serious. If I'm right, Oakmoss is no longer being targeted by ill-wishing. I think that pie was poisoned.'

28. AN OFFER OF KIPPERS

Oakmoss awoke from a very vivid dream, sweaty and terrified. He was glad to be awake, and that a monster was not about to eat him.

But his heart was thundering and something was pressing on his chest. Something was making it difficult to breathe, and there was a rumbling, roaring like . . . Nightshade snoring.

And Pudding had snuggled in too, her snowy puffball bottom right in Oakmoss's face.

He slid out of bed, unsuccessfully trying not to

disturb the sleeping cats, and left them to finish their prolonged morning stretching routine as he headed to the kitchen in search of breakfast. As he bounded down the many polished stairs, his feet slowed as he remembered that last night someone had tried to poison him.

But there was no time to take that in properly, because today was full of ambitious plans that were almost certain to go wrong because they relied heavily on him, the unluckiest boy in the world. Success hinged on him getting a favour out of Trapmole, and he'd lied to Stormforce about having already arranged things with the snarky apprentice.

Even the sight of Hyacinth bustling around, calling a cheery greeting, and the welcome smell of kippers and toast didn't make him feel any less like someone had run over him. Should anyone ask, his nose was fragile, he was covered in scratches, bruises and semi-healing scars, even in bits you couldn't see, and he squirmed to find a comfortable position in his chair. Hyacinth asked if he wanted kippers and made a comment about trying not to hurt himself today.

Should he interpret her words as some sort of threat? Oakmoss hated himself for even thinking it. It was terrible to suspect everyone. He slumped at the kitchen table, wondering if there was any way he could slink out of taking part in any of the frankly terrible plans for the day, from breaking into the workshop to the whole fairy-tale gala.

All he wanted was to spend the day fishing quietly and seeing if he could spot the kingfishers again.

As Hyacinth placed kippers in front of him, miraculously Nightshade and Pudding were there, looking up at him expectantly with hungry eyes. A bit for Nightshade, a bit for Pudding, a very little bit for him. The kippers didn't last long. Oakmoss got up to make himself some scrambled eggs and toast.

Moving made him feel a hundred years old.

He gave a wide yawn just as Dexter Stormforce strode into the kitchen looking fresh and damp from a shower, managing to look dashing, as if he'd been up for hours.

'Hello. I've been up for hours,' he said. 'I went out for a run around your grounds – everything is hotting up for later,' he said chirpily, helping himself to one of Oakmoss's freshly made slices of toast the second it popped out of the toaster. 'How are you?' he asked, reaching for the butter. 'Nice black eye you've got.' He looked closer. 'Black *eyes*, I should say. What time does your fairy-tale gala start?'

'For some of us, it started the minute the first

delivery lorries arrived,' said Hyacinth wearily, offering hot drinks as Stormforce sat down in the chair Oakmoss had just vacated.

Oakmoss wanted to ask if someone attempting to poison him last night would get him off asking Trapmole to divulge security details for the Hornbeam Workshop as he didn't rate his chances. Trapmole seemed to want to devote his life to the workshop and to pointing out Oakmoss's many shortcomings at every opportunity, presumably in the hope that his parents would never let their son anywhere near the family business.

It was easy to imagine Trapmole slipping poison into that pie.

And to imagine him realizing their unexpected guests, including Veena, might now eat a slice, and smashing it on the floor, leaving feuding cats to take the blame. But how could they prove anything?

Nightshade was under the kitchen table, teasing out a lot of white fluff from among her black glossy fur. But the second Oakmoss placed his plate of scrambled eggs down on the table, she leapt to her feet and up on to the table, pointedly ignoring a lot of loud miaowing from Pudding, who was too small to jump that far.

Oakmoss put a saucer of egg on the floor for

Pudding and went to crack a load more eggs after receiving a hopeful glance from Stormforce.

'You are going to have to keep that cat out of here,' said Hyacinth, looking red-faced and stressed already as she swept Nightshade, a piece of toast clamped in her jaws, from the table. 'I do hope you have not brought this stray in permanently.'

Nightshade blinked at her and the end of her tail twitched, but Hyacinth was already on her way out of the kitchen, so Nightshade escaped any punishment.

'I need to keep you more under control!' Oakmoss grinned at her, and Stormforce took the chance to pinch the remaining slice of Oakmoss's toast.

Oakmoss's breakfast should have incorporated kippers, toast, scrambled egg and more toast, but his stomach knew different.

'I wasn't the only one taking a look around bright and early this morning,' said Stormforce through munching. 'There was someone wearing their hood up and trying to look unobtrusive, spying with a pair of bird-watching binoculars, slipping between all the deliveries and taking notes.'

'Veena was here already this morning!' But Oakmoss wasn't really surprised.

'One blue van was being loaded rather than

unloaded,' went on Stormforce, adding more butter to the toast, 'with boxes stamped with the words Hornbeam Workshop. Guess they are full of your dad's bestselling toys – those black cats with the waving paws and tails.'

'Fortune cats, yes.'

Oakmoss looked out into the courtyard. Trapmole was right there barking out orders to a driver. Oakmoss's stomach squirmed and clenched at the thought that Trapmole might have tried to poison him and now the plan was that he be nice and ask Trapmole for a favour.

'Perfect opportunity,' said Stormforce, his eyes glittering as they rested on Trapmole. 'Find out about those extra security measures. Extra security for a toy workshop – does make you wonder.'

Wonder what? thought Oakmoss.

Dexter's good looks and lazy charm made everyone like him. But maybe that was a superpower. He was simple to dismiss as easy-going and not at all dangerous. Yet today Stormforce's laid-back manner barely concealed that he was excited to be on the case and Nightshade had described him as one of the best magical investigators in the business. Oakmoss tried to remember quite how the magical investigator had talked him into helping.

Was taking a shrewd magical investigator like Dexter Stormforce into the family workshop really a good idea?

But they just made toys, Oakmoss reminded himself. He reluctantly accepted he had little choice but to go ahead. He knew exactly why he'd agreed.

'Once we get inside, we can prove any claims Mr Mustard is making are nonsense, can't we? Then you can get rid of him, Stormforce? Today? Before he does anything to mess up the fundraising gala?' Or make another attack. Next time Oakmoss might not be so lucky.

Stormforce clapped him on the shoulder. 'One thing at a time. The first step is to get Trapmole to reveal all the secrets. Let us know what we're in for, eh?' Dexter finished his last mouthful of Oakmoss's toast, turning to where Trapmole was ordering people about importantly. 'I'd say now's as good a time as any. It's up to you, Oakmoss – we are all relying on you to make sure we don't get caught.'

29. A Practised Liar

'You want to have a tour of the Hornbeam Workshop *now*?' Trapmole sounded exactly as Oakmoss had imagined. 'I can't possibly do it now. Are you joking? Are you insane? I am way too busy.'

It was true that the whole of Hornbeam Hall was preparing for this afternoon's festivities. Marquees and gazebos fluttered on the main sweep of lawn leading up from the front gate. But it was nothing compared to the fluttering in Oakmoss's stomach.

'What exactly are you doing?' Oakmoss couldn't help but ask.

Trapmole looked like he was attaching a wheeled box to the front of an ancient and rusty bicycle. He'd started barking at Oakmoss the second he'd arrived, blaming him for there no longer being a decent bicycle around since Oakmoss had ridden it into its fatal accident. Now he went a little quiet.

What would Stormforce say? 'Yes, a tour now, please, Trapmole. I don't know enough, you know, if people have questions about the business today,' tried Oakmoss, wishing he was a more practised liar. Stormforce would have made a much better job of this. Stormforce, he felt sure, wouldn't let something like a small lie stand in the way of his investigations.

'We all want this to be a huge success for Mum and Dad,' he continued. 'We don't want to let them down. I need to be prepared.'

'I suppose the Hornbeam Workshop is highly interesting and hugely successful,' frowned Trapmole grudgingly. He was now fixing a jaunty sign to the trolley attached to the bike. It read: STOP ME AND BUY LEMONADE. 'Of course, people across the world are envious of our success. There are trade secrets in there that you really cannot let on to anyone about.'

Were there? Trapmole's caginess was a little unsettling, although the apprentice was always full of his own importance.

'What exactly are you doing?' Oakmoss asked again.

Trapmole's ears went a little pink as he fiddled with the rusty bike and looked ready to make a wobbly effort to cycle off. He explained he'd be cycling around selling glasses of lemonade.

'It sounds a brilliant idea, Trapmole,' Oakmoss enthused. 'I'm sure your lemonade cart will be a big success for the fundraising.'

Trapmole gave an uneasy chuckle. 'Do you know, I think it might bring quite a flood of donations. Your parents will be very pleased.'

Oakmoss thought quickly, 'You're right, you're too busy. Dad was so keen that I have a tour. I'll just tell Dad I asked but of course you didn't have time.' Oakmoss rolled his eyes, as if the request was nothing to do with him.

Trapmole stopped. 'No, no, no, no, no – now is absolutely fine if that's what Mr Hornbeam wants, although why he couldn't have said . . .' He looked up at the sky. 'Do you think this weather looks a bit Christmas for a gala?' He gave a weak smile.

'What?'

'It looks like reindeer.' Trapmole nodded at the dark clouds brewing far on the horizon. 'You know,' Trapmole snapped, losing his feeble attempt at a smile, 'rain, dear? It's like a play on words.'

Trapmole had made a lame joke. Oakmoss belatedly leapt in to manage a really forced chuckle to show how well they were getting on. He felt just like one of Flanagan's cronies on the Dogberry Academy bus. 'Rain, dear! Very good, Trapmole.'

And with that, Trapmole bustled across to the small door in the whitewashed wall. It took a moment for Oakmoss to realize he was expected to follow.

Trapmole gave a little chuckle himself as they stood by the door, not able to stop himself boasting about how nobody would even notice the workshop was here. 'No one can see how big it's become,' he said proudly, leaving Oakmoss feeling Trapmole had been responsible for the glimmer.

Trapmole pushed aside a frond of ivy that was concealing a sleek number pad. The first security measure. Oakmoss had to be alert – he needed to watch carefully so he could report back every detail to the others. They were relying on him.

Trapmole punched in an impossibly long number that made Oakmoss blink.

Then he winced. That wasn't fair, that wasn't even a magical trap, that was . . . just a very long number he couldn't possibly remember. There wasn't a chance he'd get the others past even this first bit of security for the Hornbeam Workshop. This plan was going to fail.

There was a click, and Trapmole pushed open the door. Oakmoss braced himself for whatever might come next.

30. NOT A RAT'S GALA

I was on the boathouse veranda, sitting perfectly still alongside Veena. I was mesmerized by some little silvery fish darting about in the lake below. She was tapping her lucky pen against her notebook, fidgeting and swinging her legs impatiently.

At first sight of Oakmoss, she leapt up. 'What took you so long?! We need to talk to our prime suspect before that idiot police officer Truffle tries to move him along again.'

'Sorry, Veena. Trapmole said he didn't have a

moment to spare, but once he got started the difficulty was getting him to stop. He takes his work way too seriously. I've lots to tell you. Do you know that the fortune cat is now so successful it's the only line we do? And that we're forecasting double-digit sales growth for this quarter?'

Veena crooked an eyebrow at Oakmoss. 'I don't think that's the sort of information Dexter wanted. Now, please can we go and find out exactly what's brought our prime suspect to Hornbeam Hall.'

I could tell Veena was excited and nervous in equal measure about her forthcoming interview and I was ready to pad after her. She hadn't abandoned all hope of finding a story she could print on her front page that didn't involve magic.

'Maybe we should wait for Dexter,' suggested Oakmoss. 'Where is he?'

'I don't know. Doing his hair, probably.'

'Also, I stopped to get these.' Oakmoss laid a few pieces of wood at the door of the boathouse.

'What are they for?'

'We need to fix the floor.'

'But that's going to take ages.' Veena began to bounce on her toes impatiently.

'It won't. And with all of us here, crowding in, it'd

only need someone to step backwards at the wrong moment . . .'

The thought of plunging into the lake did the trick and Veena agreed to wait. We watched as Oakmoss did something deft with his hands, and just like that the wood was in place and the floor was as good as new. It really had taken him seconds.

'Oakmoss, you really are amazing,' said Veena.

Oakmoss blushed. 'I'm really not, I don't even know how I do it. I just kind of concentrate and it happens. Honestly, it's not a big deal. Come on, let's get this interview done. Mr Mustard's really not going to admit he poisoned that pie, is he? Are you going to ask him?'

'We'll just have to see what we can persuade him to tell us.'

We fell into step following the slow-moving river, turning away from the house to reach the perimeter wall. We'd decided it was a good idea to approach Mustard from the side, rather than through the front gate.

Oakmoss was looking even more thoughtful than usual, blinking owlishly behind his glasses. I sensed seeing inside the workshop had given him plenty to think about, and that was troubling. I longed to ask more, but it was probably right to wait until we were all together.

Veena began musing over whether they might get more out of Mustard if he believed his attack had been successful and Oakmoss was dead. 'Or at the very least in hospital, seriously ill,' she said, leaping down from the wall and looking sideways at Oakmoss. 'Maybe you need a disguise. Otherwise it rather blows our cover, doesn't it? Because if you'd eaten the poisoned pie rather than Grimalkin, you'd hardly be wandering around spying and asking for newspaper interviews, would you?'

'I'm not wearing a disguise.' Oakmoss reached nervously into his pocket and popped a soothing zingtasco into his mouth. 'Especially to prove that I'm dead.'

'When I said disguise,' she said, 'I don't mean a false beard or anything. Maybe just a hat and sunglasses?' Oakmoss was unmoved. She rolled her eyes. 'OK, fine! I can't believe you're grumbling about a simple hat and sunglasses after you telling me I'd make a good Maleficent. And a hat and sunglasses would be a better look than crusty swamp monster having a day off, which is what you were happy to look like yesterday.'

'Who said I was happy about it?'

Veena was trotting alongside the grey wall at quite a chirpy pace. 'Who could have guessed that I'd be off to interview a person camping out on your doorstep, accusing your family of . . . something?' she said. 'Your family is so interesting, Oakmoss.'

'You can't put Mr Mustard on your front page.' I could tell Oakmoss was trying to sound insistent, but he rather ruined the impact by having a mouth full of sweet and then tripping over his own feet. He teetered, grabbed hold of something to steady himself. Unfortunately, the something was a thick patch of tall stinging nettles.

'But Mr Mustard is the only story I can print that doesn't involve magic, Oakmoss,' said Veena, offering him a steadying hand.

I sensed an argument brewing, and now was really not the time. 'We all need to concentrate on what's important,' I reminded them as I padded along. 'We need to make sure he's got no plans to threaten the RATS gala.'

'We're not calling it the RATS gala,' said Oakmoss. He swallowed his sweet a bit too early. I could almost see his throat bulge. He turned back to Veena. 'I'm not letting you into a whole load of my family secrets because I'm giving you a newspaper exclusive,' he reminded her. 'But because you're my best friend.'

Veena bit her lip then opened her mouth to respond, but didn't quite manage to – we'd rounded the corner to the front of the house, and the sheer number of people gathered in the road outside Hornbeam Hall was enough to silence anyone.

A final few delivery lorries were waiting, still and silent in the road, but around them milled a crowd that brought such a festive atmosphere you might think the fairy-tale gala had begun already. Some had spread picnic blankets or were perched on the parched grass sharing crisps. Standing in a line, waiting patiently by the gates, was a line of people clutching cake boxes or tins. Perhaps there wasn't a great deal to do in Dogberry on a Saturday morning.

Above the black entrance gates a big banner was draped advertising the fairy-tale gala. But across it were daubed the words: HORNBEAM WORKSHOP ARE CHEATS. And beyond the crowd was Mr Mustard's bright-blue tent. It remained zipped, as if he was waiting for the right moment for his entrance to have maximum impact.

As one of the dark black gates began to swing inwards, a gasp of anticipation rose from the crowd.

It was like watching a long-closed tomb start to open. There was a lot of squeaking of hinges and a few 'oohs' from the waiting locals. Then Hyacinth

Privet stepped out, her ginger plaits tied neatly on top of her head. I think everyone had been expecting at least an Egyptian mummy, not a woman carrying a clipboard and a harassed look.

'Got a Cinderella for you,' called the first lorry driver, crooking his thumb backwards at his delivery load.

Hyacinth peered at her clipboard. 'Yes. One Cinderella fairy-tale bouncy castle, but there should be an underwater one too.'

'I got no order for any of our underwaters,' the driver frowned and turned his head sideways to read the clipboard too. 'One Cinderella, with additional turrets. All I was told to bring.'

I heard Oakmoss draw in his breath sharply. But he wasn't looking at the gates. He was looking at a girl on the grass verge opposite.

She had incredibly long, straight hair almost down to her waist. Dark and glossy. Not often I get hair envy, but this was hair you couldn't ignore. She also had the sort of long nose that was good at looking down on people. Her whole air said she felt everyone else should look up to her, even as she sat on a picnic blanket, grinning as she watched all the action.

'Oh no,' cried Oakmoss in a strangled voice. 'Flanagan!'

Veena mumbled. 'Taking more bets, most likely.'

'What?'

'I told you. She's taking bets on everything – from who is going to win the Puss-in-Boots throwing to the fancy dress prize. Even about how long Mr Mustard is going to camp here – I heard last night that the smartest money's now on a month. And she's making a mint.'

This was not good news for Oakmoss's nerves, or for the Hornbeam family.

'Give me the disguise now,' said Oakmoss grimly. He held out his hand. 'If you suggested a disguise you'll have brought something with you. I'm going to slip in behind her and see exactly what she's up to.'

With a sigh, Veena took out a bucket hat and a pair of dark glasses. But the hat was bright yellow and the moment Oakmoss replaced his normal glasses with the dark ones, he tripped over his feet.

And the second we crept a little closer to the waiting crowd, a voice rang out: 'Oh, hello Oakmoss! What's with the hat?'

'Hello, Flanagan,' said Oakmoss, hurriedly dragging off the hat and losing the dark glasses as a rosy blush spread over his freckled face. 'It's, er, I thought...'

Before he could bumble out a response, there was an unzipping sound and, seizing his moment, Mr Mustard sprang from his tent.

31. Involving Some Shouting

Mustard sidled up alongside the lorry. I wasn't sure of his plan, but was impressed with the way Hyacinth did her best to ignore him as he loomed closer.

Believe me, it's not easy to ignore a small man with a big moustache who is hopping from one leg to another shouting: 'They robbed me!' Robbed him? Mustard really did seem angry.

Hyacinth's face slowly turned red. Oakmoss looked like he wished he could turn into a bird and fly away.

'What are you going to do about it?!' yelled Mustard.

But the biggest surprise was reserved for Mustard himself, as Veena tapped him on the shoulder, distracting him from his aim of causing maximum annoyance at the gate. He turned in startled surprise as she announced herself as editor and chief reporter of the *Dogberry Academy Times*.

'We want to give you the chance to tell your side of the story.'

Mr Mustard put his head on one side. 'Are you offering money?'

'Money?' repeated Veena, sounding shocked. She had to raise her voice over the hiss of brakes as another delivery vehicle arrived. And the discussion about the incorrect bouncy castle delivery now involved some shouting. 'I'm offering a chance to get your voice heard. You can't put a price on that, can you?'

'I probably could. This *Dogberry Academy Times* – is that a school newspaper?' quizzed Mr Mustard, stroking his big moustache thoughtfully.

'It is, and with a loyal readership and a rising circulation,' said Veena proudly.

The line of Dogberry townsfolk with cake tins and other offerings for the tea tent began to snake past.

Mustard sighed and looked longingly at the shifting crowd. 'People are losing interest in my story,' he said wearily. 'No one's even brought me food today. Everyone seems more interested in this blasted fairy-tale gala.'

'You need to get your side of the story into print. And can I just point out that is a better way of drawing attention to your complaint than attacking Oakmoss.'

'Who's Oakmoss?'

Veena rolled her eyes at Mr Mustard's attempt to pretend he knew nothing. 'Are you planning to disrupt the fundraising gala too?'

'I hadn't thought about it, but thanks, that's a very good idea. All right, I'll give you my story. For the price of a coffee and a bacon butty from Marge's,' negotiated Mr Mustard.

Veena failed to cover her surprise at these terms. 'You expect me to buy you breakfast?' She drew herself up and I could tell she was thinking of her principles. I quickly trotted forward, feeling she might need my support. 'That's bribery,' she said scornfully.

'That's hunger, lassie.'

I pawed at Veena's leg and got her attention. We were up against the clock. I gave her a look that was clearly saying there are times when principles have to be shelved. One of those times is when you've got a magically protected toy workshop to break into in the middle of a fairy-tale gala. And a rudimentary sorcerer to protect.

Veena looked down at me and then back at Mr Mustard with narrowed eyes: 'It'll be an exclusive?'

'If you throw in a doughnut I can guarantee it'll be all yours.'

Veena beckoned in Oakmoss. They had a quick, quiet conversation, during which there was some fumbling in Oakmoss's pockets. I heard, *'We'll go and borrow some from Uncle Erasmus.'*

Veena looked at Mr Mustard. 'OK, deal.' They shook on it.

32. A Prime Suspect

Erasmus didn't cover his surprise to see us. 'Thought you'd be way too busy with the gala to visit me. I said the same to Trapmole.'

'Trapmole was here?' said Oakmoss. 'I'm here to borrow some money. Why was Trapmole here?'

'Well, you've come to the wrong place for money.' Erasmus chuckled and made a lazy gesture that took in the shop crammed full of unspeakable junk. 'Luckily, Trapmole wanted a book – I can help with books, sometimes.'

I'd stepped inside cautiously. *Cat.* I could detect one. We might be one orange monster down with Grimalkin on a long visit to the vet, but I hadn't forgotten he had a brother. And he was right here. Somewhere.

I stayed where I could be certain of a quick exit, lifting my nose, my whiskers trembling on high alert.

'What book did Trapmole want?' enquired Veena, examining the tightly packed bookcase.

'One that he'd received as a gift, I think. But he's lost it and wondered if your mother ditched it in one of her frequent clear-outs. He couldn't find it.' He squinted at Oakmoss. 'Actually, now I think about it – you took a couple of books, didn't you?'

Oakmoss shuffled and looked embarrassed. 'Sorry, but *Best Book of Birds* ended up in the lake, along with me and a bag of zingtascos.'

'That wasn't the one. I can't remember . . .'

Veena opened her mouth and I nearly interrupted as I guessed she was about to let slip she'd been reading *Mind-bending Meld Magic*. Luckily she stopped herself just in time. I'm pretty sure Oakmoss's family weren't quite yet ready for the fact that he'd shared the whole existence of magic with Veena.

Erasmus rootled around beneath the counter and offered a fresh bag of the purple sweets, saying that at least there were some other things he could help with and he asked how much money Oakmoss needed.

There he was. Gisborne was curled in the same chair I'd settled into the day before, the one with its stuffing spilling out on to the floor. Asleep? Or just craftily lulling me into a false sense of security? I tensed, ready to flee as he turned his big head slowly. I got a spiteful look from one yellow eye that put my paws on alert. But he didn't twitch so much as his tail. And he looked smaller and a whole lot less threatening without his big brute of a brother by his side.

'We need enough money for a bacon butty and a mug of coffee from Marge's,' explained Veena, as if that explained anything.

'And a doughnut,' said Oakmoss through his sweet.

Erasmus crooked an enquiring eyebrow at them both, but didn't ask questions. He went to the old-fashioned till and a bell chimed as he opened it and extracted a pile of coins, which he handed to Oakmoss.

'Thanks, I'll see you get it back,' said Oakmoss, bundling Veena out. I slipped out with them.

The bribery items were procured and the three of us headed back for our interview. I was interested to see if Veena managed to get our prime suspect to admit he'd got it in for Oakmoss. And what exactly was behind his accusation of being robbed and tricked.

There was still a party atmosphere on the scrubby grass verge outside the front gates of Hornbeam Hall. I could count three more families who had rolled up and brought chairs, offering around lunchtime sandwiches from plastic tubs.

The Flan was doing a roaring trade taking bets and offering a free peppermint with every one placed. The crowd were getting a good performance from Mr Mustard. He was taking advantage of the fact that most deliveries were safely stowed inside the black gates. One final delivery remained, leaving the crowd with less to entertain it and more chance for Mr Mustard to get his complaints noticed.

'The toys!' Mustard shouted, stepping up the show with a wild gesture to the picnickers. He pointed to the gates of Hornbeam Hall. 'The toys are evil. We have to stop them!'

Veena walked right up to Mr Mustard and handed over a brown paper bag and a takeaway cup of coffee. He sensibly decided to take a break from being the main attraction, removed his blue waterproof coat and spread it carefully on the ground to sit on. He opened the bag, taking a sniff.

'Why are you here? What exactly are you accusing the Hornbeam Workshop of?' asked Veena, not even waiting for him to take a mouthful of butty before taking out her red pen and notebook.

'Did you remember mustard?' enquired Mr Mustard, squinting with one eye into the bag.

'We wouldn't forget mustard,' replied Veena.

Mustard rummaged, took a squeezy yellow sachet from the depths of the brown bag, tore it open and lifted the lid of his butty to dollop the sauce inside. He waved his coffee cup. 'Is there sugar in this?'

Veena squinted. 'Do you want there to be sugar?'

'We weren't sure so we just put in half a teaspoon,' said Oakmoss helpfully, nudging Veena to Get On With It. They had a lot to do today. 'And we remembered the doughnut.' He handed over another bag. 'It's got jam in it.'

The black gates of Hornbeam Hall slowly closed, leaving nothing more to watch. The air had grown very still and I sensed even the picnickers were chewing more slowly to earwig what was going on.

'I am here because,' Mustard bit hungrily into the butty loaded with rashers of bacon and took a slurp of his coffee before he was ready to speak. 'They never answered my letters.'

'This is about letters?' squeaked Veena. 'I thought

it was going to be about tricks or fraud and the toys being evil.'

'The letters were about money they stole. I went to the police. They dismissed me as some sort of crazy person. That's why I'm here.'

'Because bringing a tent and camping outside the gates of Hornbeam Hall hurling accusations are the actions of a sensible person?' said Oakmoss, earning a withering look from Veena that warned him she was conducting this interview.

'And how do you think it looks to hurt Oakmoss?' said Veena.

'Oakmoss?' responded Mustard.

Oakmoss persisted. 'Why do you think the Hornbeams stole money from you? You told me you bought a fortune cat as a gift for your wife. Sorry, but I'm not surprised the police dismissed your complaint.'

Mustard wiped a smear of yellow from his chin. 'I'm trying to tell you. My wife and I had a day out at the seaside and it rained—'

'You were at the seaside and it rained?' Veena's pen tapped the side of her nose as she watched the last mouthful of butty being eaten. 'I have a feeling I wasted my money. This is not going to make the front page,' she muttered.

'My wife donated to the RATS charity.'

'Well, that's very kind of her, it's a popular cause,' said Veena impatiently. 'There's this fundraising gala and everything. Lots of people are making donations, Mr Mustard, not just your wife. That's not stealing.'

'Oh, making a charity donation is fine.' He reached into a pocket and took out a big red handkerchief and wiped his face. 'But she made so many donations.'

It was at this point, just as things were getting interesting, that I noticed someone was lumbering in our direction.

I nudged Veena as a tall and wide uniformed police officer approached. He had hair cut so short you could see his sunburnt scalp showing through. He wore a crisp white shirt and thick belt around his waist that appeared to contain assorted weaponry. He had the look of someone who had joined the police, but whose real ambition was to be a commando. I guessed this was Dogberry's PC Truffle, and that meant our chance for an interview was almost over.

'Oh no,' I heard Veena say quietly.

'Don't worry,' I said reassuringly. 'I think at least one of those canisters attached to his belt is actually a thermos of coffee.'

Veena turned back to Mustard, her pen scribbling furiously. 'So, your wife made donations? How many exactly?'

'Too many to count. It was my bank who phoned to tell me how fast the money was disappearing. And it was all connected to that fortune cat. My wife loved that cat – it sat on her bedside table next to her alarm clock and she got into this habit of making its paw and tail wave every morning. It was me who smelled a rat, or RATS. They're both right here at Hornbeam Hall, did you know that?' He waved his arms around. 'Am I the only one to see the connection? Everyone dismisses me as a fool.'

'I'm not sure I really understand what you're saying, Mr Mustard.'

'To be honest,' he wiped his face with his big red hanky, 'I don't really get it myself, but that's your front-page story.' He tapped Veena's notebook with a slightly mustardy finger.

'Front-page story?' Veena put away her pen crossly. 'Your wife making donations to RATS is not a front-page story. And it's certainly not a reason to attack Oakmoss.'

PC Truffle had almost finished his ponderous walk. The crowd seemed to have stopped crunching its crisps and were waiting to see if their patience was going to be rewarded by seeing Mr Mustard get arrested again.

I could see more money changing hands as the Flan adjusted her odds.

Truffle announced loudly (mostly to the crowd) that he was here to make sure Mr Mustard was not planning to disrupt the afternoon's festivities.

Mustard started jigging about and waving his arms. 'Disrupt?' Mustard yelled in the officer's face. 'I'll do more than disrupt.' He started hurling accusations loud enough so the crowd could hear. 'Call me a fool if you like, but I'm going to make the thieving swindling Hornbeams pay. I'll make them regret the day they sold me that fortune cat,' he raged, flapping his arms wildly and even shaking his fist at the closed black gates.

'I don't think I can print any of this,' said Veena. 'Still no front page!'

'They chose to mess with the wrong man when they messed with Mustard. I will get my revenge.'

'Are you making threats against the Hornbeams?' asked Truffle.

'Too right I am.'

And so the inevitable happened, and PC Truffle arrested him.

33. EXPLAINING THE TRICKY BITS

They found Dexter in the boathouse, slouched in a corner, his long legs outstretched so that they draped across the prow of the boat.

He looked like he'd been snoozing while Oakmoss had been sent on exhausting missions trying to prise useful information out of Trapmole and Mr Mustard.

'Just how difficult is it going to be to get past any magical security so Stormforce can do his under-cover magical investigation and prove there's

nothing sinister about the fortune cats?' Veena said to Oakmoss. 'Nearly impossible, or just plain impossible?'

Stormforce didn't look as if he was in a race against time to plan a break-in during a fairy-tale gala. He looked like he was taking a short nap, his long fringe covering his face. Perhaps Dexter had gone off the whole idea, Oakmoss allowed himself to hope. Was Stormforce still going to insist the undercover investigation was the only way to prove Mr Mustard was hurling false accusations about?

'The gala starts soon and who knows what attacks Mr Mustard might be planning,' went on Veena. 'You need to tell us what you've learnt. I hope you got everything out of Trapmole.'

Oakmoss hovered in the doorway uncertainly. There wasn't much room for tall people like Dexter in the boathouse. With Stormforce, Veena, Night-shade and Pudding squashed in there, it felt as if the boathouse had shrunk. Oakmoss had often sat on the veranda watching the silvery flashing fish and flitting birds, wishing he could share this exciting place. Right now, he mostly wanted everyone to go away and leave him alone.

'Can we do it?' Veena moved towards Oakmoss. 'Investigate. Find answers. Get out. Not get caught.

Get Mustard out of the way and stop these attacks on you or the gala.'

Oakmoss guessed he'd reluctantly go along with whatever Stormforce suggested if it meant getting rid of the man camping outside, particularly if that man had tried to poison him and was planning some sort of attack on the gala.

But when Oakmoss pictured them slipping into the workshop, it ended with PC Truffle arriving, startled looks, tricky questions and an arrest. Oakmoss would be carted off for interrogation, Trapmole standing there looking smug, arms folded, explaining to Oakmoss's disappointed parents how he'd always told them their son wasn't to be trusted with anything, least of all the family business.

After everything he'd already done this exhausting morning – the tour, listening to Trapmole, trying to remember everything, trying to make sense of Mustard's accusations, what he most needed was a biscuit. There weren't that many left. From memory, one ginger nut and a chocolate bourbon cream. That ginger nut was his, even if had to step over everyone to reach a shelf in the farthest and driest corner where the biscuit tin was stashed. But he supposed he was going to have to offer them round. Another reason to want everyone gone.

This had always been his secret place. He came here most days, even through the winter when icicles hung over the doorway like knives waiting to get him.

Stormforce's long legs were between Oakmoss and the biscuit tin and he suddenly had an urge to try something. He felt certain he could use his magic to levitate it out of the corner.

The biscuit tin was just floating above Stormforce's nose (it really was incredibly easy) when the investigator stirred and looked straight at Oakmoss, who only narrowly avoided dropping the spell and sending the tin crashing down on Dexter's head.

But Oakmoss kept control and the tin successfully moved right into Oakmoss's hand. Stormforce roused himself from whatever deep thoughts (or sleep) he'd been having.

'How do we get in? Let's start with that,' said Stormforce. So this terrible breaking-in plan was still on.

Oakmoss offered around the biscuits. At least there was one more than he'd remembered (lucky), but it was an unwanted plain one that didn't even have any sugar sprinkled on the top. A definite also-ran in the biscuit stakes. He hoped neither Pudding nor Nightshade were going to be difficult and want one, but he wouldn't put it past either of them.

'So, Oakmoss, don't keep us in suspense.' Stormforce lazily bit into Oakmoss's favourite, the ginger nut. 'What have you learnt – what will we face? And how do we get past it?'

Oakmoss soothed himself by having two zingtascos at once. Mistake! His head shot backwards, only narrowly avoiding hitting the shaky boathouse wall. It felt like steam was coming out of his ears.

'It's stifling, can we go outside?' he suggested, gulping thirstily from a bottle of water.

He felt better after he led everyone out on to the wobbly veranda, even though it felt like the boathouse seriously wanted to dump its load of three people and two cats straight into the murky water. They sat in a line, legs dangling, and he explained how Trapmole had taken him through the old door in the whitewashed wall that looked more like it should lead into a secret garden, not to a toy workshop.

'Was there magical protection on that door?' interrupted Veena, her face frowning with her particular look of concentration.

Oakmoss shook his head.

'But . . . ?' prompted Nightshade. 'I can always tell when there's a *but* coming.'

Oakmoss pushed his glasses up his nose. 'If it was a magical lock, Stormforce might stand a chance, but opening that door's going to be impossible.' He paused. 'Trapmole's worried about two things,' he explained carefully, feeling the pressure of everyone relying on him.

'He's not imagining anyone magical is going to break in. He thinks a gala-goer might get curious. But what he really suspects is that Mustard's going to do exactly as we're planning – use the gala as a distraction to slip in. So he's got the door set up so if anyone even tries to gain unauthorized access, extra security will be triggered.'

'Sounds bad,' said Veena.

'It is bad. You mess around with that door and it will set off an alarm. The only way to open it is if you know some really long number code you have to punch in. Trapmole was smug about it and said it's twelve digits and very hard to break a code like that. I kept thinking of excuses why I'd need to know the number, but he absolutely refused to tell me. That door's sensitive. The merest hint of anything suspicious and a metal grille slams into place and bolts get fired across the door. There's no other way in. I'm sorry.'

'Or out,' drawled Stormforce 'A really crucial part

of any plan is not just getting in, it's the getaway.'

'Well, actually,' puffed Veena, 'getting past that twelve-digit code might be pretty straightforward.'

Oakmoss stared at her.

'True. I reckon I've a few unlocking spells I could try,' said Stormforce easily.

'Actually,' said Veena, sounding rather smug, 'you can leave that door to me. All the deliveries gave me great cover to do some investigating this morning when you were still in bed. I spied on Trapmole when he punched in the code.'

'You managed to remember a twelve-digit code?' said Stormforce admiringly.

'Er, well, I just wrote it down. In my notebook.' She turned to Oakmoss. 'You probably want these back.' She produced his bird-watching binoculars from her pocket.

'That's brilliant, Veena!' said Stormforce, making Veena blush.

'That *is* great, Veena, but I haven't finished explaining the tricky bits,' Oakmoss cleared his throat, just as everyone started getting to their feet and paws. 'That's not an end to our problems.'

'Right.' Stormforce seemed eager to be off. He rubbed his hands together impatiently. 'But at least we're in. And the fact that Trapmole's gone to such great lengths to protect the workshop makes me even more curious.'

'But Dexter,' began Oakmoss. He dug into his back pocket and unfolded a sheet of paper, 'Look, you need to see this. I've sketched out what I can remember.'

He smoothed out the drawing. Everyone pored over his sketch of what they'd find if they got inside, until Pudding decided to park her bottom right in the middle.

'It's a cat thing,' sighed Nightshade apologetically.

'At the end of the production line, here,' Oakmoss pointed, moving Pudding out of the way, 'the fortune cats disappear into a sort of tunnel that leads to another room that is accessed by this door here. This door has got a big "No Entry" sign on it. And it's locked, similar deal to the main door – anyone tries to breach it, the alarm goes off.'

'And if the alarm goes off, that shutter comes down sealing the front door,' muttered Dexter.

Veena frowned at Oakmoss. 'Is there another twelve-digit code for the no-entry door?'

'No. This one's even worse. I asked what was behind that door. It's the packing area. I had to insist Trapmole show me. I've still no idea what's behind that door as he slammed it shut again before I could see anything inside. But at least I saw how it opens. Trouble is, he opens it by pressing that big silver skull ring he wears into a pad. Maybe it's even a charm, I don't know. All I noticed was there is a kind of strange smell from that room, then he said he really had to go and sort out his lemonade bike.'

'Perfect. Good job, Oakmoss,' said Stormforce easily. 'Needn't be a problem. A locked area inside a sealed workshop disguised by magic. Sounds like you've identified the bit we need to look most closely at. That'll save us time. Let's get started,' he said, as if everything was decided.

'We can't do it, Dex,' protested Oakmoss, wondering if he had not explained well. 'Not without the skull ring. We even try to open that door without Trapmole and we get trapped inside.'

Stormforce considered a moment, then began walking.

'You're sure you can tackle it if the lock's magical?' asked Veena, sounding a little impressed and a lot nervous. 'You know a spell that will open it? Will you have enough time to break any charm? We don't want to get stuck,' she finished uneasily.

'Don't you worry,' answered Stormforce.

'But Stormforce,' protested Oakmoss, 'I think there's some kind of magic about how that ring works.'

'Oh, we don't need to work out how to get past the magic. We don't need Trapmole. We just need to pinch his silver ring. Simple.'

34. When a Plan Comes Together

'But Trapmole always wears that ring,' said Oakmoss. 'It was a present from my mother. He's not going to hand it over.'

'I reckon you're the best person for this job, Veena,' I said.

'He won't hand it over to me!' she protested.

'Actually, that's not a bad idea, Nightshade. Trapmole really likes you, Veena,' said Oakmoss.

'He does not!' protested Veena, blushing furiously.

'Yeah, he does. He really does like you,' insisted

Oakmoss, with a straight face that looked as if it was disguising a little chuckle.

'Veena, we need that ring,' said Stormforce, who was clearly itching to be off. 'And I may have mentioned once or twice that we are running out of time. The gala is going to start any moment.'

'Whether he likes me or not, he's never going to just hand it over to me,' protested Veena. 'Not a secret key to the no-entry room in the workshop that may even be magical.'

So we all sat back down on the veranda, staring at all the little silver fish.

'We just have to make sure he loses it,' I said.

'You mean Veena's going to have to pinch it,' grinned Oakmoss.

Veena's face was a mixture of shock and reluctance, but before she could even begin to protest I suggested he would take the ring off if his hands got mucky.

'Oakmoss, any chance you could find something suitably mucky in this old boathouse for Trapmole to stick his hand in? Veena – tell him you've dropped something precious right in the muck. I bet he'd love to rescue it for you.'

'That's a terrible plan, Nightshade!' said Veena.

'That doesn't matter. Plans never work perfectly,'

drawled Stormforce. 'That's when you improvise.'

'This is what being a magical investigator involves, is it? Just coming up with terrible plans and going with them anyway and then making it up as you go along?' said Oakmoss.

Dexter and I exchanged an amused glance. 'Pretty much,' we said in unison.

Oakmoss took his glasses off and rubbed his eyes anxiously. 'Veena, say you dropped your lucky pen in the bottom of the boat. It's already half full of mucky water and I'll add a bit of weed and grime. With a bit of work I reckon I can make it look extra uninviting.'

'I don't have a lucky pen,' said Veena unconvincingly.

'Yeah, you do. You're always telling me it's the one you took the notes with that led to your big exposé of the Scrabble Scandal. You always use it.'

Veena took out her smart red pen with the gold nib and stroked it fondly. 'Do we *really* have to drop the pen into the muck?'

'We all have to make sacrifices in search of the truth, I'm afraid,' said Stormforce. 'As a journalist, you know that better than anyone. Sometimes investigating involves just a touch of deceit.'

'This really is the worst plan ever,' mumbled Veena.

'Oh no, I've worked with much worse plans than this,' said Stormforce easily. 'But it's best not to forget the improvising bit, just in case.'

'But your plans always come together OK in the end?' asked Oakmoss, filling a bucket with particularly smelly, dark and sludgy water to tip into the boat. I felt he might be enjoying his part of the plan a little too much.

'Not always, no,' replied Stormforce. 'But sometimes they do.'

We made our way back towards the hall, winding our way between the rows of soon-to-be-open stalls. We spotted Trapmole near the courtyard with his bicycle, jaunty sign and box on wheels, which he was filling with bottles from a crate. Two of the bottles looked like the weirdest lemonade I'd ever seen, with a pinkish tinge and a smoky look.

Oakmoss veered off towards the bouncy castle, avoiding his mother as she was testing a microphone to make her welcome speech. Stormforce slid around the back of the Baba Yaga tea and cake tent. I hoped this was a part of the plan he hadn't told us about, and not a shameless attempt to skip the afternoon-tea queue.

I trudged towards Trapmole behind a dour-looking Veena. He grinned stupidly at her and started over-explaining how Mr and Mrs Hornbeam were trusting him to raise money doing mobile refreshments and wasn't he doing a great job of the fundraising.

'Only, right now I'm thinking cold drinks aren't going to be the thing. The weather looks a bit, well, a bit . . .' He looked up at the sky.

We looked up too, and he wasn't kidding. In the distance it was dark and glowering with angry clouds. Typical that after days of endless sunshine, those rain clouds chose the day of the gala to show up.

Veena barely had to do more than mention how her lucky pen was missing and how that was ruining everything as she was supposed to be taking notes and writing up the event for the *Times*.

'I don't suppose you'd do me a huge favour and come and look with me. I definitely last had it in the boathouse,' she asked pleadingly. 'Oakmoss and Dexter have vanished. Typical! This fishing competition's going to be a washout, not like your lemonade cart; that's such a great idea!'

Trapmole gladly abandoned his lemonade cart to help Veena. Soon enough we were back at the boat-house and, with hardly a grimace, he was groping around in a lot of very smelly sludge in the bottom of the rowing boat. There was one major hitch, though – he hadn't taken the ring off. Clearly keeping it on was more important to him than keeping it clean. He triumphantly retrieved the pen and held it out. Veena accepted it delicately and offered him a towel from Oakmoss's stores, even insisting on helping Trapmole dry his hands, and distracting him by asking questions about his apprenticeship at the Hornbeam Workshop.

He didn't notice that she was subtly removing the silver skull ring.

Now *that's* improvisation.

I had a feeling Trapmole could have spent all day telling Veena how marvellous he was, but all it took was a little nudge to remind him that Mrs Hornbeam was just about to give her opening speech and finally he scooted off, but not without a promise from Veena that she would come and get a lemonade from him later.

Stormforce and Oakmoss rushed in the second Trapmole was safely heading back to his lemonade cart.

Veena held up the skull ring triumphantly.

'Stage one of the plan complete,' grinned Stormforce to the sound of a distant rumble of thunder.

'Worst plan ever; best improvisation ever,' crowed

Veena triumphantly. 'I've done my bit brilliantly. He didn't suspect a thing. I reckon from here it's going to be a picnic!'

PART FOUR

35. Moulded Cats and Security Traps

The extensive and perfectly green Hornbeam Hall lawns were now fully transformed, not only by colourful fairy-tale-themed stalls, but with too many princesses to count.

'Now that's a wolf,' I commented on one costume. 'I'm all right with wolves and those people in red cloaks carrying baskets. But I can't tell a Snow White from an Elsa.'

'Don't worry,' said Oakmoss good-naturedly. 'I don't think anyone can. Mum and Dad will be so

pleased so many people are here and so many in fancy dress!'

I lost count after twelve white rabbits, three Gruffalos, a couple of Zogs, several Alices and a vast Winnie the Pooh, complete with a jar of honey that looked as bad an idea as Mr Hornbeam's Humpty Dumpty suit.

'People really aren't very clear on what a fairy-tale character is,' said Veena as we passed at least three Spider-men queuing for the chance to throw the Puss-in-Boots welly.

'It's great how people enjoy putting their own interpretation on things,' said Stormforce, edging out of the way of a short guy with a long white beard carrying a tiny spinning wheel. A nylon dinosaur was crackling its way to join the end of the already long line to win a coconut.

'I think Mum may have been right that a hundred scones isn't going to be nearly enough,' said Oakmoss, staring at crowds still streaming through the front gate.

'Half of Dogberry have been baking cakes,' said Veena as we wove our way through the busy stalls in the direction of the huge Baba Yaga tea tent that had been positioned to obstruct the way to the courtyard and deter any prying eyes.

We threaded our way through the guy ropes and round the back, the familiar courtyard almost eerily silent after the bustle of the gala, with just the distant babble of chatter and the occasional cheer. Then we were standing by the ivy-covered door, nervously glancing over our shoulders. This was it.

I doubted any of us were really ready. Except Stormforce, who, with a hasty glance, took out his tiny dagger and cast a shimmer of blue light over the gate.

'I've been dying to have a really good look at this glimmer,' he said, peering into the handle of the dagger.

'Are we going to be able to do this?' asked Oakmoss.

I knew he was nervous. He had his hopes pinned on Mr Mustard being the source of all his problems, of being at the bottom of the ill-wishing and the poisoning of the pie. I could tell he'd told himself that if he could just help Stormforce, he'd be able to persuade Mustard to disappear and all his problems would disappear with him.

Everyone was focused on sneaking into the Hornbeam Workshop without getting into trouble. But I suspected nothing was going to be as simple as we hoped.

Stormforce asked if Veena was ready with the code. Veena took out her notebook, looking very uncertain. But, after a moment's hesitation, she carefully punched in the number she'd copied down.

There was the softest of clicks, and the door opened about three centimetres. We all braced ourselves for an alarm to sound and give us away. But all we heard were encouraging cheers from the boot throwing. Stormforce pushed the door open fully with one hand, hesitated just a second . . . and nothing bad happened.

'Do you know,' said Veena, 'I think this plan is going to work.'

We all stepped through the door and found ourselves straight into the manufacturing room with a series of peacefully empty conveyor belts. It was weird to think that outside it was all lemonade and princesses in sparkly dresses. Stormforce closed the door and I guess with their human eyes they found it difficult to see as Oakmoss cupped his hands together and created a small ball of magical light.

'Wow, Oakmoss, I never knew you could do that. You're pretty impressive!' said Veena, open-mouthed. 'We don't even need my torch.'

Oakmoss responded by increasing the light, but it was still dim and shadowy in the corners. 'If we'd come here when the workshop was up and running, there'd be hundreds of fortune cats flying around – it's pretty impressive. This way.'

They all started tiptoeing awkwardly past the empty production line. I always walk on tiptoe, so I didn't look awkward at all.

'Trapmole takes health and safety very seriously. There are vents and things up in the roof.' Oakmoss waved vaguely with his ball of light. 'Let me know when we've seen enough and can tell Mustard we've investigated,' he said, as Stormforce began to send shimmers of magical blue light across the machinery.

Veena craned her neck to peer around at everything, and stared up at the beamed roof high above. 'When we prove there isn't any truth at all in Mr Mustard's claims, I can put that on my front page, can't I, Oakmoss? I won't need to mention magic.'

'I suppose he should get what he deserves if he tried to poison me,' responded Oakmoss.

'What are you looking for when you wave that blue light around?' Veena asked Stormforce.

'It's difficult to explain, but sometimes the only way you identify magic is from the ripples it leaves in the air, which only experts can detect. Sometimes magic is very dangerous and it needs more than investigating – it needs stopping. Telling the difference is the trickiest bit.'

'What kind of dangerous?' asked Veena nervously.

'The sort of dangerous that only sorcerers can really invent,' replied Stormforce, taking another reading and sending a shimmer of cornflower blue right up to the ceiling.

'But there are no magical ripples in here?' Veena asked.

'I can't detect ripples,' I said, 'but I can detect a smell. Is it me, or is there a strange odour in here?' Everyone sniffed. 'I know my super-senses mean I detect these things before humans, but it's getting stronger.' The smell was growing as we crept around the conveyor belts, heading deeper into the workshop.

'Kind of like decay and dead flowers,' announced Stormforce, pulling a face.

'Is that evidence of a spell being used?' asked Veena, wrinkling her nose.

'It might be,' I said.

Stormforce answered by sending a darker and heavier shimmer of blue light methodically around each machine, the floors, walls, even reaching the high ceiling again. He didn't speak. We all watched closely, and after he looked at the handle of the dagger again, he dashed off into one of the dark corners.

'Well, this was unexpected,' he said, when he reappeared out of the gloom dragging something behind him.

'Have you found something magical?' asked Veena.

Stormforce was dragging a sack. He opened it and we all peered inside. It was stuffed full of money. I don't think any of us could believe it, let alone explain it.

'I wonder if this might be the donations,' Oakmoss said hesitantly.

'Hyacinth did say a sackful of donations arrived yesterday,' I said, 'and that she'd put it with the others. Your mother must work incredibly hard on getting people to donate.'

'People are incredibly generous with their donations to RATS, aren't they?' Stormforce sounded baffled as he dragged the sack back to where he found it.

'Er. Well, I think—' began Oakmoss.

'Frankly, I'm amazed she has so much time to raise all that money, what with her garden room and her orchids and lilies and redecorating and sending all her old bits to Erasmus,' I added.

'There isn't a repair centre for these toys yet, is there?' asked Veena.

'It's got to be planned carefully.' Oakmoss bit his lip thoughtfully, muttering something about feeling sure his mother probably did work very hard.

I wondered if we were all thinking the same thing . . . the tightened security, the elaborate glimmer to stop people even knowing the workshop was here . . . and that smell was getting stronger, even with all the ventilation and the high ceiling. Things about the Hornbeam Workshop were all starting to look a bit strange.

I began to feel mighty nervous about what we were going to discover.

'I think we're done in here,' declared Stormforce. Even his voice held a slight tremor of nerves. 'Let's go see where the fortune cats are finished off and packed. Then we can get out of here quickly,' he added under his breath.

Oakmoss looked relieved to be away from the main room and that curious sack of money.

He led us along a short corridor, dark, except with my super-sense night vision I could detect a kind of pinkish glow coming from beneath a door. There was no doubt about it, the smell of decay was stronger here.

We were approaching the room Trapmole had not wanted Oakmoss to get a good look inside. This was the door that could be opened only with Trap-mole's silver skull ring. Why did a packing room need such elaborate security?

Now perhaps wasn't the time to remember Trap-mole had been at Erasmus Collectibles trying to track down a book about magic that tricked the mind. Or to find yourself thinking how that glimmer fooled people into not noticing a whole building was there. And I remain convinced Oakmoss had been under a powerful ill-wishing. And someone had tried to poison him.

'Did Trapmole say anything else about what was in here, Oakmoss?' asked Stormforce, who was dithering; this made my whiskers twitch. Dexter has always been more your rush-into-dangerous-situations-and-ask-questions-later sort. He'd been cagier than usual about this whole plan.

Oakmoss was shaking his head. 'With everything else he droned on for ages, but all he showed me was how genius it was that it only opens with this skull ring. Then he shut it again really quickly and said he had to go and sort out his lemonade bike.'

'See, sometimes having a plan is a great idea,' said Veena, grinning as Stormforce took the skull ring out of his pocket and looked for where to slot it in. 'Lucky I got that ring so we don't set off an alarm that will bring PC Truffle racing along to arrest us.'

Stormforce hadn't slotted in the ring. Instead, he had his dagger raised, and cast a shimmer of blue light over the door and then frowned at the end of the instrument.

'Is it safe?' asked Veena.

Stormforce trained a focused beam of light around the edges of the door.

'Dexter is one of the most skilled in S3 at getting into magical places,' I said reassuringly, but I was feeling increasingly uneasy.

My whiskers were telling me there was something odd here. What had Mustard said exactly? Something about his wife making a lot of donations to RATS after he'd bought a fortune cat. That the cat had tricked him. That the toys were evil. And then there was the fact that Trapmole had sealed this door. You add that to the existence of the workshop concealed with magical trickery. And that terrible smell. And what was that strange pink light? What did it all add up to?

We all stood staring at the door, at Dexter frowning silently at whatever reading he was getting from his magical investigations and hesitating. And I could see that everyone else could see that shimmering pink glow beneath the door.

I could not help but ask myself – what if there was something in the outrageous claims of annoying Mr Mustard? What if they were even a little bit true? What if something was terribly wrong with the toys made in the Hornbeam Workshop?

We were all waiting and hoping Stormforce would tell us nothing seriously bad was going to happen to us if we opened that door. But he held the silver skull ring loosely, looking as if he was having difficulty deciding.

Oakmoss started fidgeting. 'Can we just go in so we can get out quickly before anyone realizes we're here?' he snapped. 'If my dad discovers I've secretly led an investigation into his workshop, my parents will be even more disappointed in me than they are already.'

'On your cue, Dexter,' I said. 'We're ready. Oakmoss is right. Let's do it and get out of here. No sudden movements, stay close to Stormforce – he can investigate and we can be out of here quickly. It'll be fine.'

But it didn't feel fine, and the sudden smell of peppermints told me that if things were already going wrong, they were only about to get worse. We heard a very familiar, very piteous miaow.

Oakmoss was the first to turn.

'Flanagan!' he said in a choked voice.

I turned too. 'Pudding!' I cried crossly.

And we both said together: 'What are you doing here?'

36. NOTHING SINISTER OR ILLEGAL

'Wu-hey! This is *craaazzzy*,' said Flanagan, stepping out of the gloom.

Oakmoss could only look on in horror as his worst nightmare stepped towards him at exactly the worst moment.

He had the presence of mind to cut the magical ball of light he was holding in his hand. This plunged them into almost complete darkness, apart from a surreal pink glow, until Veena switched on a torch. Stormforce and Nightshade slipped

backwards further into the shadows.

The Flan approached along the corridor, eyes gleaming and an excited smile fixed on her face as she glanced all around, drinking it in. The three people (four if you included Nightshade) not out in the sunshine raising money at the fairy-tale gala, but here in the almost-dark, guiltily outside a door with a huge no-entry sign.

'This is totally amazing!' said Flanagan. 'You can't even see this from the outside. Just that wall and the tiny door. Why the disguise? Why all the secrets? Are your family doing secret work for the government, Oakmoss?' She loomed closer, bringing the hated smell of peppermints. 'Or investigating aliens? Or is it something to do with that Mustard guy? He was raving about those awful cat toys and saying your family are crooks.' She rattled off questions right into Oakmoss's face. 'Are you taking a look around where you shouldn't?' Her lips curved into a cruel smile. 'How interesting.'

'Er . . .' responded Oakmoss, hating the way his voice came out so strangled.

In the blurry light cast by Veena's torch, Flanagan looked even taller and more menacing than on the school bus.

There was a tiny miaow from Pudding before the

Flan went on. 'And this is where they're made? In this secret workshop? What's the truth then, Oakmoss? Is that what we're investigating? How very, *very* interesting.'

'Er . . .' repeated Oakmoss. He was unable to think of anything to say, any excuse or explanation, or even to do anything but watch as Flanagan walked right up to the no-entry door with its ethereal pink glow and that terrible stench.

'How did you get in?' demanded Veena; finding her voice.

Flan chuckled. 'I noticed you lot all sloping off somewhere looking ridiculously sneaky, so I thought I'd follow and see if you were doing something a bit more exciting than eating cake dressed like an idiot. But hey – wow! I never guessed you'd be breaking in here.'

'We're not breaking in,' said Oakmoss hastily, fighting to make his voice seem not just normal, but unusually confident. 'I own this place, don't forget.'

'Heh, heh, yeah right. You're not sneaking in, just creeping around in the dark looking shifty. So, is this where the secret stuff happens?' She gestured at the no-entry door, pushing past Veena to get even closer.

Oakmoss was aware of Stormforce and Night-shade having a muttered argument further along in the shadows, Dexter saying something under his breath about her not being much of a lookout.

'No one specified a particular role,' Nightshade muttered back.

'But you're always lookout.'

'Just because I'm the best at climbing. No one asks me if I *want* to be lookout.'

'Flanagan, I was just giving my friends the tour,' said Oakmoss, speaking loudly to cover the conversation. All they needed now was for Flanagan to realize they'd brought a talking cat with them – she hadn't seemed to register Nightshade shouting at Pudding. She would never believe there wasn't anything strange or sinister about the Hornbeam Workshop if there was a talking cat inside.

'And your friends include a cat, do they?' she sneered.

Nightshade turned, her green eyes reflecting brightly in the torchlight.

'Well, you brought a cat with you too.' Veena pointed at Pudding. 'How did you get past the twelve-digit code?'

'That was *eeeasy*,' Flanagan smirked, flicking her exceedingly long hair. 'I missed you on the school bus yesterday, Oakmoss. And when all you sneaked away looking all furtive I was kinda sad you didn't invite me along, because I really hoped you'd missed me too. So I hid behind a big plant pot in the court-yard and I just watched.'

'You just watched and remembered a twelve-digit code?' said Veena in disbelief.

'Oh, I'm *amazing* with numbers.' Flanagan shot a triumphant look at Veena. 'Some people are almost proud at being bad at numbers. Doesn't stop them placing bets though, which works out really well for me.' She gave a huge grin. 'Yeah, I just punched in that old code and strolled in the door after you. I knew none of you would notice! I'm better at sneak-ing around than you are,' she crowed. 'So, time to spill. What are we all here for?'

She wrinkled her nose thoughtfully, looking sideways at Oakmoss.

The very last thing he needed was the Flan. But how could he get rid of her?

Dexter Stormforce stepped out of the shadows. 'I'm Dexter, but all my friends call me Dex. You've joined this tour a bit late, I'm afraid, we were just leaving.'

Normally people responded to Dex's charming manner by immediately being friendly back, but not Flanagan, oh no – she was staring too fixedly at the no-entry door.

'So what does go on in here? We've got this far, may as well find out.'

'This is a toy workshop.' Oakmoss tried sounding confident. Not for the first time, he really cursed the Flan for always somehow managing to make things in his life go wrong. 'You're always telling me how lame it is that my family make toys.'

But Oakmoss could see it all through Flanagan's eyes. More powerful than the smell of peppermints was the scent of flowers rotting. It was strong here, right next to the door to the packing room from where the fortune cats were sent around the world, from where the weird pinkish glow was spilling under the door.

'I never knew this was where all those hideous fortune cats were made. It's really weird, because when I followed you into the courtyard, it took me a while to realize it was even here. It's disguised, isn't it? Which is so interesting. Are there some kind of mirrors on the outside? Is that how it works?'

'It's very dull,' insisted Oakmoss, pushing his glasses further up his nose. 'I wouldn't bother. You could head back and try to win a coconut.'

'I won one once and it was pretty dire. This looks a long way from lame.' Flanagan stepped even closer, so her long nose was almost pressed up against the no-entry door they were all clustered around. 'It's all kind of hidden, isn't it? And that tricky code on the door. Makes me wonder what you're hiding in here.' Flanagan gave an awful smile. 'I'd *love* to stay around and get the tour. Particularly of this room, where it looks like you're keeping an alien or something. What's that pink?' She sniffed. 'And that terrible smell, like something's dying?'

Oakmoss had been desperate to get behind that door and have Stormforce cast his investigative magical light around, desperate to prove all Mr Mustard's claims were false and there was nothing sinister going on here. There was no connection between the fortune cat he'd bought for his wife and her making so many donations to RATS.

But the Flan was ruining everything.

Mustard might never go. The ill-wishing and the attempts to hurt Oakmoss would never stop. He had to manoeuvre her out.

'Are you going to show us where they dissect the aliens?' insisted Flanagan.

'Flanagan, they just make stupid toys,' snapped Oakmoss.

'I don't know about you, but I can never resist a no-entry sign.' Then she reached for the handle.

'Don't touch that!' cried Dexter.

She rattled it.

'Flanagan, don't—' began Oakmoss.

Too late. Before he could stop her, Flanagan gave the door a hefty shove.

The door shook and did little more than give a protesting squeak. But immediately a terrible wail rose up and quickly turned to a warning siren that blared around them.

Flanagan's eyebrows shot up, but she was no longer looking interested, she was looking scared. 'What's that? What's happening?'

The piercing sound of the alarm wasn't the only noise – bolts were slamming home and something heavy was dropping into place, something that sounded awfully like a big metal guard shutting off their means of escape.

'You've done it now, Flanagan,' cried Oakmoss. 'You've set off the security measures. We're trapped.'

37. Trapped

'Well, cheers, Flanagan, things were going fine until you turned up,' said Veena. She had to speak loudly over the wailing siren.

'We can't be trapped!' said Flanagan, her voice fearful. 'I don't like enclosed spaces and being underground.'

'It's not that much of an enclosed space,' pointed out Veena. 'And it's not even a little bit underground.'

'Oakmoss will know a way out.' Flanagan turned to him hopefully, her dark eyes huge in the shadowy

gloom. 'Quick – alarms are usually linked to the police station. We can't be arrested, we need to get out of here.'

With the alarm screeching, and faced with Flanagan, it was impossible for Oakmoss to think. There must be another way out of here, some sort of getaway plan.

PC Truffle could be on his way, expecting to arrest a gala visitor who had got too curious. Trapmole would be with him, never imagining anyone would be smart enough to breach that twelve-digit code on the main door and be caught inside. Trapmole would probably assume PC Truffle could be relied on to be so excited about making an arrest he'd fail to notice he had been summoned to an invisible building.

But they were going to find Oakmoss captured here with five others (including two cats). That could not happen. They needed to escape.

Flanagan unceremoniously shoved a fistful of cash into Oakmoss's hand. 'If the police are coming, maybe you should have this.'

'What is it?'

'I found it. It was in one of the big sacks near the entrance.' Flanagan gestured vaguely. 'There was absolutely loads, I didn't think anyone would miss a bit. But I don't want the police turning up and accusing me of being a thief.'

'You are a thief,' pointed out Veena. 'All those sacks are the charity donations.'

'Well, they shouldn't be left lying around.'

'They are in a locked building with high security,' said Veena, managing to sound scathing even above the noise of the alarm. 'And now, thanks to you, we are all going to have to explain exactly what we are doing here.'

'Aha! I *knew* you weren't supposed to be in here! You're just as guilty as me!' cried Flanagan.

Think, Oakmoss told himself. He put his fingers in his ears.

Breaking in was supposed to get his life back. He'd wanted to stop the raging man hurling accusations from a tent, the ill-wishing, the accidents, the poisoning. He'd convinced himself this was the way to get back to being ordinary. Well, as ordinary as you could manage when you belonged to a magical family.

But, as ever, anything Oakmoss was involved with was simply cursed to go as wrong as could possibly be imagined. But he could not let the ill-wishing win. Nightshade had told him bad luck was mostly in the mind. He needed to think. He'd done the tour with Trapmole. It was up to him to find a way out. There had to be a way.

Because if PC Truffle did turn up here, even Truffle would notice that weird pink glow and the terrible smell. You didn't need Stormforce's blue light or even Nightshade's whiskers to see something here was wrong. On the other side of the no-entry door was a spell, Oakmoss was sure.

Then Veena gave him some scrunched-up tissue to stuff in his ears, and that helped a bit. The noise was no longer drilling right into his head. She did the same for them all, including Nightshade and Pudding. But the dulling of the siren only seemed to allow the Flan's curiosity to overtake her fear.

'That stench has got worse since that door moved a bit. You'd better tell me what's going on?' Flanagan folded her arms. 'I've got nothing to worry about. I just saw you all breaking in here and followed to stop you going into this weird and suspicious place.'

Even Stormforce was looking startled when faced with Flanagan. Oakmoss knew how he felt. The important thing right now was not to give someone smart like Flanagan the chance to confirm there was anything strange about the Hornbeam Workshop. The longer they stood here with that strange pink shimmer leaking out from the door and the terrible stench, the more difficult that was going to be.

Through the noise of the alarm, Oakmoss focused. It wasn't too much of a stretch to imagine there might be a magic spell in that packing room, one that was cast over the fortune cats that were sent all over the world. A spell that worked on the mind. Was it connected to donations flooding into RATS by the sackful? Especially to a charity that was insanely popular without actually doing anything.

But now was not the time to think about that. He could dissect all those thoughts later. Now they needed to get out and not be arrested. Oakmoss needed to prevent his father finding out he'd led an official magical investigator right to the heart of what looked horribly like a family secret. And, most important of all, he needed Flan to forget everything she'd seen. He needed a plan. Even a terrible plan was better than standing here.

'I think there's another way out through here,' he said, seizing Flanagan's arm and gesturing to Stormforce that he should go ahead and use Trapmole's skull ring to get the door open.

It was a risk. Stormforce hesitated, but there was no time for questions. All they needed was for the Flan to be confused enough to not be sure of anything she'd seen. And on the other side of this door was some kind of mind-meld magic, something that confused people. It was their only hope.

Oakmoss managed to convey to Veena over the sound of the alarm that she needed to hold her breath as long as possible once that door was open. Stormforce, it appeared, had come prepared. Stormforce had probably guessed a lot of what Oakmoss was only just working out, because Dexter brought out a scarf and wrapped it around his mouth and nose.

The smell of decaying flowers grew stronger as the skull ring opened the door. They were running out of time and the panic and the noise in Oakmoss's head made him practically shove the Flan into the packing room and hope Stormforce had some idea of how long an exposure to the spell would be just enough to confuse her.

Oakmoss bent to gesture to Nightshade that she was to come with him.

'I've got a plan, Nightshade. It's not a very good one, but it's going to need you.'

'Yes,' sighed Nightshade, 'like always.'

38. AMAZiNG PAWS

'I'd like to say that you're filling me with confidence,' said Nightshade, pausing briefly to polish her whiskers as they made their way back to the conveyor belt, 'but actually you're doing the opposite.'

Oakmoss ignored her, stopped and pointed upwards. 'Trapmole talked about ventilation. There are a couple of windows but they don't open, so that vent must lead outside.'

'Yes, all very interesting,' responded Nightshade her green eyes gleaming as Oakmoss brought a little

ball of light into his hand to show the tiny vent up near the ceiling. 'Trapmole talked about a lot of things. I don't know about you, but I think Trapmole's been having far too much fun experimenting with mind-meld magic.'

'The vent has to lead to fresh air,' insisted Oakmoss, 'so anyone in this main workshop won't get exposed to whatever confusion magic is in that smelly pink haze.'

'Ah yes, confusion magic, I agree. Remember the book you took from Erasmus's shop?' said Nightshade, peering upwards. 'Reckon it must be the one Trapmole was looking for. Confusion magic is a branch of mind-melding. Glimmers are just a type of confusion too. A low dose probably gives a general effect of haziness and people slightly losing control over their thoughts. Which is what I guess you hope will happen to the Flan. I believe the use of confusion magic is restricted by the Elysee.'

'Yes, well, I guess you shouldn't really use magic to compel people into doing something you want them to,' muttered Oakmoss.

Whenever he'd imagined being magical it had always led to an urge to send some sort of bad magic over the Flan. Now it looked like he'd done just that.

'MagiCon and S3 operatives sometimes use it to

convince non-magical folk they haven't seen something magical,' went on Nightshade. 'But using it to get people to send you money. *That* would be illegal magic.'

'That vent—' Oakmoss tried to get back to the urgent matter in hand.

But Nightshade continued, speaking loudly over the continuing scream of the alarm. 'If it gets out that the fortune cats are exposing people to illegal magic, it won't only be Mr Mustard camping out on your doorstep hurling accusations. The Sinister Speculation Services, MagiCon and the whole of the Elysee will come down on the Hornbeams like a tree falling.'

'Yes, well. We can't do anything to put things right from in here,' said Oakmoss, feeling increasingly distraught. 'That vent is the only way out.'

'Hang on,' said Nightshade, following Oakmoss's pointing up the ceiling. 'I know where this is leading. I may be an extraordinarily good climber, but even my amazing paws can't manage a sheer wall. That's not so much as climbing as flying.'

This was true, Oakmoss agreed. 'But it's the vent, or we're all doomed.'

'I'm sure Stormforce included a getaway in his plan,' said Nightshade hopefully.

Oakmoss knew Stormforce hadn't been at all straight with him about this whole plan from the start. Of course a magical investigator wouldn't simply turn up to save a magical family the inconvenience of having a one-man protest on their doorstep – Stormforce must have had his suspicions all along. But he'd deal with his feelings about that later.

Veena's voice rose from the shadows. 'Flanagan wants to make a donation,' she announced, joining Oakmoss and Nightshade next to the conveyor belt and dropping her hand from covering her mouth. 'Think she's a little confused. She might not know exactly what's happening. If we could get out now,' Veena said pointedly, 'she might not remember things very clearly. She's a bit fixated on—'

'Where did you say I can make my donation to RATS?' Flanagan asked, looking around dizzily.

Pudding appeared behind them, distressed and miaowing incessantly. Oakmoss wondered if the spell also affected cats. How long might it last? Oakmoss picked up the troublesome kitten and folded his T-shirt to make a small nest for her to cuddle into close to his chest. He tried to ignore that terrible shrill bell, which must have been sounding loud enough to summon the entire fairy-tale gala, and quickly outlined his plan.

'I think it's a good plan,' said Stormforce, squinting up as he arrived from his investigations. 'But who will ever fit through that tiny hole? Have we got a rope?'

Even Stormforce seemed a little confused. Oakmoss guessed he hadn't been able to avoid ingesting a little bit of the spell.

'I can't climb a rope,' pointed out Nightshade.

Oakmoss was waiting and hoping for Dexter to say something decisive. Something helpful.

'Well, that doesn't matter, we don't have a rope anyway,' said Stormforce.

The S3 agent must have inhaled more of that pink spell than Oakmoss had realized – he clearly wasn't thinking straight.

'But it's good of you to volunteer.' Dexter was having to shout above the sound of the alarm. 'All you need to do, Nightshade, is shimmy up there, go through that narrow tube and into whatever system of air vents is up there. You get outside and slip round to the door in the wall and punch in the code. I bet it'll override the alarm. It's actually a good plan.'

'Shimmy? Up there?' said Nightshade. 'It's not happening.'

'You can do it, Nightshade,' said Stormforce. 'You'll just need a little magic to get you started.'

39. WE COULD USE MAGIC

What other options did they have? The vent really was very high up, and Oakmoss had a sickening feeling in his stomach that it was a very dangerous plan – dangerous for Nightshade.

'Dexter, you are not using magic to haul me up there,' said the cat.

'You're right,' said Dexter. 'I do have amazing magic and a number of magical talents, but flying is not one of them.'

'The plan is doomed,' protested Nightshade. 'The

number pad will be too fiddly with paws. It is, possibly, the worst plan ever. Glad we're definitely not doing it.'

Oakmoss could practically feel Trapmole getting nearer and nearer, could feel the apprentice breathing down his neck. But that might just be Pudding stirring.

That spell wasn't going to leave Flanagan in a docile daze for long. It was going to wear off and she'd be back to her sharp and snarky self.

Stormforce had his head tipped back, still staring at the small dark hole way up above them. 'Ah you shouldn't let that put you off, plans never going according to plan anyway,' he said to Nightshade.

Flanagan said nothing as she stared into the middle distance. She muttered about wanting to make a donation every now and again, but it was the least dangerous Oakmoss had ever seen her.

'I think this is our only chance,' said Oakmoss, even as he felt his resolve crumble.

'It'll work,' said Veena unexpectedly. 'It's a good plan. And I'd do almost anything to shut off the noise from that alarm.'

'Right,' breathed Oakmoss, shooting a wary look at Veena. He hadn't expected her of all people to be that easily convinced – perhaps a little bit of the confusion charm had got her after all. 'Then let's do it. You get the air moving underneath her,' he said to Stormforce.

Stormforce crooked a grin at Oakmoss. 'The ability to manipulate the air might well be one of my amazing talents,' he shouted above the alarm. 'But why am I doing it when Nightshade tells me you're the most natural rudiment she's seen in a long time?'

'Me do it?' Oakmoss responded in horror.

'You can do it, Oakmoss,' said Veena. 'Nightshade's been telling you that you're one heck of a sorcerer. It's time you believed her and believe in yourself.'

It was one thing to glow in praise while people (or cats) said you possessed powerful rudimentary magic, but quite another to even imagine yourself manoeuvring a friend all the way to a high ceiling using only the air and magic.

'I'm not going to be levitated up to a high ceiling by a novice sorcerer reckoned to be the unluckiest boy in the world,' said Nightshade.

It was a fair point.

'Dex, you have to do the actual magic,' pleaded Oakmoss.

'When I said he was one of the best rudiments

I'd ever seen, at no point did I ever mean I wanted him to dangle me from a high ceiling,' went on Nightshade.

'There won't be a lot of dangling,' coaxed Veena. She looked upwards. 'It's a small opening – I don't think you can guide her through from down here, you're going to have to carry her, Oakmoss.'

'It would play havoc with my fur,' Nightshade carried on protesting. 'And how am I going to remember a twelve-digit code? And the paws! Don't forget the paws!'

Flanagan shot her a suspicious look that made Oakmoss think the confusion was wearing off already. What would she say if Nightshade's ability to talk penetrated her brain fog? And if they both started flying? Oakmoss tried to focus.

Throwing that tree had simply been a reflex. How had he done it? He didn't know, and that meant he wasn't sure he could do it again.

'Once we're out, you promise I can make this donation?' said Flanagan.

'We'll be on the other side of the door.' Veena bent to speak closely to Nightshade. 'We'll call the number out to you. You're our only hope.'

'I realize that. It always is me. I say this is a terrible plan and I'm always right.' Nightshade gave a big sigh. 'All right, I'll do it. But the next time the only chance of escape is through a high-up narrow tunnel, everyone needn't look at me. Next time it can be someone else who saves the day.'

'Right,' said Oakmoss, letting out a nervous breath. 'I don't want to drop you.'

'I don't want you to drop me either.'

Oakmoss pushed his glasses further up his nose and wiped his sweaty hands on his shorts. He looked at Nightshade. 'Together. Ready?'

'Of course I'm not ready, would anyone be ready to allow a totally inexperienced sorcerer levitate them to the ceiling of a high building? But you're going to do it anyway. You should ask me if I've any last requests.'

'I'm not going to drop you.'

'Good. That was my last request.'

40. Adventure To The Ceiling

Nightshade shot about three metres in the air.

'Whoooooa! Give me a warning why don't you!'

Oakmoss had been focusing on the feeling he'd had when he'd been in the lake beneath the boathouse, tangled with weeds. Then, things had happened so fast he hadn't had time to even take a proper breath before disappearing under the water. But somehow he'd found a way to reach for his magic and use it to shoot up and out of the water. He was trying to do the same thing and move the air.

He concentrated, reached within himself and slowed her ascent, feeling exceedingly pleased with himself as she floated gently back to his eye level.

'Wow, this is actually amazing!' she said. 'I feel like a floating bubble or a butterfly.'

Oakmoss now had the air confidently under his control and moved her up and down like a puppet.

'Right, I'm coming up with you so I can see what you're doing.'

Oakmoss pointed one hand down at the ground and raised an arm towards the ceiling and floated upwards more gracefully than he could possibly have imagined. 'Have you ever wanted to fly, Nightshade?'

'Of course. Would be such a surprise to birds.'

'I wonder if I could get all the way to Dogberry Academy like this,' said Oakmoss. 'I would never have to get on the school bus again. I'd never have an accident on a bicycle.'

'Stop messing about!' yelled Veena. 'Concentrate on getting her level with the escape vent before PC Truffle or Trapmole or your father or all three turn up!'

But Oakmoss couldn't quite resist sticking himself to the ceiling like a giant spider, throwing his arms and legs wide and experiencing a sudden elation. He'd never realized before that magic could be such enormous fun.

Then he spotted Flanagan's face, giddy and confused as she frowned upwards. 'That looks like Oakmoss.'

And Oakmoss lost control of the spell and he and Nightshade plummeted down several metres before he pushed at the air again and recovered, his heart thundering as he narrowly stopped them smashing into the floor.

He heard Veena mutter some excuse about him being Spider-man for the fairy-tale gala. Oakmoss concentrated on doing what he was supposed to be doing and manoeuvred himself and Nightshade to the vent. He peered along it into darkness and he was struck once more by what a terrible plan this was. What if Nightshade got stuck? What if there was no way out? But the vent had to lead some-where, didn't it?

'I'm not sure about this,' he hesitated.

Pudding miaowed, reminding Oakmoss the fluffy white kitten was still snuggled into his chest and that she'd come on the adventure to the ceiling as well.

But having got this far, Nightshade seemed keen to scramble against his magic to get all her four paws safely inside the narrow vent. Once she was in, he let go of the spell. He moved right to the entrance of the vent and was about to wish her luck, hoping this wasn't going to be the last time he'd ever see her.

Then there was a sudden movement from his chest, and before he knew what was happening Pudding had scrambled in after Nightshade.

Two tails disappeared into the vents. Oakmoss gulped noisily.

From far down the echoey vent floated the words: 'Oh, cheers. Whose brilliant idea was it to chuck the furball in here? This was definitely not part of the plan.'

41. THE WORLD'S LOUDEST MIAOW

It was dark up here, slippery, and it smelt as if pigeons had been partying. I couldn't walk upright; it was more an undignified crawl on my belly. I moved carefully, my claws scraping and rattling and giving me no grip whatsoever.

I had no idea what was going to be at the end of this long, metal tunnel. The worst I could imagine was there being something heavy and impossible to pass, because turning around and going back was not an option. Or would this vent end with some big

whirry fan thing? That could be worse. I could at least hope (while I dragged myself along on my belly, trying not to focus on my doom) that today any fan would be turned off, just like the conveyor belts far, far below. If I was wrong, I was going to be rapidly turned into pigeon food.

I wasn't really able to focus on anything, because the worst thing about an already dire situation was the annoying miaowing coming from behind me, and the irritating fluffball that kept giving an undignified nudge to my tail.

The very last thing anyone needs on a dangerous mission – where it's essential to have all senses alert and focused, whiskers twitching to give warning of the slightest bit of danger – is to have the whole space echoing with anxious whimpering.

One piece of advice – if you ever have to save the day by crawling through an air duct with very little hope of anything working out well, do not do it accompanied by a really annoying kitten with the world's loudest miaow.

There was only one way I could think of to make this any better, and that was to manoeuvre Pudding in front of me, so I could nudge her along with purrs of encouragement.

This I achieved with such great difficulty it made

me think the rest of the mission was going to be easy. But when she was finally squeezed in front, I realized there *was* one way the whole situation could be worse.

If you are ever trapped in a nasty, dirty air vent faced with the likely prospect of being turned into pigeon food – don't do it with a kitten's bottom right against your pink nose.

'Don't you dare do any bottom burps, young Pudding,' I said sternly.

She was putting too much energy into the miaowing and too little into moving, so I picked her up by the scruff of the neck. As well as having to practically crawl on my belly like a commando, now I had two of us to move along and a mouthful of straggly fur.

I guess Pudding stopped me worrying about things, like whether this was going to turn out to be less of a vent and more of a chimney. If I had to start going upwards, that would be the end. No way did I have the claws to scrabble up sheer metal and dirt.

I'm not normally what I'd call a fretty sort of cat, but moving along with the fluffball, I couldn't help pondering that I was the twin of destiny of calamitous Oakmoss, the unluckiest boy in the world.

Even so, maybe I was heading towards a square of daylight. With an extra-determined effort, I pressed on. The light got bigger as I scratched and wriggled my way towards it. We reached the end. I was right, there was an extractor fan. Switched off and silent. *Lucky, then.*

My whiskers informed me there was room for manoeuvre and I trod carefully as I stepped between the still blades, carrying my irksome companion. Then my pink nose was through and I tasted fresh air, freedom and triumph. And my paws were on something solid.

Next tip: never have anyone join you uninvited on a tricky, vital and dangerous mission if you have not first assessed how lousy their jumping and climbing skills might be. Or if they have a head for heights. Even if they are a cat.

Us cats are exceptionally good at jumping – that's something people get right about us. But we got to the edge and stood next to a couple of pigeons and when she looked at the ground far below, Pudding's piteous mewling started up again. It was all very well for those pigeons to coo happily. They had wings.

This leap was going to be less of a jump and more like flying.

I dropped Pudding, spitting out a mouthful of

fur. 'Well, no one asked you along.'

I'd said this was a plan doomed to fail. There was still a very high chance I was going to end up as a snack for the pigeons. Pudding must have had the same thought, as her mewling reached a crescendo.

My best hope of achieving the impossible was a stack of crates, which would lessen the chance of me breaking my neck, as well as every other bone in my body. The crates were only a little less far below than the concrete path leading to the courtyard.

I tried to encourage Pudding to watch how I did it, and make the leap after me. Her eyes just became bigger, wider, more piteous and her miaowing was at a peak that was hurting my ears.

I didn't have time. I was about to attempt a jump no sane cat would make unless it was from a burning building and your life depended on it. But others were relying on me. So I picked Pudding up and made sure she was secure in my jaws. There was only one way down. Ignoring her increasingly frenzied miaows, I leapt.

PART FIVE

42. Really Annoying

I was heavier than usual and unbalanced, and it was not my most elegant landing. Nevertheless, I wished there had been someone there to see it, because it was amazing. It deserved a round of applause.

We'd reached the ground and were alive and able to tell the tale. But this adventure was by no means over.

I'm really not joking about cats and superpowers. I have extraordinarily sharp hearing that some bats

would envy . . . I could go on. From the roof I was pretty sure I'd spotted PC Truffle's extra-white starched shirt and his close-cropped hair moving among the gala crowds. It was no surprise that he was heading this way.

I raced around to the courtyard, orientated myself and spied the door and the number pad. I had to find a way to key in the numbers with my paws if I was going to get the humans out, but first I had to reach it.

No one had taken my objections seriously that this part of the plan was doomed to failure, but they really do not design those number pads to be used by cats.

And I knew my luck was running out, as my super-hearing picked out two familiar voices from the background noise of the gala in full swing and the still-wailing alarm. The police officer was close and a second voice told me Trapmole was with him.

'I expect it's a false alarm,' PC Truffle was saying. He must be closer than I'd realized. 'I just queued for half an hour for that welly boot throwing and I was almost at the front. I'm sure this is a waste of time, but it'd be rather unprofessional of me not to take a look. Entrance this way, is it?'

'I almost predicted this would happen,'

responded Trapmole. 'Inviting hundreds of people into Hornbeam Hall means there's a greater risk of prying eyes wanting to learn the secrets of the Hornbeam Workshop. And welly boot throwing, really? Shouldn't you be there keeping an eye on Mustard? I thought you were supposed to be keeping him locked up.'

'I don't take orders from you,' responded Truffle huffily. 'And so far Mustard's done nothing more serious than be a nuisance.'

'Well, if you get a move on you'll have something to charge him with all right. That alarm means someone's trying to get past the security I've set up.'

'Security for your toy workshop, huh?' Truffle didn't sound impressed.

'If you catch Mustard, or any spies trying to break into my building, I may very well buy you a cup of tea. Or even a lemonade.'

'Cup of tea? I was in line to win that welly boot throwing. I bet the prize will be more than a lemonade.'

I was looking around in desperation. Someone had placed a few plant pots here and there on this side of the courtyard. None of them were beneath the keypad. My only chance was to move one of them to help me reach.

'You suspect Mustard. Or rival toymakers after your secrets. I suspect a pigeon got inside,' PC Truffle said. 'Pesky birds, those.'

'Yes, I spotted a couple pecking around and eating my toast only yesterday, but we don't get a lot of trouble with birds,' said Trapmole flatly. 'We have a big ugly killer cat that stalks anything feathery with a merciless accuracy. Unfortunately, it was poisoned last night.'

'Poisoned?!'

'Yes. I wondered if that was Mustard too – you don't seem to have been exactly successful in stopping him making threats against the family.'

I had my shoulder to the pot nearest the keypad, but it was not budging. Those things are heavier than they look, and they look pretty heavy. Then I felt the first splash of rain on my fur. Like most felines, normally at the first splash of rain you'd find me dashing for cover. Now I was going to have to utterly save the day and do it with wet fur.

Pudding's usually beautifully snowy coat was streaked with dirt and quite probably pigeon poo from inside that pipe. Yet she still looked glamorous, and glanced up fearfully at the already steadily falling rain. Utterly useless.

'Sounds pretty suspicious,' began Truffle. 'Yesterday

your cat's poisoned and today pigeons make a flap inside the workshop.' I could hear him perfectly clearly now above the crowd, that must mean he and Trapmole were close. 'Maybe it was the pigeons poisoned him.'

'What?' said Trapmole.

'Just a joke about the pigeons,' said Truffle rather acidly. I could tell he wasn't exactly delighted at having interrupted his day at the gala to investigate. 'Maybe it was them same birds who were hanging around after your toast. Maybe they were casing the joint. Could you identify the criminals, maybe?'

'I do hope this is still part of your joke, because I could not identify two particular pigeons.'

'No. No one ever can. You would not believe how often, when alarms go off, the supposed dangerous burglars everyone suspects of making off with their goods are actually little feathery fellows looking for a nice place to nest.'

I didn't need my super-senses to hear urgent voices coming from the other side of the door as I heaved and pushed at the flower pot.

'Nightshade, are you there yet?'

'What's taking you so long?'

'Long?!' I was panting and exhausted and that pot was not moving. 'I'd like to see any of you –' I pushed with all my might – 'crawl through a narrow dirty air duct and pop out to face a jump high enough to kill you, all while carrying an annoying fluffball.' What I really needed was Oakmoss's ability to use the air to move things. But Oakmoss was trapped on the wrong side of the door.

'I've lost count of the number of times I've been called out on false alarms,' said Truffle. 'But you only get one chance of winning a Puss-in-Boots throwing at a fairy-tale gala. I think I deserve a slice of cake to take the edge of my disappointment at not being able to win the prize, you know.'

I couldn't see them yet, but they had to be close.

'I'm very good at throwing,' went on Truffle. 'Do you happen to know what the prize is?'

'Truffle and Trapmole are nearly here,' I panted. 'We're never going to do this. You'd better start getting your excuses ready.'

At that moment, Pudding shuffled up next to me and joined in, shoving her tiny shoulder against the plant pot that I was trying and failing to shift.

I didn't think we could do it. But actually, I'd never have done it without her.

I felt the pot move.

43. CRIMINAL MASTERMIND PIGEON

With two of us, even if one of us was Pudding, we actually had just enough oomph to slide that pot and get it shifting. Then it was the work of a moment to get it positioned under the keypad. I think the rain helped a little too, as everywhere was quickly getting slick with the stuff.

I rested a paw lightly on the wall and pinged out a sharp claw. 'Hit me with the code,' I said loud enough to reach the people inside.

It's always a complete miracle when a plan actually

works. Seconds later, the alarm stopped its annoying bleeping, and there was the sound of a metal grille and bolts retracting. Oakmoss, Veena, Stormforce and the Flan staggered out into the rainy courtyard and Dexter slammed the door shut behind them.

I turned. Trapmole and Truffle were just rounding Baba Yaga's tea tent, slowed by stepping through the ropes. Of course they were going to spot us all lingering suspiciously by the small door where the alarm had been going off for a good ten minutes. We weren't in the clear just yet.

Dodging raindrops, Pudding scampered over to the new arrivals as the break-in team and Flanagan attempted to saunter away from the door as if they hadn't been anywhere near it.

PC Truffle exclaimed: 'Oh, look! Isn't that the cutest kitten in the world?' He bent down to ruffle her ears, even though she was both soggy and filthy.

Now that's what I call a cat person.

I spoke quickly to Oakmoss. 'Say you saw a pigeon pecking at the keypad and the alarm went off. You would have called Trapmole and the police, but you saw the pigeon fly away again and then the alarm shut itself off.'

'Say I saw a what?'

I sighed, wishing people would keep up.

'Medium-sized birds, grey, quite tasty.'

'Yes, I— Never mind.' Oakmoss turned as PC Truffle strode across the courtyard, flexing his fingers around his utility belt. 'Erm, glad you've arrived. The alarm's been going off.'

'What are you doing here?' demanded Trapmole.

'We thought we saw a pigeon pecking at the keypad. Of course we don't have the code to shut it off,' said Oakmoss, with a sideways glance in my direction, checking he was getting it right. 'But we saw the pigeon fly off again and I think everything is OK.'

PC Truffle peered at the tiny door in the whitewashed wall, a touch confused. 'Hornbeam Workshop's underground, is it?' He seemed satisfied with his own explanation, and had been completely fooled by the glimmer.

Trapmole was frowning with suspicion at our little group. Rain was starting to drip off the badger-like white stripe in his hair. I could tell he was unwilling to swallow Oakmoss's unlikely excuses involving pigeons.

But PC Truffle was already turning. 'See! Told you. Those pigeons are always causing false alarms.'

'I'll need to take a look around,' Trapmole said. 'You haven't seen any signs of that Mr Mustard hanging about?' he asked us through narrowed eyes.

Officer Truffle hitched up his utility belt. 'You do what you want,' he said. 'D'you think they'll let me to the front of the queue for that welly boot throwing? Perhaps you could have a word,' he hinted to Trapmole.

I was just feeling there was a real chance we were going to get away with this when Flanagan began tugging at Veena's sleeve.

'I really want to make a donation.'

'Not now, it's not very important,' said Veena.

'That RAT society is so worthwhile,' went on Flanagan.

Veena managed to get Flanagan to shut up and resume just staring around, as if not even sure where she was. If we were lucky, her memories of the entire episode would be one big haze and she would never know for sure what she'd seen. Perhaps Oakmoss's luck was finally turning, because PC Truffle was already striding off back through the guy ropes.

'I shall look forward to that lemonade later,' he said ponderously. 'This weather's getting a bit Christmas, isn't it?' Truffle looked upwards. 'You know—'

'Yes,' groaned Trapmole. 'It looks like rain, dear –

I've heard it before. We can do without the lame jokes and forget about side stalls and prizes,' he spluttered. 'That's not what you're here for. Where is Mustard? He's your prime suspect. You were supposed to be keeping an eye on him.'

'I told you I don't work for you,' the officer responded. 'You, who thinks the same pigeon is responsible for the break-in as the poisoning of your cat.' PC Truffle gave a look that warned Trapmole not to push it.

'I did not—'

'I can put it in a report that you're suggesting we are dealing with some sort of criminal mastermind pigeon here, make an announcement to the press . . . round up possible suspects and do an identity parade. Or we can just call it a false alarm. And – you can have a word to get me to the front of that queue.'

'I don't think . . .' began Trapmole, drawing himself up. 'I didn't mean— What I mean is . . .' he tailed off.

Trapmole was definitely the sort who enjoyed making life uncomfortable for other people, and particularly making himself look good by pointing out the mistakes of others. It was quite pleasant to see him failing to manipulate PC Truffle. I'd also award him points for being able to tell when he was beaten.

Trapmole sighed. 'I'll have a word with the Puss-in-Boots stall. You're right, we've both got better things to do. I need to go and sell lemonade.' The apprentice straightened his shoulders and was about to stalk off with as much dignity as he could muster, but not without first giving Oakmoss a particularly malevolent stare, his eyes glinting dangerously. 'My lemonade will ensure that I bring in far more money than you today, and that I am far better suited to running things around here.'

PC Truffle shuffled in a little closer to Trapmole, looking up at the rain, which was now bucketing down (I think that is the technical term humans use).

'Are you two having a competition about who can raise the most money? Then a friendly word of advice: ditch the lemonade. Shame you aren't selling tea. The smart money will be on getting a hot drink somewhere warm and dry. I've experience of these things and it always does rain.'

PC Truffle turned to us. 'Same way as I knew it'd be a pesky bird. Told him, I've seen it before. Now, if all's tickety-boo, then I'll just toddle back. Does anyone know what the prize is for the boot throwing? Don't think there'll be much of a queue now. A bit of rain is always lucky for some.' He grinned.

'Thank you, Officer, for your concern, but I do

302

always have a Plan B,' sneered Trapmole, attempting to maintain his dignity, but looking anxiously at the rain.

'Plan B? Too right,' nodded the officer.

We watched him move ponderously away and the apprentice stomping off after him, looking as keen as I was to get somewhere dry. Pudding's bedraggled white coat clung to her tiny shape like a bird plucked of its feathers. Fur and water do not mix.

Before Trapmole got very far, Stormforce nudged Flanagan and pointed to the ground, muttering an instruction under his breath that she obeyed without a murmur.

'Hey, think you dropped something,' she called, making Trapmole turn.

Flanagan dug the apprentice's silver skull ring out of the dirt, where Stormforce had just dropped it. Trapmole stomped over and snatched it from her with a look of intense suspicion as he cleaned it on his trousers.

'I'm far too busy to worry what you lot have been up to,' he snarled. 'People are relying on me to raise money.'

'But Trapmole,' said Veena gently, 'I really don't think it's going to be worth you cycling around selling lemonade.'

His only reply was a snort as he stalked off.

We may have got away with the break-in. But my whiskers were telling me our problems at Hornbeam Hall were far from over.

44. Sort of Pink and Hazy

Truffle disappeared in the direction of the Puss-in-Boots throwing and the chance of a prize. We watched the apprentice vanish into the crowd. Now, if only dealing with Flanagan would be so easy.

But I think the confusion magic had done its work. She was still looking around vaguely and saying how deserving the RATS was. I did hope it would wear off before she handed over too much cash like Mr Mustard's wife had done.

My own thoughts went: get out of this rain, tea

tent, dry, warm, cake, milk and then an enormous nap, then worry about Mustard and Oakmoss's ill-wishing.

I guessed we needed to think about what we'd discovered in the workshop. How could we stop the Hornbeam Workshop casting any more mind-meld spells on the fortune cats, and do it before the whole family was arrested for illegal use of magic?

'We should go to the tea tent,' suggested Oakmoss to Flanagan, starting to steer her that way.

'Mr Mustard was telling the truth all along, wasn't he?' said Veena, watching Oakmoss persuade Flanagan that what she really needed was a cup of tea and a scone and not to make a donation.

'Or maybe a lemonade,' suggested Oakmoss.

'Oh, no,' I said.

'I'm afraid it has to be true, Nightshade,' Veena protested. 'It's clear there's been some magic cast over those fortune cats in the packing room. I wonder if somehow Mr Mustard's wife got a rogue fortune with an extra-strong dose of that magic, one that made her keep on donating? Not everyone who's bought one can be doing that, or more friends and family would be camped out with Mustard! But I think we need to put a stop to anyone else getting put under that spell. I think the Hornbeams have got a bit too fond of that easy way to make money.'

'Whiskers and white mice!' I stopped heading towards the tent, even in the rain, even with my fur soaking up water like a giant sponge. Even within sniffing distance of an awful lot of cake. I was a detective cat and wouldn't run for cover and cake at the first sign of trouble (or was this the tenth sign of trouble? I'd lost count).

'What?' asked Stormforce and Veena together. Pudding didn't stop or ask any questions, just continued into Baba Yaga's tea tent, ducking through a tiny gap in search of dryness, warmth and as much cake as a cat could eat.

'Lemonade!' I said. 'You're right – Trapmole's found an easy way of impressing the Hornbeams by bringing in cash by the sack full. But he also keeps boasting about how he's going to get the biggest fundraising donations today. Did you see that lemonade earlier?'

'I didn't particularly notice the lemonade.' Veena wrinkled her nose. 'I was panicking about whether I could get that ring off him at the time, remember?'

'What are you trying to tell us, Nightshade?' asked Stormforce, water dripping off his fringe and the end of his nose. 'It's something bad, isn't it?'

'I saw him loading up that little wooden cart attached to his bicycle. I thought some of the lemonade bottles looked strange. Weird, sort of pink and hazy.'

'Pink and hazy, as in exactly like the spell that was in the packing room?' said Veena nervously.

'Exactly. I think Trapmole's trying to go around and give a bit of that spell to as many people as possible. We've got to stop him putting a confusion charm on anyone who drinks a lemonade. We've got to find Trapmole.'

My paws started working quickly as I led a dash through the guy ropes.

'You mean,' said Veena, eyes widening and sounding appalled, 'he's going to cycle around selling lemonade corrupted or bewitched or whatever with that spell?' She was following nimbly through the guy ropes. 'And that spell is going to give everyone here an overwhelming urge to donate to RATS? That has to be breaking several magical laws all at once.'

'Don't panic,' said Stormforce, striding with his long legs to keep up with my pace. 'I doubt he'll make many sales cycling around in this rain.'

'Yes, everyone's probably sheltering in the tea tent,' said Veena.

Stormforce wiped rain from his face with his sleeve. 'Even so, we should find the lemonade cart and make sure any magic is destroyed.'

'To think,' went on Veena, struggling to get through the guy ropes as quickly as me, 'he wanted me to have some!' She turned to Stormforce. 'You can do that, right, destroy it? What happens to illegal magic?'

'There's an Elysee department that specializes in that kind of thing. We just need to find the cart. Did anyone see which way Trapmole went?'

We finally rounded the far end of the tea tent.

The lawns and most of the stalls were deserted. Just a few stragglers were making their way to where the tent bulged with babbling customers. The aroma of cake was just edging ahead of the smell of damp grass and drenched fairy-tale costume.

Stormforce was thinking out loud as we stood there looking out at the grounds. 'That spell must be a pretty lucrative line for Rescue All Toys. Most people probably donate once and forget about it. Kind of lucky a rogue batch got out there, otherwise I don't think we'd have got on to them.'

Veena shook her head with a rueful smile. 'I have to say, it's clever, isn't it? What will happen? Will you have to report them to the Elysee?'

'All I do is catch the bad guys. I track down the wrong kinds of magic being used on non-magical people. It's not up to me what happens after.'

'But what do you think will happen?' she asked. 'To the Hornbeams, I mean.'

I led them to where I'd seen Trapmole loading up his cart.

'Trapmole might be acting alone, thinking that adding illegal mind-meld magic to things is a good way to impress the Hornbeams,' answered Stormforce. 'Proving whether or not they knew about it will be tough. Investigating magic is tricky.'

Oakmoss must have successfully abandoned the Flan in the tea tent, because we found him waiting for us, right by Trapmole's lemonade wagon. The handwritten sign – STOP ME AND BUY LEMONADE – was lying in a puddle, barely readable as the lettering had run.

'You've worked it out too? He was going to bewitch the lemonade,' breathed Oakmoss. 'I knew I'd seen that strange pink stuff before. It was in his cart.'

'But where is he?' asked Veena, looking around frantically.

'More importantly,' said Stormforce, 'where are the strange bottles of pink haze?'

Stormforce was right. The cart was still full of lemonade, but there was no sign of the illegal spell.

I saw a flash of Trapmole's badger hair threading

its way towards the crowded tea tent, and pointed with my paw. 'Whiskers and white mice, he's not giving up,' I said urgently. 'He must have taken that spell.'

'He told PC Truffle he had a Plan B in case it rained,' said Veena.

'You don't think Trapmole's Plan B is to add it to the tea?' said Oakmoss.

We all stared at the huge queue for hot drinks, a happily babbling line of patient people clutching prizes and coconuts. The queue reached right to the edge of the tent, where people were doing their best to avoid the rain cascading in a sheet.

Stormforce had a look I seldom saw on him – it was one of panic. 'That's exactly what he's going to do. We've got to stop him.'

45. Don't Drink The Tea

'He might have already put that mind-meld spell in the tea, we might already be too late.' Stormforce could not have sounded more urgent. 'I think we need to make sure no one drinks anything.'

'But how?' asked Oakmoss.

'Oakmoss, you look for Trapmole, in case we've got to him in time. Get that spell off him if possible. Veena and I will warn everyone not to drink anything,' said Stormforce, looking like he wanted to race around, but the overpowering crush of damp

bodies meant it was almost impossible to move anywhere at all.

Oakmoss looked down at Nightshade. 'This is no job for a cat. You'll get crushed. Leave this to us – and if things go well, I'll bring you out some cake.'

'Go well?' responded Nightshade grumpily, diving under a tent flap.

Oakmoss thought he heard her saying the chances of that were pretty much zero.

Oakmoss was trying in vain to see Trapmole in the crowd. He could see Mum in full flow, a cup of tea in one hand, a slice of cake in the other. And the same with Dad. In fact, it looked like every single person had a cup of tea in hand.

He was distracted by a roar from behind. And there in the rain stood Mr Mustard, his blue windproof jacket zipped up to his walrus moustache, yelling, 'Hornbeam, you coward, where are you?' He put up his fists and gave another roar. 'Have the courage, man, to come and face me.'

'On second thoughts,' said Stormforce, 'Veena, you track down Trapmole. Oakmoss, you stop anyone drinking tea. I'll deal with the man who wants to give your dad a bloody nose.'

It was impossible to hurry through the packed

throng in the tent. It was impossible to look for Trapmole. It was impossible to come up with any sort of a plan.

Oakmoss looked around wildly. From the Little Miss Muffet who was feeding squash to her pet spider, to Alices with damp hair and glasses of milk, to a shiny-looking stegosaurus, every single one looked to have a drink in their hand.

'Think I'm just going to try to stop anyone drinking anything,' said Oakmoss to Veena, who was still close behind him, eyes darting, jumping up and down, looking for a sign of Trapmole.

'Er,' Oakmoss began hesitantly, walking up to one of his teachers from school, who was dressed like Robin Hood and sipping appreciatively at a mug of something hot. 'Hello, sir, maybe you shouldn't drink that.'

Rain drummed on the canvas roof, and there was a terrible humid atmosphere. Robin Hood — aka Mr Broad (maths) – just put his head enquiringly on one side, as if he must have misheard. And then took another sip.

Short of making the tent collapse on them, how on earth was Oakmoss going to stop hundreds of people drinking? All he could hope was that they'd been quick enough and Trapmole hadn't yet had chance to do his dirty work and give everyone a taste of the rogue spell.

Oakmoss started frantically delivering his warning not to drink anything to as many people as possible. But they looked bemused and chuckled faintly, as if he was joking. No one took any notice of him, just carried on drinking.

'Don't drink the tea,' Oakmoss tried again, to a man in wolf's clothing and also wearing a Little Red Riding Hood dress. The fact that there were so many people in ridiculous fancy dress made the whole thing feel unreal. It was as if he had stepped into a nightmare, where every way he turned, everyone seemed to be mocking him, raising their cups, determined to drink. No one was ever going to take his warning seriously.

He heard a yell and another threat from outside, and could tell Dexter's mission to calm down Mr Mustard was proving just as unsuccessful. Oakmoss could not believe that only moments before he'd actually been congratulating himself that, so far, the day hadn't actually gone half as badly as he'd expected.

Now it was difficult to see any way to avoid this afternoon ending in the sort of headline Veena was going to be proud of. Probably involving the word *carnage*. She was going to achieve her dream of writing for a national newspaper rather than the *Dogberry Academy Times*.

He finally battled his way to the trestle tables at the back of the tent. This was the front of the queue, where yet more people were buying yet more cups of tea poured from a giant urn.

'Stop!' he cried. His voice too weak and the tea just carried on being poured. He even received a couple of snide looks, as if he was simply trying to jump the queue.

Oakmoss cleared his throat. There was only one thing he could think of. He summoned the air, imagining how a loud-speaking charm could at least make him shout a warning to everyone all at once.

'This is an official announcement,' he said desperately to the crowd. He could tell no one really knew where the carrying voice was coming from, because no one was looking at him. There was a lot of staring around in search of speakers and looking to the roof of the tent where the rain drummed heavily. But the loud general hubbub lowered to a whisper. People were listening. This was going to work.

'There has been an unexpected difficulty with refreshments this afternoon. Please do not drink anything.' All sound seemed to stop, except for the incessant rain. 'Sorry about that.'

Oakmoss held his breath.

Everyone had listened. There was even a halt to the number of drinks being sipped as everyone stared about. Oakmoss could now clearly hear Stormforce trying to reason with Mustard outside, which was slightly better than the sound of punches. He had lost all track of Veena and Trapmole.

And just when he thought he'd been successful, the low murmur of background noise simply began to grow again, people sipped their drinks, smiled at each other, shook their heads and carried on as if nothing had been said.

Oakmoss summoned his charm again, this time making it louder. 'Warning! This is serious! Do not drink anything.'

This time there was less silence, more of a puzzled whisper that went around. And Stormforce could clearly be heard saying: 'There's no need for violence. Your claims are being fully investigated!'

Oakmoss shouted: 'This fairy-tale gala is under attack. DO NOT DRINK ANYTHING. We think the drinks might be poisoned.'

This time there was barely a second for the words to register before the first screams. Then there was a rush of fairy-tale characters, as everyone fled in one movement to the exit in a large jam of colourful costumes, abandoning not just their drinks, but cakes, scones and pots of clotted cream. And not just abandoning – plates, cups, cakes and cream all got thrown in the air or trampled underfoot in the headlong rush to escape.

It seemed impossible to empty a place as big as Baba Yaga's tea tent quite so quickly, but within seconds not a single person remained. China mugs rolled, plates had been crunched and shattered, plastic beakers were tossed to the ground.

A sea of costumed gala-goers fled Baba-Yaga's tea tent, making straight for the black entrance gates. They were stopping for nothing, not even an angry man spoiling for a fight. They kept on running. A man dressed as a pig led the frenzied stampede; at his heels was a small but sprightly velociraptor.

Cake wasn't the only thing that had got squished underfoot in the race for safety – Oakmoss ran after the crowd and looked back to see Stormforce offering Mr Mustard a hand up from where he lay, face down in the mud, flattened by the fairy-tale retreat.

Oakmoss followed in the wake of everyone streaming out of the gates, heading for the street outside, until there was only one final guest, an elaborate Tin Man who looked as if his costume was difficult to run in. His spray-painted silver face looked surprised but also a little hopeful as he stepped beyond the gates, just as the downpour finally abated and a weak yet hopeful sun returned shyly from behind the heavy clouds.

The Tin Man looked around and asked no one in particular: 'Who *did* win the fancy dress competition?'

Oakmoss gave a half-hearted shrug and, once the Tin Man was safely beyond the grounds, he slammed the big black gates shut behind everyone, and locked them.

46. NOT QUITE AS HE HOPED

Oakmoss dashed to a part of the wall where he could climb up and watch the fairy-tale crowd slowly vanishing in a bedraggled line in the direction of Dogberry town. He enjoyed the feeling of calm descending and a final spray of rain, gentle now, on his face.

He took his time before he finally returned to the crushed and broken remains of Baba Yaga's tea tent. He found himself quite alone, apart from a substantial amount of uneaten cake in sugary towers on the

trestle tables. He was pleased that the rain had eased, the sun appeared to be blinking back into view and nothing too terrible had actually happened, apart from the unfortunate squashing of an immense amount of sad-looking strawberry tarts.

At least there had been a headlong rush to the gate rather than to make forced donations – he guessed they had got everyone out before Trapmole could taint all the drinks with his confusion spell.

Oakmoss guessed everyone must be up at the house. He had no expectation of what might happen next, apart from the obvious of loading up a plate with abandoned cakes – well, why not? It took him a while to get a decent stash balanced to take indoors to share.

He half expected someone to seek him out and ask what he was doing, or maybe come to find him, or report on what was happening, but it appeared everyone had vanished. Only the fluttering colourful bunting seemed to be trying to attract his attention.

He took his time, trod carefully through the wet grass, leaving behind the abandoned stalls and staggering between the guy ropes and trudging to the kitchen, looking out for signs of Veena, Storm-force, Trapmole, Nightshade, or even his parents or Hyacinth. Where was everyone?

He munched on something gooey that stuck to his teeth pleasantly, thinking how one minute the whole of Hornbeam Hall had been packed and now it felt as if he was the only person left in the world.

Not quite the only person. When he reached the kitchen he was surprised to find a tall man where Hyacinth normally stood, boiling the kettle. This man wasn't dressed as a fairy-tale character – he was dressed in a closely fitted silvery suit – but Oakmoss guessed he must be one of the gala-goers who had taken a wrong turn.

The man helped himself to a thick slab of sticky toffee and banana cake from Oakmoss's loaded plate, uninvited. Oakmoss was too surprised to stop him.

'Shame to waste them,' the man said, taking a bite.

'Are you lost?' Oakmoss asked.

The man chewed thoughtfully, looking at Oakmoss through round glasses that reflected the light and made it difficult to read his expression. 'This is Hornbeam Hall?'

'Yes.'

'Good, then I most definitely am not lost. Did you miss lunch?'

Oakmoss put down the towering plate and was halfway through the first of several coconut macaroons as he tried to remember. 'I think I did.

But I don't think that's the point. I think the point is that you are in my kitchen. Were you at the gala?'

'Me? No. I've only just arrived.'

Nightshade strolled in, closely followed by Pudding, whose fur had returned to a fluffy halo of white.

'Inspector Pewter!' cried Nightshade, rushing towards the man and rubbing around the bottom of his smart trousers. 'Oakmoss, you didn't tell me you knew Inspector Pewter.'

'I don't know Inspector Pewter. He's just eating my cake.'

Nightshade explained that this tall person helping himself to tea and cake was an inspector from MagiCon.

'You mean a bit like PC Truffle, but with the Elysee magical police? Wow!' Oakmoss stopped halfway through his mouthful. 'Are you here to arrest someone?'

With everything that had happened, Oakmoss hadn't had a chance to consider what would happen next. Stormforce had investigated. Would Mr Mustard no longer haunt the doorstep, flinging out his accusations? And then his insides panicked. 'Is Mr Mustard OK? He looked pretty flattened last time I saw him. Is he leaving now?'

Inspector Pewter looked particularly tall standing in the low-ceilinged kitchen, his hands in his pockets. 'I'm delighted Nightshade has been giving a helping hand, even though if Nightshade's here there'll be some sort of havoc involved. Probably means a whole stack of paperwork for me. That's how it usually ends. One thing cats don't understand is paperwork.'

Pewter and Nightshade started chatting in a way that make Oakmoss pleased Veena wasn't here to see yet another example of magical people gathering together. He had completely failed to answer any of Oakmoss's questions.

Oakmoss decided to put the time to good use and tackled the abandoned cake mountain, challenging himself against a tower containing a slice of sticky date cake, a strawberry scone and a very large chunk of lemon drizzle cake balanced on top.

The inspector hardly paused in catching up with Nightshade to swoop in for the lemon drizzle.

'No one is expecting you to eat every last bit of the leftover cake,' said Hyacinth, arriving with another plate loaded with treats and also addressing the inspector as if she knew him. She swiftly set about making tea.

Inspector Pewter thanked Hyacinth as he took a

chair, sliding his tent-pole legs under the kitchen table. He drummed his fingers on the table and looked at Oakmoss in a way that made him worry that maybe the inspector was here to arrest him. He was suddenly filled with thoughts of him levitating Nightshade, getting those leaves to fly, using his magic to shout out loudly across the tea tent. Somehow, from barely having used magic before, he seemed to have used it quite lavishly. And he didn't know enough to feel sure none of it was illegal use of magic.

'You asked if I was here to arrest someone,' said the inspector.

Oakmoss heard himself give a dry swallow.

'You are right, I do arrest people.' The way the inspector was looking at Oakmoss made him fidget uncomfortably, completely sure he was about to receive at the very least a stern reprimand about his magic. 'We do need a few rules about how magic is used and the choices people make.'

What had Stormforce said about the punishments the Elysee could dish out to sorcerers who made bad choices about how to use their magic? Limiting the use of magic was one. Being sent to prison was another.

Oakmoss felt himself turning red, as if it was written on his face how badly at one time he had wanted to explore his magic to make something bad happen to Flanagan. Not very bad, just a little bit bad.

'Accidents do happen, of course,' Inspector Pewter went on.

Oakmoss knew something awful was coming. Was he going to receive one of the worst punishments the Elysee could give? Was the inspector going to invoke the power to prevent him using his magic? And where were his parents and Trapmole?

'I'm going to have a little chat to a few people around here,' said the inspector quietly. 'Starting with your parents, who I know will be helpful in clearing up a couple of small matters.'

Oakmoss felt himself breathe again at the mention of small matters.

'And I really do like clearing things up, even with all the paperwork it brings.' Pewter munched on his last mouthful of cake. 'And chatting to people about how they've been using their magic.'

'I don't think there's anything I can tell you,' said Oakmoss weakly. But even as he said it, he knew it wasn't true and he guessed Inspector Pewter would also be asking him some uncomfortable questions.

Like about those sacks full of donations.

Like how the charity had plenty of money coming

in. Yet his mother always found another reason why the toy hospital couldn't get started. If Oakmoss were a MagiCon inspector, his questions might include: Why did so much money generously flood into a charity that didn't even do anything yet? Why was none of the money that flooded in ever spent on repairing any toys?

'Where are my parents?' asked Oakmoss.

Mum and Dad surely had suspicions. Had they noticed that so many of their fortune cat customers sent in donations to RATS? Sure, most only donated once, but what about Mrs Mustard, who hadn't been able to stop?

And that pink haze in the packing room? Did they notice or question that every single fortune cat left here with a spell cast over it?

'Where's Dexter?' Oakmoss asked nervously.

'Ah yes, young Dexter Stormforce is very useful. He is skilled at spotting where a little unauthorized magic is leaking out where it's not supposed to!' said Pewter heartily. 'He does have a nasty habit of then calling me in to finish the enquiries and do the clearing up. Your parents have both very kindly agreed to assist MagiCon in the clearing up,' he said in a tone that made it sound as if they'd just won a ten-day cruise.

'By MagiCon,' said Oakmoss, pushing away his plate and suddenly not feeling at all hungry, 'you mean you?'

'Yes.'

'What enquiries are they going to help with?'

Hyacinth, who was never anything less than bustling, was suddenly very still. Oakmoss was aware she was standing at the kitchen sink and only pretending to do something.

'MagiCon might be quite interested in magic being used, shall we say, irresponsibly.'

'Irresponsibly?' That didn't sound too bad. That didn't sound so bad as illegally, for instance. Because it sounded as if the inspector already knew all about Dexter's investigations into the workshop, already knew about the mind-meld charm. And even Oakmoss already knew that was illegal use of magic.

'Has Dexter gone?' Stormforce's work was over, the undercover case he'd been sent to investigate had been investigated. Stormforce would have called in Pewter to do the tidying up and the paperwork. 'By irresponsibly, you mean illegally, don't you?'

'Yes.'

Oakmoss breathed heavily. 'So what's going to happen to Mum and Dad?'

'Hopefully nothing.'

A small chink of optimism rose in Oakmoss's chest. 'That's good. Apart from the *hopefully* bit. They won't go to jail, will they?'

'It may just be a rap over the knuckles,' said Nightshade, hopping on to Pewter's lap, angling for a piece of cake, and he fussed her ears.

'That would be the most positive outcome from a range of possible outcomes,' said Pewter, sneaking the last coconut macaroon which Oakmoss had abandoned.

'I'm not sure that sounds all that good or very hopeful,' commented Nightshade.

'I'd have to agree with you,' nodded Pewter. 'That is why your friend Veena has gone to fetch Uncle Erasmus. I'd quite like to meet him. It's good to have all the family around at a time like this.'

Oakmoss slumped down in a chair and was pleased when Nightshade leapt from Inspector Pewter on to his lap and snuggled into him.

He should have seen this coming, right from the moment Stormforce had said he was here to investigate and round up the bad guys.

Oakmoss had only wanted to help. He'd thought he was doing the right thing in helping to get rid of that pest Mustard. It had seemed that letting Stormforce check out if Mr Mustard's ridiculously outlandish accusations had any truth in them was the best way to get things sorted. In fact, that's definitely what Stormforce had allowed him to believe he was doing.

But, of course, Oakmoss had never dreamt Mr Mustard's ridiculous accusations about the toys being evil and the fortune cat tricking him were true. Those fortune cats brought a lot of fortune, but it was all for the Hornbeam family.

And Oakmoss . . . Oakmoss had done it this time, hadn't he? He really was the unluckiest boy in the world. Because he was the one who had led Stormforce right to the truth. Because Oakmoss had never stopped to properly consider that his parents might actually be the bad guys.

'But it was all Trapmole, wasn't it?' he said hopefully to the inspector.

'That is one of those interesting questions we hope to get answers to,' replied Pewter.

Oakmoss feared he knew already that Trapmole showed off every small change or improvement he made to impress Dad. Surely this one Trapmole must have kept to himself? Dad would have stopped it, all that money pouring into Mum's charity . . . wouldn't he? All that money arriving every day. So much that it had to be kept in sacks.

Oakmoss stroked Nightshade's silky fur, haunted by everything Dexter had said about what happened to sorcerers who were found guilty of using magic illegally, particularly on people who didn't even know magic existed. Dexter had been here to carry out a covert magical investigation into the Hornbeams all along, alerted by Mustard's complaints that a magical crime was being committed.

'Afternoon, all. Looks like things are clearing up out there,' said Erasmus, bounding in through the back door. Oakmoss's heart lifted at the sight of his uncle, especially when he was closely followed by Veena.

He breathed a sigh of relief. Surely together they would be able to sort out this horrible mess. His uncle would be able to deal with everything. There was still a chance they could put it all right.

47. NOT VERY FAR AWAY

Erasmus had arrived dressed smartly for the second time in two days, wearing the same crumpled linen jacket he'd worn to Mum's posh dinner, along with an air of undisguised curiosity.

'What's all the excitement? Veena wouldn't tell me anything.'

He had also brought an enormous basket with him, for which he apologized as he placed it on the long kitchen table. 'Veena said to be prepared for anything so I didn't like to leave this old fella alone.'

A low hiss issued from the basket. 'He's not been the same since his poor . . .'

'You've brought Gisborne?' said Oakmoss as he felt Nightshade tense on his lap.

Pudding had popped her delicate nose into the kitchen, but one look at the malevolent yellow eyes of Gisborne staring out between the bars of the basket sent her scuttling away again.

The end of Nightshade's tail began to swish ever so slowly.

Erasmus pushed back his fringe, took off his jacket and dumped it on the chair next to Oakmoss. 'Anyway. What's this all about? All I was told was that I'm needed here on an urgent mission and I can already see one source of trouble. You clearly need help to eat up all this cake.'

'The trouble is . . . Well,' Oakmoss began, feeling it was up to him to explain, 'this is Inspector Pewter of MagiCon and he's . . .' Oakmoss swallowed hard, suddenly overwhelmed by the awfulness of the situation, 'asking Mum and Dad a few—'

'How's it all going?' Stormforce interrupted as he strolled through the back door.

'Dexter!' cried Oakmoss, 'I thought you'd either gone or been trampled in the fairy-tale stampede.'

'Oh, it takes more than a few princesses to knock

me off my feet. Ah! Cake!'

Stormforce seized a strawberry tart from the plate Hyacinth had brought. Oakmoss had felt he'd brought more cake than they could possibly need back from the Baba Yaga tent. He might be wrong about that. He was very probably wrong about quite a lot of things.

'Erasmus Hornbeam, welcome,' began Inspector Pewter, taking over the explanations. 'We are just discussing the ways in which your brother, Mrs Hornbeam and their apprentice, Trapmole, have been quite busy and rather innovative. They have kindly agreed to explain exactly what they have been doing, as unfortunately it looks as if they may have put their efforts into something not entirely allowed.'

'It's possible they might have broken a few magical laws,' said Stormforce, reaching for another cake.

Erasmus looked puzzled as he nodded a thank-you at Hyacinth, who was sliding mugs of tea in front of everyone. 'Well, that all sounds like a mis-understanding,' he said, absent-mindedly taking a slice of the sticky date cake.

'A misunderstanding, that's exactly right,' nodded Oakmoss eagerly, breathing a sigh of relief. Perhaps his parents and Trapmole hadn't known they were breaking magical laws.

'Thankfully, MagiCon are here. We can trust MagiCon to get to the bottom of things,' said Erasmus.

Oakmoss lifted Erasmus's jacket to make room for Veena to sit down next to him. He slid her a slice of lemon drizzle. Veena gave Oakmoss's arm a comforting squeeze.

He was trying not to feel angry at Stormforce for tricking him into helping – now his parents were going to be dragged off for questioning. But Erasmus would make sure they came back soon. There had to be a way of clearing up this misunderstanding.

Pewter got to his feet. 'Well, you are half right. You can certainly trust MagiCon to get to the bottom of any misunderstanding. But the bottom of things is that there is no misunderstanding. I've asked you here as we need to make a little plan about what happens next.'

'A plan?' echoed Oakmoss. 'But plans never work out.'

'There might be something in that,' nodded the inspector.

Oakmoss looked at Erasmus, hoping he'd step in and disagree. But Erasmus just kept eating his cake.

'The Elysee have been keeping an eye on the Hornbeam family, ever since your grandfather made the same mistake and used magic for something it very definitely should not be used for,' said Pewter to Oakmoss.

'My grandfather used magic illegally?' asked Oakmoss, feeling there was really rather a lot about his own family that he didn't know.

'More than once, I'm afraid,' answered Pewter. 'And at least three times very badly.'

'Is that why Dad doesn't like talking about magic?'

'Your grandfather had some seriously bad ideas about what magic can be used for and what he thought he could get away with. I cannot speak for your father, not until we've had our little chat.'

Erasmus rubbed the back of his head. 'I didn't know that. That does explain why my brother was always so bitter and scathing about magic. I thought it was because his own magic wasn't very good.'

'It's often less about power or even skill, and more about the choices made,' nodded the inspector.

He clapped Oakmoss on the shoulder. 'Glad you have a few friends and family around you, young Oakmoss. None of this is in any way your fault. We can't help the families we're born into.' Inspector Pewter bent to look at Oakmoss closely, his eyes suddenly shining a very bright blue behind his glasses. 'One day I hope you will see that bringing these illegal happenings to an end is entirely the right result.'

Oakmoss did not know what to say. He just stroked Nightshade's silky fur without meeting anyone's eye.

'One day I hope you will see that – but I'm sure today you are very probably not going to see things that way.'

Oakmoss had so many questions he wished he was Veena, demanding an exclusive interview with Pewter. Perhaps he was just a lot more afraid of the answers.

Avoiding questions might be why the inspector had done little except eat two cakes and drink three cups of tea but was now making what looked like a cautious exit.

'And is Mr Mustard . . . ?' floundered Oakmoss, wanting to stop the inspector before he could disappear, taking any chance of an explanation with him.

'Ah, indeed. Good question!' cried Pewter, reaching the back door with just a couple of strides. 'I've had a little chat with your Mr Mustard already. He's not in too bad a shape and has been quite forgiving, despite the trampling. He is also looking forward to heading home. That's some good news I can offer you at least. His decision to leave was probably helped by your father returning every penny that was stolen from him.'

'He has? Oh, that's great news!' Or was it? Didn't that confirm that what Mr Mustard had said was true, and his wife had been conned by their fortune cat into giving a lot of donations to RATS. 'I'm so glad Dad offered to pay him back,' Oakmoss stuttered.

'Not offered, not exactly,' said Pewter, sticking his hands deep in the pockets of his silvery suit. 'But he came around to that point of view. I can be surprisingly persuasive. So, Mr Mustard has unpitched his tent and will not be troubling you any more.'

48. Taking The Boat Out

Hyacinth gave Oakmoss a hug. 'Look, not a bit of dried blood or mud on you, things are looking up.'

Oakmoss tried a smile. But all of a sudden, the inspector had gone and there was too much quiet in the kitchen and Oakmoss's thoughts buzzed too noisily.

He needed some fresh air. He had never wanted to go fishing more. Even better, he could take the boat out. No one ever wanted to go out in the boat

with him. It felt like years since he'd been out on the lake. Maybe if his bad luck truly had left with Mr Mustard then someone would even come with him.

'Who's for fishing?' he tried. 'Hyacinth, you could come. You've got a lot less work if it's just me for dinner. And you'll be up for anything,' he said to Nightshade and fussed her ears. 'As long as there are fish involved.'

Erasmus clapped him on the shoulder in a way that was less reassuringly friendly and closer to an assault. 'You go out and enjoy yourself. The Hornbeam Workshop will be in safe hands until your parents and Trapmole return. There really isn't anything to worry about.'

This wasn't entirely true, but Oakmoss tried a smile. Then he worked out what his uncle was saying. 'You're going to take over until my parents and Trapmole come back? But you'd hate it. You'd have to give up your lovely shop.'

'Someone needs to take over the success story that is the Hornbeam Workshop and make sure the Hornbeams bounce back. I'm up for it, even if it means closing up the shop. Just in case . . .' It felt as if Erasmus was trying to avoid Oakmoss's eye. 'You take your friends and go out in the boat. I'll have closed up the shop and my flat above it and moved in here by the end of the day.'

Erasmus got up to leave, and Oakmoss reached to hand over his uncle's best jacket. As he did so, he noticed there was a deep-orange stain on the shoulder that would have been planted by the annoying hothouse lilies. Erasmus must have walked past them yesterday evening.

'I don't think I care all that much for the workshop,' admitted Oakmoss. 'Maybe you could close it and keep your shop?'

Erasmus was grinning reassuringly. 'You're far too young to be worrying about business. Someone needs to take over and run things.'

Oakmoss handed over the jacket,. 'You'd do that for me? You want to come and live here? That's really great!' And it was, even though part of him knew this meant Erasmus didn't think his parents were coming back any time soon.

He guessed he was pretty much surrounded by people who well-wished him – that had to outweigh any amount of ill-wishing, right?

Hyacinth shook her head. 'No fishing for me, Oakmoss. There's clearing up to do. All those delivery vans will be back to collect the tents and chairs and everything else they dropped off. I for one will be glad if we never host a fairy-tale gala ever again. At least you prevented the whole of Dogberry from drinking tea doctored with magic. You prevented a complete disaster.'

'You did, Oakmoss,' said Stormforce. 'Hope this means your bad luck is over. I'm going to help Hyacinth take down everything and get it ready for loading, so no fishing for me either.'

'You could help, Oakmoss,' said Veena, the first thing she'd said in a while. She was staring at Erasmus as if she was lost in a little dream world. 'You could take tents down really easily, couldn't you?'

Oakmoss answered with a shrug, his mind couldn't seem to get interested in tents, but he wanted to help. Perhaps fishing could wait, but no one seemed in much of a hurry to begin all the hard work of dismantling the surviving wreckage of the failed gala. Veena suggested she pour everyone another cup of tea first. Oakmoss had many questions, and pretty soon Stormforce would leave too.

'The poisoned pie – that was Mr Mustard?' muttered Oakmoss, still fussing Nightshade's ears. Stormforce telling him his bad luck was over reminded him how the cat had insisted someone was ill-wishing him. 'Was there an ill-wishing?'

Maybe it hadn't been Mustard at all – he

genuinely didn't seem to have known who Oakmoss was. So had it been Trapmole?

Trapmole, presumably, had the magic to do the glimmer and set up the other magical security. And he had been illegally infusing the fortune cats with a mild mind-meld spell (and getting Mum and Dad into serious trouble with MagiCon). Had he been behind the ill-wishing all along? When the three of them returned from answering questions, would Trapmole be offered his old job back? Oakmoss could never quite tell with Mum and Dad.

'Don't worry about any of that,' said Erasmus affably.

But it was difficult not to worry. Because he felt his uncle was only offering to move in and take over the running of the Hornbeam Hall and the workshop because his parents and Trapmole would be answering for their magical crimes for rather a long time. The future felt very uncertain, and it kind of made it worse when Hyacinth came across to give him another hug – clearly she was worried too.

'I never satisfactorily got to the bottom of your accidents, Oakmoss, I'm sorry,' said Stormforce, taking tea from Veena. 'If they carry on I'll come back and look into it.' He reached in to pilfer the very last strawberry scone.

'You know we've always disagreed a little about covering the news,' Veena said unexpectedly.

It felt as if everyone was trying to distract him from his very dark thoughts and there was still very much the question of what Veena might put on her front page.

'I understand, Veena. You try to always tell the truth. You think everyone should be honourable and interested in things like truth and justice. I know you find it difficult to cover things up.'

Veena nodded. 'Sometimes you cause a lot of fuss by pointing out bad behaviour. But you're only pointing out the truth. It's never your fault that those wrong things were done in the first place.'

'Is this your way of telling me you've got more bad news about what's going on your front page?' asked Oakmoss.

'I'm just saying it's better to face the truth than to believe in a lot of lies.'

'You're telling me that you don't want me to blame Stormforce?' said Oakmoss slowly.

Stormforce gave a small shrug. 'It is my job to stop illegal magic being used on the non-magical. I never know who's going to turn out to be the magical bad guys.'

Veena groaned and put her head in her hands.

'You're right, Oakmoss. I can't believe after everything that's happened, I *still* don't know what I'm going to put on the front page! Being on the inside track about all this top-secret magic has made my job and my whole life about a hundred times more complicated.'

'Welcome to the magical world,' said Nightshade gruffly to a hiss from Gisborne, still trapped safely behind bars in his basket.

Erasmus turned to Nightshade in surprise. 'The cat just talked? That happened, right? And none of you so much as flinched, so you all knew? And I'm guessing Veena knows about magic too?'

'Sorry, sorry,' said Nightshade. 'It's hard not to speak and sometimes I lose track of who knows and who doesn't.'

Erasmus dragged his hands through his hair. 'It's been quite a day, hasn't it? I'm sure Gisborne will be quite at home here when he learns he's living with a magical cat.'

Nightshade made no comment, just looked at Erasmus steadily with her big green eyes. Gisborne hissed in his basket.

Oakmoss finished his tea and considered eating more cake. 'All right, I'm ready for it. Veena, tell me the worst. What terrible news story will be all over the front page? I'm sure you could even find a way not to give the game away about magic. Stormforce said non-magical folk often find ordinary explanations for extraordinary things, because no one ever dreams any of it is really down to magic.'

Erasmus muttered about heading home, going to put on his jacket, then noticed the bright-orange stain on the shoulder. He started rubbing at it frantically. 'Don't you worry about anything, Oakmoss.'

Nightshade extended her claws. 'Stormforce arrived here to investigate the Hornbeam Workshop. But I was always interested in solving the mystery of your ill-wishing, Oakmoss. I'm not ready to go yet.'

'You've stopped all those people being tricked by the fortune cats, Oakmoss,' said Veena. 'It was the right thing to do, but Nightshade's right . . .'

'She usually is,' said Nightshade.

'Who poisoned your pie?' asked Veena, narrowing her eyes and shaking her head. 'Someone was trying to do more than ill-wish you. Someone had a pretty good go at trying to kill you. We still don't know for sure who that was.'

Nightshade looked at her with her big green eyes. 'I'd say the answer is not very far away.'

49. A Better Name Than Rats

'Wasn't it Trapmole?' said Oakmoss into a kitchen that suddenly felt way too silent. 'Or Mr Mustard?'

'Trapmole's magic turned out to be better than I thought,' said Stormforce, who lingered, a cup of tea in one hand and yet another slice of cake in the other.

'With magic it is always difficult to tell,' put in Nightshade.

'Trapmole was so desperate to impress my

parents. He worked out how to do at least one illegal mind-meld charm,' said Oakmoss thoughtfully, considering everything, including if, after all, he could manage another cake of any variety. 'I don't think he'd stop at putting me right out of the picture.'

Erasmus cleared this throat. 'Yes, well, Trapmole's magic surprised us all. He was always asking me questions about learning more. I may have left one or two unsuitable books lying around that might have given him ideas. But, as you say, er, Nightshade,' he said, trying to make talking to a cat appear normal, 'I didn't spot his magic was way stronger than I thought.'

'The question I am asking myself,' said Nightshade, licking a paw, 'is why Trapmole would want to poison you, Oakmoss.'

'He wanted to run the workshop, and not have me take over.'

'But you made it pretty clear you never wanted to spend your life making those horrible fortune cats anyway. You were never in his way.'

Oakmoss winced. 'What I want doesn't come into it – Dad expects me to take over, however much Trapmole tries to impress him. If Dad left it to me I wouldn't make those cats.' He felt Nightshade shudder.

'What would you do?' asked Veena.

'Erasmus, you said you'd move in here to keep the Hornbeam Workshop going. I'd do the opposite,' said Oakmoss, stroking Nightshade thoughtfully.

Erasmus looked confused.

'I – I think Mum has been spending the charity donations on all the improvements to Hornbeam Hall. I don't think,' he admitted, hanging his head in shame, 'that she ever intended to build a toy repair hospital. So that's what I would do, that's what people have donated money for. I know some were tricked, but not all. People turned up to the fairy-tale gala wanting to donate, didn't they? Raising money to repair toys rather than throw them away is a really good idea. We should properly do it.'

'Oakmoss!' cried Veena. 'That is so honourable.'

Erasmus's face furrowed with concern. 'Don't let's be hasty. I'm not sure a repair service would be anywhere near as profitable. You're a little young to understand business. Hornbeam Hall is an expensive place to run. It needs careful looking after.' He spread his hands. 'I don't mind taking on all that responsibility.'

'Hornbeam Hall will cost a lot less without Mum changing her mind, making changes and buying new things,' insisted Oakmoss, feeling unexpectedly stubborn.

'Changing the Hornbeam Workshop into a repair shop is a great idea,' enthused Veena. 'You love fixing things, Erasmus, and Oakmoss's astounding sorcery means he is utterly brilliant with his hands. He could fix anything, I think. You'll need a better name than RATS, of course.'

Erasmus was staring at Oakmoss, his face a picture of shocked disbelief. 'Oakmoss's astounding sorcery . . . ? There's a lot I need to catch up on.' He cleared his throat. 'We'll talk later. Plenty of time once I've moved in. I really should go and pack.'

'Yes, I'm sure you'd rather spend your life fixing broken things in your junk shop than lazing around Hornbeam Hall and finding someone else to do all the work, Erasmus,' said Nightshade.

'Getting advice from a talking cat. There really is no end to the surprises.'

Oakmoss blinked at this uncle and pushed his glasses up his nose, rubbing Nightshade's ears just as she liked it. 'I'm really not sure about the astounding sorcery.'

'It must be true,' said Veena, her arms folded and her expression steely. 'It's why the ill-wishing didn't kill you. You just kept bouncing back!'

Erasmus gave a little frown at Veena. 'Suddenly you're an expert in ill-wishing? I hope Oakmoss hasn't been discussing too many things he shouldn't.'

'Lucky for Oakmoss he discussed it with us,' said Nightshade. 'All that ill-wishing would have meant a fatal accident for anyone else, but every time something terrible happened, Oakmoss managed to save himself. Veena is absolutely right.'

'I usually am,' said Veena.

'We don't need to talk about it now,' said Erasmus easily. 'I'll be moved in here before the end of the day. Oakmoss, don't go worrying. I'll take care of everything.'

'Actually,' drawled Nightshade, blinking her green eyes, 'I think you'll find Hyacinth does that already.'

Inspector Pewter, who Oakmoss thought had left, was unexpectedly looming particularly tall in the doorway. 'So good of you to step in to run things here, Mr Hornbeam.'

'I wouldn't abandon Oakmoss,' said Erasmus.

'Very honourable. Putting up with living here. Settling for a life of luxury and ease instead of your adorable shop.'

Oakmoss wasn't sure why Pewter was staring so particularly at Uncle Erasmus. His little round glasses had cleared and behind them the inspector's eyes were a piercing blue.

Oakmoss felt unexpectedly brave enough to put one of his many questions before he missed the chance.

'How soon do you think my parents will be back, Inspector?' he asked.

'All I know is that when they do return, it won't be without ramifications after the poor choices they've made,' answered Pewter.

'You mean the Elysee will be keeping an eye on us Hornbeams for ever and making sure we are using our magic responsibly?'

'I wouldn't be surprised if some restrictions aren't put on your father's ability to use magic, just like his father before him. Life might be a little less comfortable when he returns.'

Oakmoss resolved right then that he would never be like his grandfather or father and get investigated for abuse of magic, or have his sorcery restricted. Or be like his mother, and spend charity donations on herself. This, he vowed, would be the end of the Hornbeams' misuse of magic and the Hornbeams being the magical bad guys.

'My brother doesn't exactly take disappointment and setbacks well,' sighed Erasmus. 'Comes from always having life very easy. I don't mind staying on and helping out for as long as it takes.'

Pewter stroked his chin. 'By helping out, do you mean encouraging the next apprentice to take risks with mind-meld magic?'

'I think Oakmoss might do better without that sort of help,' said Stormforce.

'I mean, it's very clever and brought in a lot of money,' said the inspector. 'Just illegal.'

'How could we have known what Trapmole was getting up to?' said Erasmus easily, but trying to exit. Pewter was in his way.

'If anyone did know, they might have seen it clearing a path towards exactly what they wanted. They might have found all obstacles could be removed. They might even find a way to move in here, take control of the house, the workshop. Oh, wait a minute, yes, there is one thing standing in the way of you taking total control. Your nephew, Oakmoss. And you very nearly got away with it.'

Oakmoss had been busy enjoying a little dream of how fun living with his uncle might be. How rewarding it might be to fix toys. Now he found himself startled out of that pleasant dream. What was Inspector Pewter saying?

Stormforce lazily placed something small and purple on the long kitchen table. A zingtasco. Stormforce had once accepted one, but Oakmoss had noticed him politely putting it in his pocket. They *were* a little strong.

Stormforce reached for the dagger he kept in his inside pocket and jetted out a haze of blue light which settled on the sweet. The air fizzed and crackled around it, like lightning looking for a conductor in a storm.

Erasmus gave a dry chuckle. 'Interesting.' He was looking uneasily at the zingtasco as it finally stopped fizzing.

Oakmoss remembered what Veena had said about the truth and how it was better to know it than to find yourself living a lie. Nightshade stirred in his lap, reminding him to keep stroking her ears as he watched the last shimmer of the fizzing blue light fading from the zingtasco.

Oakmoss didn't need Stormforce to tell him what that little experiment meant. The truth was, those sweets that his uncle was always giving him were ...

'Bewitched,' said Veena, staring as the last fizzes of magical blue light died away. 'That sweet was bewitched.'

50. I'VE ALWAYS BEEN UNLUCKY

'The ill-wishing spell was in those zingtascos all along?' said Veena.

I shuffled from Oakmoss's lap and padded up to her, rubbing around her legs. She really was a smart girl.

'Oakmoss was lucky he kept his supreme sorcery from you, Erasmus,' I said, licking a paw. 'But it must have really confused you when he survived every attempt at ill-wishing.'

Erasmus looked at Oakmoss, then at Inspector Pewter and Dexter Stormforce. Then he darted,

making a swift move to pick up the incriminating zingtasco from the kitchen table, but Stormforce was blocking his way.

'If you hadn't become impatient you might have got away with it,' I went on. 'You gave up trying to get rid of Oakmoss by making it look like an accident and resorted to good old-fashioned poison in the cherry bakewell pie.'

'It was a brilliant plan to take over completely,' said Pewter admiringly. 'You had to get a lot of people safely out of the way. First, you convinced Trapmole his boss would be impressed if he cast a little magic over the fortune cats and brought in a lot more money – that was a great start. Mr Hornbeam might have taken a bit of convincing, but when money poured in and no one asked questions, what's not to like?'

Erasmus darted a look around the room and flicked his tongue over his lips. 'It wasn't my idea. Trapmole never stopped bending my ear about how desperate he was to get Oakmoss out of the picture. I may have suggested he use a little magic to impress my brother.'

I pounced on a little bit of cake on the floor. I didn't mind that everyone had forgotten to feed me and I was reduced to dining on scraps. What I did mind was having to listen to Erasmus's weak excuses.

'Yes,' said Pewter, rocking on his heels. 'Getting Trapmole to actually do all the magic. Sheer genius.'

Sheer *evil* genius, I might have said. But Pewter had it right – Erasmus hesitated for just a moment, but could not resist showing off how clever he'd been.

'It wasn't easy, believe me. The number of times I left the right books out, open at the right page, steering him towards mind-meld magic. I thought he'd *never* work out which spell to add to the fortune cats. The hints I had to drop! While my brother and his wife lorded it over here. And then Trapmole did it and it worked – then they were raking in the money. But no one ever suspected a thing. There were never any questions. They just kept getting away with it. And making more and more money.'

'But it was all your idea,' I said. 'That must have really hurt.'

'You needed the illegal use of magic to be uncovered,' said Veena, tapping a foot. 'Mr and Mrs Hornbeam and the whole Rescue All Toys Society would be implicated, and you'd be in the clear, ready to take over. If you could get rid of Oakmoss as well, the whole of Hornbeam Hall would be yours. Not to mention all that money – pretty hard to work out how much was genuine and how much came from the spells. So much cash – very hard to track.'

'If I influenced Trapmole into upping the dose to ensure it drew attention to their illegal activity, I was only doing my duty,' said Erasmus loftily.

'You must have been thrilled when Mustard was suddenly making a helluva fuss about it,' said Pewter.

'You were nearly home and dry,' I said, leaping back on to Oakmoss's lap. The boy had gone very quiet. 'But it was the ill-wishing and the poisoned pie that put me on to you.'

'I've always been unlucky,' wailed Erasmus, brushing at the orange pollen stain that had ruined his best jacket. 'Unlucky that according to the Hornbeam legacy, the entire family fortune went to my brother – the younger son gets absolutely nothing,' he finished with a snarl.

'I bet no one ever asked if you wanted to live in that horrible junk shop, taking boxes of Mrs Hornbeam's thrown-away old things and fixing other people's terrible furniture,' I said. 'It can't have been easy.'

'Easy!' cried Erasmus, thumping the kitchen table. 'I hate junk! I can throw together a few low-level charms and curses. But what's the point? Who seeks out sorcerers for spells any more?' He gestured around him. 'And my brother gets all this.'

Oakmoss stroked my fur and I hoped my being there was giving him some comfort.

Erasmus responded with a dry chuckle. 'Anyway, I know you can't prove any of it. Magical investigations are very tricky.'

'Erasmus!' cried Oakmoss, unable to keep quiet any longer. 'This is all a joke, isn't it? Explain what really happened.'

Erasmus was gripping the back of one of the kitchen chairs. He quietly pushed his fringe out of his eyes, looking straight at Oakmoss. 'It was never anything personal, Oakmoss.'

'Nothing personal!' cried Veena, outraged. 'You tried to kill him.'

'You did try to poison me,' said Oakmoss quietly. 'And actually, I can prove it.'

51. Anything To Do With Fish Is Fine By Me

'I find that difficult to believe,' said Erasmus quietly.

'Nightshade's brilliant at detecting magical crime.' Oakmoss looked down at me and I purred in reply. 'She's been explaining all sorts of things to me.'

'I have,' I agreed.

'I'm pretty sure Stormforce is on to whatever spell you've been feeding me in those zingtascos,' said Oakmoss. 'But what's given you away is that you poisoned the pie. I don't want to believe it, but I

know, because of the lily pollen on your jacket.'

'This?' said Erasmus, looking at first puzzled and then disdainful as he pointed at the orange stain on his crumpled jacket. 'I don't think it proves anything.'

'Oh, but it does. Those lilies mark you if you go into the garden room. You could only have got that stain by being in there. And it had to be before dinner, because you took off your jacket the moment you came into the dining room.'

I thought Erasmus was going to sink heavily down, defeated, into the chair he'd been holding on to, but at the last second he moved swiftly. He opened the cat basket and Gisborne leapt out, a snarling ball of marmalade fur and teeth, and launched himself straight at me.

I've been in many highly dangerous situations, but I'm a quick-thinking and very agile cat. I can normally rely on my wits to keep me out of trouble. But I hadn't seen this coming and I was trapped on Oakmoss and part-wedged under the kitchen table. No escape, no way to evade the monster that was heading towards me, claws unsheathed.

I scrabbled to untangle myself from Oakmoss's lap, probably causing the boy to get a little bloody in the process, I don't doubt. I tried to dart underneath the kitchen table, even knowing there were far too many legs between me and the door.

Gisborne had been wanting to give me a bloody nose and this time nothing was going to stop him.

Pewter moved. I thought he was darting to stop Erasmus, who had caused the distraction and was making a bid for the door and freedom.

But Pewter moved to throw something – a spell. And the hissing stopped.

I had closed my eyes, but no monster leapt on me, there were no ripping claws. I dared to turn. And behind me, where there had been nothing but muscle, sinew, sharp teeth and claws, there was now the tiniest cutest orange-coloured kitten with slightly confused yellow eyes.

Even as I tried to work out what had happened, Pudding strolled back in and the two kittens started mewling at each other and making friends.

'What's happened to Gisborne?' asked Veena, picking up the tiny ginger kitten and giving it a cuddle. 'If this is him he's a lot nicer this way.'

'Apologies,' said Pewter. 'A spell was the only thing I could throw that would reach in time.' Somehow he also had Uncle Erasmus in a firm grip. He stood at the door. 'You haven't any other family, have you, Oakmoss? Only, er, I seem to have now arrested all of them. I don't want to leave you on your own.'

'I may not be family, but I'm still here,' said Hyacinth, drawing Oakmoss to her in another crushing hug. 'We will run things fine.'

'Yes, a troublesome family,' said Pewter. 'Luckily, I like a challenge.'

'Not all of them are bad,' said Hyacinth, and Oakmoss gave her a grateful smile.

'Don't go blaming Stormforce now, will you, for bringing all of this to my attention and it all resulting in rather a lot of arrests,' said Pewter as he steered Erasmus away. 'I know things look pretty grim, but that's often the way with truth and justice, you just ask Miss Vale.'

Oakmoss blinked owlishly. 'My parents and Trapmole are swindlers and I've got a murderous uncle who made several attempts to kill me. I think anyone would call that pretty grim.'

Pewter looked at him, nodding. 'All I can say is that things often look better after—'

'An ice cream,' I interrupted.

'On it!' said Hyacinth.

'And I'm still here,' said Veena, playing with not one but two kittens. 'You're really not on your own, Oakmoss.'

'Perhaps, Oakmoss, you could give a little help with the tents,' suggested Hyacinth, squeezing Oakmoss on the shoulder as he stood, unmoving. 'Inspector Pewter made a start, but I think he's leaving now. Ice cream after clearing up?'

I was still shaking, not quite able to believe I was still in one piece.

'Right!' said Stormforce. 'I can help and then Oakmoss, you can show me where the kingfishers are nesting. And then some fishing. Even if you've got a terrible leaky old boat, I'm up for it.'

'Well, he's certainly got one of those,' said Veena.

'It's fine,' said Stormforce. 'Now that I understand Oakmoss has been keeping it afloat with magic all this time.'

'You all worked it out before me, didn't you?' Oakmoss said, bending to fuss my ears.

'Of course I did,' I said. 'But it wasn't the easiest thing to have to tell you.'

'Let's clear up first,' said Oakmoss. 'Then fishing.'

'And ice cream,' I reminded him.

'Good plan.' Veena was nodding enthusiastically. 'And I really want to see where the kingfishers are nesting too, please.'

'Why are you suddenly so interested?' Oakmoss's eyes narrowed.

'My front page,' she wailed. 'I need something!'

'Come on, we've loads of good news. Oakmoss didn't die,' said Dexter. 'The ill-wishing will stop now his uncle has been arrested, the troublesome Hornbeams will be a lot less troublesome. But, ah right, I get it – you can't print any of that, can you?'

Veena shook her head. 'All of that involves magic, and I made a promise to Nightshade. I think the fact that kingfishers are nesting is ... well, it might be the only thing I can print,' she finished.

'Kingfishers nesting really is great,' responded Oakmoss, heading outside. 'I shall love explaining to you and all your readers why it really is very good news.'

I followed, and was immediately reminded what a truly terrible mess the grounds of Hornbeam Hall were in. The Baba Yaga tea tent had given up after all the excitement and had slumped in on itself. Oakmoss was going to need to do wonders with his magic to get it all cleared away before dark.

As everyone slowly began to work, I turned to take a last look back at the gaunt grey house.

'You know, we should have worked it all out sooner. There was a big clue that Mr Mustard might be telling the truth and that there was something bad at the heart of the Hornbeam family,' I said.

'What did we miss?' asked Veena, gathering smashed plates. 'What?'

'Those turrets! Honestly, practically screaming out a warning about the Hornbeams.'

'Not all of them,' Hyacinth reminded us.

'Let's get cleared up quickly so we've got time to go fish,' said Stormforce.

'Well, sorry, but I'll have to see you down at the boathouse,' I said, leaping ahead. 'Sadly I won't be any good at packing away tents, not with paws.'

'But fish . . .' said Oakmoss, pausing folding a tent in mid-air to stop and fuss my ears. 'Anything to do with fish is fine by you, isn't it, Nightshade?'

I turned, pleased. The boy had learnt much.

'How very true, Oakmoss Hornbeam, anything to do with fish is fine by me. Particularly if I get to eat them.'

ACKNOWLEDGEMENTS

It has been such a joy to have worked again with the talented team at Chicken House. I have so many people to be grateful to, including Rachel Leyshon for her forensic red pen, and Fraser Crichton for making me think harder about things like the operation of cats' paws.

To Héloïse Mab for the beautiful yet quirky jacket illustration and the coolest cat to appear on the cover of a book.

There are so many hard-working parts of publishing and I am grateful to you all and the way you strive to make this book the best it could be. I am ridiculously lucky to be part of a unit that works so brilliantly.

I have had amazing support from booksellers during a very challenging year. To everyone in essential jobs in schools, libraries and bookshops who have enthused about my books and got them into the hands of readers – thank you. Your efforts to support books, writers and readers is critical to helping young people uncover stories that will open so many doors. I'm constantly in awe of your dedication.

I would be nowhere without getting the space and support to write. So thank you to Mark, Alex and

Tim who are brilliant people to share my life with. And particular huge and grateful thanks to my mum, Noreen Miller, for stepping in so brilliantly and without whose generous help this year would have been a bit of a disaster to say the least.

And thank you to all at St Ethelwold's house in Abingdon, for peace and beauty and for giving me space to work.

My final thanks goes to readers everywhere, particularly those that take the trouble to contact me and tell me how much they like my books! A very big thank you from me. And do keep on reading. Always.

THE LAST CHANCE HOTEL

Seth is the oppressed kitchen boy at the remote Last Chance Hotel, owned by the nasty Bunn family. His only friend is his black cat, Nightshade. But when a strange gathering of magicians arrives for dinner, kindly Dr Thallomius is poisoned by Seth's special dessert. A locked-room murder investigation ensues – and Seth is the main suspect.

The funny thing is, he's innocent . . . can he solve the mystery and clear his name, especially when magic's afoot?

'This mystery is a worthy prizewinner . . .
a jolly, atmospheric mystery.'
THE TIMES

Paperback, ISBN 978-1-911077-67-1, £6.99 • ebook, 978-1-911490-41-8, £6.99

THE PECULIAR TALE OF THE TENTACLE BOY
by RICHARD PICKARD

Marina meets William while exploring the haunted pier in her seaside town. But William is not like other boys. He's ... different – with crab claws for hands and tentacles that stretch from his head. What he needs from Marina – if she's ready – is a friend who can help him to unravel the fishy mystery of his past ...

> 'A whimsical adventure stuffed to the flippers with fish puns and fun.'
> SAM SEDGMAN

Paperback, ISBN 978-1-913322-39-7, £6.99 • ebook, ISBN 978-1-913696-10-8, £6.99

MIDNIGHT HOUR by BENJAMIN READ & LAURA TRINDER

Emily's parents have vanished into the secret world of the the Midnight Hour – a Victorian London frozen in time – home to magic and monsters. Emily must find them in the city of the Night Folk, armed only with a packed lunch, a stowaway hedgehog and her infamously big mouth. With bloodthirsty creatures on her tail, Emily has to discover the truth to rescue her parents. What family secret connects her to the Midnight Hour? And can she save both worlds before she runs out of sandwiches?

'Anarchic humour, rich imagination and poetic writing, interspersed with elegant line drawings, add up to pure delight – with a stowaway hedgehog as a bonus.
GUARDIAN

Paperback, ISBN 978-1-911490-90-6, £6.99 • ebook, ISBN 978-1-911490-91-3, £6.99